PUCKING HEARTS COLLIDE
PUCKING DARK HEARTS
BOOK 1

MAGGIE ALABASTER

Copyright © 2024 by Maggie Alabaster

All rights reserved.

No part of this book may be reproduced in any form or by any electronic or mechanical means, including information storage and retrieval systems, without written permission from the author, except for the use of brief quotations in a book review.

Cover design by Artscandare

Edited by Lily Luchesi

Proofread by Nora Hogan

TRIGGER WARNINGS

Hey lovely reader, in order to help you to look after you, I'm here to warn you about the violence and light bullying in this book.

There is an HEA and all the juicy smut too.

1

CATALINA

"And, go!"

My feet sliced, skates sliding faster and faster, until I flew across the ice. Upper body forward, hands behind my back, eyes forward, laser focused.

I leaned hard to my left. My gloved hand grazed the surface of the ice to steady me while I took the bend. I straightened up as I came out and sped up, skating faster still.

I flew around the second bend, past my coach who stood with a stopwatch in his hand.

"Two laps to go."

I didn't acknowledge his words, merely took mental note of them as I sped around the rink.

"One lap to go."

I bent forward, skating harder, attention fixed on the ice and the angle of my body and feet.

On the third pass, my coach signalled the end of this

round of practice laps. His arm was a flash of movement in front of me. Only when I'd passed him did I straighten up and gradually slow. I skated a tight circle and skidded to a stop on the edge of the rink in front of him.

"How's the knee?" Always the first thing out of his mouth.

I shrugged. "It's okay." I flexed my right leg a couple of times.

He fixed me with a stern look. "Cat…"

"It's fine, Dad, stop fussing. You sound like a mother hen." I snatched my helmet off my head and shook out my red hair, damp from exertion.

"Don't you 'mother hen' me, girl," he said with affectionate gruffness.

"Father rooster then," I responded with a sly smile and ducked away as though he might physically retaliate. "How was my time?" As far as I was concerned, *that* was the important part of the conversation.

"You're getting there," he said. "You still need to shave half a second off your time." He made a note on his clipboard.

"Then that's what I'll do," I said. As if it was all that simple.

"Without injuring your knee again—"

I cut him off before he could start his usual, overprotective rant. Sometimes I wondered what it would be like to be coached by someone I wasn't related to. Probably just as bad. Any good coach would be as invested as he was, father or not.

"My knee is fine," I protested.

"Your knee isn't completely healed," he corrected. "I know you want to make the Olympic team, but if you do yourself a permanent injury, you'll have to live with that for the rest of your life."

I tucked my helmet under my arm. "It's been my dream since I was six years old," I reminded him. "I've let my knee hold me back for too long." Not long enough in his mind.

"I'm well aware." He held the clipboard by the edge and let it, and the stopwatch, dangle from his fingers. "I'm the one who bought you your first skates."

"So I could follow in your footsteps." I tilted my head at him.

He cocked an eyebrow like he expected me to say more, but was relieved when I didn't. "Thank you for not reminding me you want to surpass my record."

He pressed his lips together in the frustration he still clung to after all these years. He made the Winter Olympic team in short track, when I was a kid. In the final lap, he and another skater collided, letting the other three competitors get in front of them and take the medals.

Without that accident, he would have at least taken a bronze.

Instead, he walked away with nothing but a

daughter who had the same drive and stubborn streak he did. And a need to rectify the past on his behalf.

He was right, I couldn't do that with an injured knee.

"You know how important this is," I said softly. "I need to get my fitness back. We've been taking it slowly and carefully."

"Yes, we have," he agreed.

We'd moved from Victoria back to Opal Springs, in the south of New South Wales, for me to recover fully. I missed the hustle and bustle of Melbourne, but without being surrounded by other ice racers, I was under less pressure from everyone but myself. Like any good athlete, I put more of that on myself than anyone else ever could.

I exhaled softly. "But this is where you remind me I'm almost finished my degree in vet science and could be working in my field instead."

"Less risk of permanent damage to your knee," he said.

"More chance of being bitten by someone's feral pet turtle," I said jokingly.

I loved animals, and fully intended to use my degree once I was done with skating. If my parents taught me anything, it was to go after what I wanted and that I could be anything or do anything if I worked hard enough. If I was greedy for wanting to achieve both things, then too fucking bad.

No one could say Catalina Joanna Ryan was a quitter.

He sighed. "You're as stubborn as your mother was." His brow furrowed. He clung to the grief harder than his disappointment over losing his Olympic dream. She'd died five years ago, killed on her way home from work by a drunk driver. Dad hadn't dated since, in spite of my encouragement.

He insisted on giving all of his attention to me and my younger sister, Bree. With Bree busy with university, it was just Dad and me now. He should be out living his best life, in the present, not letting the past hold him back. Mum wouldn't have wanted that. Some day, I hoped he'd move on and be happy. He deserved no less.

"I'll take that as a compliment," I said.

He scratched at the side of his temple, where his faded black hair was starting to show a sprinkling of grey. According to my friends, he was a silver fox. To me he was just Dad.

"As you should," he said in his rumbly voice. He could have gone into voice acting or audiobook narration. He'd have women swooning.

Not that I thought about him that way, eww. No, for me, his voice brought back childhood memories of him reading me bedtime stories for hours. Or, more recently, reminding me to go easy on my knee.

"She'd love the idea she passed that on to you." He grimaced, but he was clearly holding back a smile. "This is what I get for living in a house full of women," he groaned. "Red haired women, no less."

"You're the one who wanted a ginger cat," I pointed out. "And the goldfish. Anyone would think you have a fetish."

He grinned and didn't contradict me.

I made a face. "That's what I thought. I'll keep an eye out for an Irish setter. In the meantime, I should go again." I glanced at my watch. "We have another ten minutes."

Renting the rink for a couple of hours a day wasn't cheap, but if I was going to get back on top, I needed to do it. It would be worth the sacrifice.

It had to be.

Dad looked like he might argue, but then he nodded. "One more time around before you cool down too much. Then I need to get to work."

"Don't want Doctor Ryan to be late." I pressed my helmet back on my head.

Dad had a small general practice clinic in town. The kind that didn't time the length of his consultations, but instead made patients feel heard and valued. Opal Springs adored him for it.

"If Doctor Ryan is late, he'll hear about it from Marley," he agreed. "My receptionist hates it when I'm late into the office. She keeps threatening to stop making me coffee." He made a face like that would be the worst fate in the world.

Marley was one of my closest friends. I could totally see her doing something like that.

"That would teach you," I teased. I skated back to the starting point, which was nothing more glamorous than an old traffic cone. The community rink in Opal Springs was nothing fancy, but it was all we had for now.

Dad was about to press go on the stopwatch, when the gate leading off the rink was opened and a bunch of guys in skates and padding shuffled onto the ice. A couple of them carried a goal between them. They glanced at us before taking it over to one end of the rink and placing it down.

I glanced at Dad, who looked as confused as I was. I shrugged and skated over to the closest of the guys.

Standing at least six-foot-five, he was a lot taller than my five foot ten. Taller still in skates. He pulled gloves onto his hands. A helmet covered what looked like brown hair, cut close to his scalp. A thin layer of stubble covered his chin.

"Excuse me, what do you think you're doing?" I asked. I planted my hands on my hips and raised my eyebrows at him. Let him know I was annoyed. His body language suggested he was confident he owned the place. I knew for a fact he didn't.

He glanced up at me. A brow twitched before his gaze slid down my body and away, like I was nothing.

"Training," he said simply. His plush lips barely moved when he spoke.

"This is my practice time," I said. "I still have time left on the clock." I pointed to the one on the wall, which clearly read 6:51.

He glanced at it and went on pulling his gloves onto his hands as though I hadn't spoken.

"You can't just come out here and set up on my paid time," I insisted. "That goal is right in my way." If I tried skating around the rink, I'd slam right into it. It was exactly in my path.

For some reason, he seemed to find that amusing. "Go ahead and move it then, Princess." He gestured toward it with one hand.

My face heated with irritation. I knew a setup when I saw one. If it took two muscular guys to carry it out here, it was going to be too heavy for me.

"You need to get it, and yourselves, off the ice until my time is done." I patted myself on the back for not swearing at him. Not yet anyway. Fucker.

He looked at me properly this time. "I don't need to do either of those things. I need to start training with the rest of my team. By the time we get the goal off the ice, it'd be time to put it back. It can stay there."

The clock now read 6:56. There I wasn't going to get in another lap or two at this point anyway. Would the universe judge me too harshly if I wiped that smug look off his face with the back of my hand? I wasn't usually given to violence, but this was my whole future here. My chance to make the Winter Olympic team. I didn't need a Neanderthal like him standing in the way.

"Next time, wait until your time starts," I told him. "Stay off the ice until then."

"This is our time now, Princess; get yourself off the ice." He made a 'go away' gesture with his fingers.

According to the clock, the time was a minute past seven.

I gave him the longest, filthiest look I could manage before turning and skating to the gate and stepping off the ice.

"Can you believe that asshole?" I said, making no attempt to keep my voice down. "Who does he think he is?"

"He's Cruz Brewer," Dad supplied. "Left-winger for the Opal Springs Ghouls hockey team."

"Opal Springs *Tools*, more like it," I said sourly. "Where does he get off muscling in on my rink time?" Not to mention the rest of the team, who were all looking at me like I was the one who did something wrong.

"I'll talk to Rhonda," Dad said. "See if she'll have a word with them."

The owner of the rink was the kind of person who took no shit from anyone, but these hockey players didn't look like they took it either. If I had to change my practice time to suit them, I'd be more than slightly pissed off.

"Please do." I tugged my helmet and gloves off. "I don't need assholes like that getting in my way." I gave the entire team a collective dirty look.

The guy standing on the edge of the rink, talking to whom I presumed was the team's coach, gave me a filthy look in return. I resisted the urge to flip him off. He was hot enough to melt the ice, but his expression would freeze it again.

More and more people in Australia were becoming interested in ice hockey, but I wasn't one of them. Especially not now. If that was their attitude, they could fuck off as far as I was concerned. I had better things to do than pander to their egos.

Dad chuckled. "If anyone could deal with them, it would be Rhonda. Or you. Go on and get showered and changed. I'll see you at dinner tonight." He kissed my sweaty cheek and headed out, clipboard tucked under his arm.

2

CATALINA

"I fucking hate hockey players." I flopped down onto the seat between Marley and Eden, my other closest friend in Opal Springs.

Marley pushed her glasses back in place on her nose, with her fingertip. "That's one hell of a declaration." As always, she was impeccably dressed. Today, in a white blouse and black pencil skirt. In heels, she was almost as tall as me.

Marley-Jane and I went to school together, all the way from preschool. When I moved back to town, we rekindled our friendship. Lucky for me, because very few people knew about the things we got up to. Sometimes I worried she'd fill my father in, but she was always professional. As far as I knew. I'd hate for him to learn the half of it.

"I'm sensing some sort of conflict." Eden tucked a strand of purple hair behind her ear. "What happened?"

A florist, she worked out of the building beside my Dad's surgery. That was where we met. Around the same age as me, we hit it off immediately.

"You're sensing conflict all right." I placed my black tea on the table in front of me and tossed my keys down beside it. I told them about my run in with Cruz Brewer and his team.

"Ugh, Cruz Brewer." Marley fanned herself. "I've seen him around work a few times. He's smoking hot and doesn't he fucking know it?"

I hummed my agreement and picked up my tea to take a sip. I preferred my coffee with milk and sugar, so it was safer to stick to black tea while I was training. "What's his deal anyway? And the rest of them?"

Marley leaned forward eagerly. If there was something she loved, it was town gossip. If she didn't know it, it probably wasn't worth knowing.

"You don't know?" she asked.

"Know what? His attitude is overcompensating for the size of his cock?" I hadn't gotten a good look, but I could tell that wasn't the case, unfortunately. Not that I was even slightly interested. I had better taste than to fall for an asshole, even a hot one.

Marley giggled. "Not as far as I've heard."

It was Eden who filled me in. "The AIHL, the Australian Ice Hockey League, is expanding. The Ghouls are hoping to be part of that expansion. They've been doing well against other teams in their division, but if they can turn professional, the AIHL will support the building of an actual arena here in Opal Springs. It'll be huge for the construction and tourism industries. Not to mention supporting grassroots sports programs for children."

"So they think that gives them the right to muscle in on my rink time?" I frowned.

Okay, an arena *would* be good for the economy of the area, but the team could have waited ten minutes. That's what polite people would have done. People who wanted to think of themselves as role models.

"They are becoming a bit of a big deal around here," Marley said. "I mean, Opal Springs is growing so fast, it's only a matter of time before we have teams in every sport you can think of. And a bunch we probably can't think of. Like, I don't know, tiddlywinks."

"I'd prefer to watch people play tiddlywinks than ice hockey," I said. "Especially after dealing with those pricks. I've met plenty just like them in Melbourne. They act as if they think they're better than everyone else because they play with a stick."

"They do some pretty incredible things with their sticks," Marley said. "All while on ice skates. Nothing you couldn't do," she added quickly.

The ability to skate didn't necessarily mean I could hit a puck for shit, but I appreciated the vote of confidence.

"It's normal for a bit of fame to go to people's heads," Eden said easily. "A place for the arena has already been picked out. A lot of local guys are hoping to work on building it. If these players can't sell their ability to the AIHL, that's a lot of dreams down the toilet."

"Are you suggesting I should have stepped right off the ice the moment they stepped on?" I frowned deeper. "I'm not the villain in this." Was I?

"Fuck no," Eden replied. "Someone needs to keep their egos in check. The last thing anyone in Opal Springs needs is guys who think they're above everyone else. You know how that ends."

I did. If there was anything Australians loved, it was bringing down someone who got too big for their boots. It was practically a national pastime, if not a healthy one.

Sometimes people were on top for good reason. Like my father was in his day. He was the talk of the sporting community for some time after the collision that ended his career. In spite of building an even more successful one after stepping off the ice, he always had that one missing thing. That one 'what might have been' moment. The wish he'd ended on a high note, not slammed into the padding on the side of the rink.

"So you agree I should have stood my ground," I said.

"Would you have done anything else?" Marley said. "I can only guess what renting out the rink costs. Why shouldn't you get your full allotment of time? After having to take a year off with your knee, you need this."

"Yeah, I do," I agreed. "I've worked too long and hard to let assholes like that push me around. My knee has stood in my way for long enough. It's fine," I added before they asked. I didn't need them fussing over me, my father was more than enough.

Marley placed a hand over mine. "I'm glad you are. I remember how you looked when you first got back to town. Like you weren't sure if you were defeated or not. I know the vet clinic would be happy to keep you on so you don't have to go back to Melbourne." She looked tentatively hopeful.

I knew she would have liked it if I committed to staying in town until the end of time, but I wasn't ready to do that. Not yet. Most of the girls we went to school with were married and had children, but I wasn't ready to do that yet either. There were too many things I wanted to do, too many places I wanted to go. And I wasn't going to settle for the first guy who wanted to marry me either. If I did that, I would have gotten married instead of going to university.

"I know," I said. Sooner or later, I'd have to commit to working somewhere, whether it was the clinic here or one back in Melbourne. If I stayed here, that would mean giving up my Olympic dream, once and for all. I couldn't, not even if it was a sensible, adult thing to do.

Fuck that. I was only twenty-five. I still had time to be young and stupid. And stubborn and driven. I wanted to win a medal for myself and for my dad. Having ambition wasn't a bad thing.

"So," Marley said slowly. She pushed her glasses back up her nose.

I took in the expression in her bright blue eyes and groaned. "Is this where you tell me I should come and watch a hockey game with you sometime?"

They both smiled.

Yeah, I was done for.

"You absolutely should," Marley agreed. "I mean, you've seen those guys up close. You know how hot they are."

"I've seen them play and I'm also well aware they know how hot they are," I said dryly. "I have no intention of becoming a puck bunny. Especially not after that asshole, Cruz. Not if he was the last guy in town." Him and the other guy who glared at me for no reason. Hard pass.

"There are other guys on the roster," Marley said. "I'm sure they're not all bad."

"They might not all be bad, but I'm still not going there with any of them," I said. "But I will come and see them play if you insist. Because we're friends and I like hanging out with you." And I liked being at the rink. It was my home away from home. Skating was as natural to me as walking. When I injured my knee and it looked like I may never skate again, I was devastated. Medal or no medal, I needed to be out on the ice. It was my happy place. The place I could work out all my frustrations and feel at peace. If those assholes disturbed my peace, I was going to… I didn't know what. Raise hell, maybe.

Marley bounced up and down in her chair. Her

glasses slid back down her lightly freckled nose. She pushed them back up and grinned. "Excellent. You're going to have the best time. Although, it'll be better when they build the arena." Her eyes were wide, slightly glazed, clearly picturing something fancy like the ones in North America. An arena like that would quickly become a landmark on par with the football stadium, which hosted rugby union, rugby league and gridiron matches. Not to mention the occasional concert.

I could hear my father now, talking about how he remembered the good old days of Opal Springs, when it was still small, and everyone knew everyone else. It was still small, but now, it was more than a former mining town. Ironically, I think more gold was found here than opals, but the name stuck.

"If," I said carefully. "It's not a done deal yet, is it? I mean, there are plenty of other hockey teams vying to join the AIHL. They might choose one of them instead."

"They might," Eden agreed. "It's not just the team, there are other considerations. They have to be able to get bums in seats. Opal Springs has to be able to deal with the traffic on game nights. And they only take a certain number of teams per state. If they choose someone else from New South Wales, then the Ghouls will be out of the running until the next expansion."

I admit, that was conflicting. I wanted this for the area, but at the same time, I wanted Cruz Brewer to fall on his face. I'd have to decide whose side I was on. I was, after all, one of those bums in seats if I wanted to be.

"Give them a chance," Marley said as if reading my thoughts. "I promise you'll be entertained." She looked thoughtful for a moment. "Maybe you could suggest an ice race before the game?"

"Challenge some of the players to a few laps?" I asked. Nothing would be sweeter than kicking their asses. On the other hand, I might get my ass kicked, and that would be embarrassing.

"I'll think about it," I said finally. "It might be more fun to get some kids out on the ice for a race." Something smaller and slower than I was used to, since the rink wasn't padded and the kids wouldn't have slice proof padding and helmets. Not unless I could get them interested in speed skating. There were worse things than inspiring the next generation.

"I can see you thinking," Eden said. "If it would help you to boost your confidence after the last year, then you should do it." She should have been a shrink. She was never *not* going to psychoanalyse us. Who needed a therapist when you had Eden as a friend?

Fortunately, she knew how far to push before she was overstepping the friendship.

"I just might," I said. I'd speak to Rhonda the next time I was in the rink and see what she thought. As long as she didn't tell me to run it by Cruz or anyone else in his team, then I saw no reason why we couldn't go ahead with it. She'd know which kids were up to a race and which weren't quite ready. The last thing any of us wanted was for them to get hurt. Not to mention that might end up with Rhonda and I being sued. I could kiss my Olympic dreams goodbye if that happened.

The café door tinkled as it opened. I glanced up and groaned. Cruz and three of his teammates stepped through the door.

3

CRUZ

I shoved the door open, making the bell above the door tinkle. Dean, Shaw and Easton followed me inside the Opal Café. Every eye in the place on us, we stepped over the worn but clean tiled floor to the front counter.

"What can I get you boys?" Henry, the owner, stood behind the counter, worn apron over his pale shirt and outdated jeans. He wiped his hands on the apron and pressed the keys on the register when we all ordered black coffees.

My gaze lingered on several cakes behind the glass to the side of the counter. Chocolate, carrot, cheesecake. Fuck, it sucked that cake was off the menu for now. There was a lot more at stake than satisfying my sweet tooth, but I could look.

I glanced around. We were used to being gawked at everywhere we went. Most people in town knew who we were. Being a local celebrity wasn't enough. The ambition to turn professional itched at me like a motherfucking rash. We were good enough, we'd prove that, shut the doubters up once and for all.

"Isn't that—" Easton. The Ghouls' right winger smirked in the direction of a table in the corner.

I locked eyes on the redhead and curled my lip. "Yeah, the little Princess from the rink."

The fucking bitch who thought a fun morning skate was more important than our training. She didn't seem to have the first clue who she was dealing with. She would if we crossed paths again. She'd know all about me and what I was capable of.

I won't lie, those soft pouty lips would look good around my cock. I thought that this morning when she was mouthing off about whatever she was on about. I wasn't really listening. My mind was on training and how to get her out of the way. Most people stepped right off the rink when they saw us coming. Five minutes, ten minutes, who gave a shit? Considering how much was at stake, I didn't.

"What's her deal anyway?" Dean asked. The goalie leaned against the counter and regarded her with half lidded eyes.

"Who gives a shit?" My eyes were still on her. So what if she could hear us? That was her problem, not mine.

"Not me," Shaw said. "Women like her think they're so fucking perfect." The team's left defenceman gave her a look like he'd happily throttle her. He had the patience of a fire ant in a jar of honey. And the bite, but he was a fucking good defensemen.

"Rhonda said something about her being Doctor Ryan's daughter." Easton shrugged.

"Really?" Dean narrowed his eyes at her. "I guess that means we better be nice, in case one of us gets injured."

I turned my attention back to him. "I'm always nice. When am I not nice?" I was very accommodating to women who wanted to fuck me because I was a hockey player. I didn't want to disappoint them by turning them down. After all, that would be rude to them and my dick.

Easton laughed. "That's some bullshit right there. Cruz Brewer, nice guy. Remind me to check the weather report, I didn't realise hell froze over."

I gave his bicep hard flick. "Fuck off. I can be nice if I want to."

"So you make a conscious decision to be an asshole?" He flicked me back.

"Sounds about fucking right," Shaw grumbled.

"I'm only an asshole to people who deserve it," I said pointedly. Easton and Shaw were both a pair of pricks. At least I owned it. Most of the time.

"So you say—" Easton was interrupted by Henry placing our coffees on the counter.

We nodded our thanks and took our cups over to the side of the café. I flopped into a chair where I could still see Princess Ryan.

"What's her first name?" I asked.

"Why do you care?" Dean asked carefully. If any of the four of us was nice, it was almost him. He had the closest thing to a conscience, if you could call it that.

I sipped my coffee and watched her over the rim of my cup. "I don't." My scrutiny was starting to get to her. I saw it in the annoyed glances she gave me every few moments. She'd shift in her chair, press her lips together and turn back to her friends.

I'd seen Marley and Eden around Opal Springs, and Princess looked familiar, but I couldn't place her. Had I fucked her at some point? It was possible, but I was almost certain I'd remember her if I had. She'd definitely remember me.

This morning I got the distinct impression she had no idea who I was. That knowledge added to my irritation. Everyone who frequented the rink, knew who the Ghouls were, and who we were going to be.

"If you didn't care, why would you ask?" Easton asked. "I think you do care." He swivelled around in his chair to scrutinise her. "She's cute."

"If you think she's so cute, why don't you go and talk to her?" I asked. Why the hell did I have the sudden urge to rip his arms off if he went anywhere near her? I gave no shits about her. If I did, it would only be because of the way she spoke to me this morning. Like a brat who was somehow better than me. That she was above me.

I'd like to teach her who was above who. It wouldn't

be a chore to do that while I was above her. On her knees or on her back, it didn't matter too much. Either way, she'd have my cock inside her, slamming into her hard enough to hurt. Hard enough to make her cry or scream. She'd fucking know who I was then. Bitch.

"Maybe I will," Easton replied. "Care to make a wager? Which one of us can fuck her first." His glance included Dean and Shaw.

"It wouldn't be you," I said. "She's seen me. Why would she settle for second best? Or third best?" I cocked an eyebrow at Easton.

"Don't fucking say I'm fourth," Shaw growled. "I don't want anything to do with her. Keep your fucking bet to yourselves."

"Scared?" Easton taunted. He cackled like a chicken.

Shaw gave him a dirty look, picked up his coffee and sipped.

"Suit yourself," Easton said, looking amused. "So, Cruzy-boy, you gonna take that bet or are you as chickenshit as Shaw?"

"Fuck off," I told him. "I'm not scared of anything." Easton gave me shit and I gave it back. We'd been like that since we started playing together. We were closer than brothers.

Dean was the younger brother who followed us around everywhere.

Shaw was new to the team, brought in to bolster the expansion application. He didn't use words to remind us of that. His glares and body language spoke for him.

Easton held out his hand challengingly, daring me to take him up on his bet.

"What are you betting?" Dean asked. Apparently he was the self-appointed arbiter of this arrangement.

Easton shrugged, pulling his hand back slightly with the gesture. "Fifty bucks?"

"What are the rules?" Dean asked. "Are we talking all the way or a blowjob?"

"All the fucking way," Easton said with a grin. "Cock in pussy."

"Consensually?" I asked bluntly. I grew up in Opal Springs caravan park, there wasn't much I wouldn't do for money. Until the team went professional, cash was light on the ground.

"Of course it would be Cruz asking that," Easton remarked.

Shaw snorted.

I sipped my coffee indifferently. "If I hadn't, you would have." Easton's childhood was only slightly better than mine. He lived in an actual house.

"Consensual," Dean said firmly. "And if she decides not to have anything to do with you, the bet is off."

"Always the respectful one." I leaned forward. "May I remind you, she was the one in our way this morning. You want the team to go professional, don't you? Because if you don't, I'm sure they can find—"

"I do," he said quickly. "She… Wasn't in our way for long."

"This morning she wasn't, but what about tomorrow

morning?" I asked. "What if it's twenty minutes tomorrow? Or thirty minutes? We have to train and then get ourselves off to work. We don't have time to mess around because of some entitled bitch." The best thing about going professional would be not having to turn up to my regular job anymore.

Being a mechanic was only who I was right now, not who I was *meant* to be. Playing hockey was in my blood. I had the skills and the drive. I could have played for one of the existing professional teams, but I believed in the Ghouls. Mostly, I believed no kid should grow up the way I had. The best thing I could do to ensure that didn't happen, was to get that arena built in Opal Springs.

I wasn't going to let anything or anyone stand in the way of that. Especially not some redheaded princess with her head up her ass. Not even a cute one.

"I guess you're right." Dean shot her a narrow eyed look. "Why do you want to screw her then?"

"Good fucking question." Shaw glared in her direction.

"Why not?" I replied. "It might keep her out of the way. She might decide to be nice to us after."

"Admit it," Easton said. "You're pissed at the way she talked to you this morning and want to teach her a lesson."

"So what if I do?" I definitely did. I wanted to teach her that I could master her body and make her do what I wanted her to do, even if we hated each other.

Watching her eyes flash with the same disdain she showed this morning, while she came around my hand or cock, would be sweet as hell.

Dean was right, it had to be consensual. Her surrender would be the sweetest fucking thing of all.

4

CATALINA

"Hey."

I was scrolling through my phone after Marley and Eden left, killing a few minutes. I stopped to look at a Booktok video when someone flopped into the seat beside me.

I glanced up half expecting to see Cruz Brewer, come to make some condescending asshole remark. It wasn't him, it was his blonde friend.

"Hey." I glanced back at my video. The universal signal for 'I'm not interested in a conversation right now.'

Like a true Booktok villain, he snatched my phone out of my hand and put it on his lap. "Don't you know it's rude to be on your phone when you're sitting at a table with someone else?"

"It only counts if they're invited to sit there," I said. I

held out my hand for him to return my phone. Instead, he shook it, grinning the whole time. Smug prick.

"I accept your invitation—" He cocked his head, clearly wanting me to provide my name.

"I didn't extend one. Give me back my phone." He was ridiculously good-looking and clearly knew it. Lean, muscular, without excess fat anywhere. He probably had a huge cock, right now he was acting like one.

"Is that how we ask nicely?" His head was still cocked, but now he threw in an eyebrow raise.

Ugh. A guy like him would be dangerous as hell to my pussy if he wasn't such a jerk. Tell that to her though, because she didn't seem to be getting the message. She was ready to rain down hell on my panties.

"I don't have to ask nicely when someone steals my phone," I said evenly. "I could always knee you in the balls and take it back." I smiled with mock sweetness.

He grinned. Of course he fucking did.

"Feisty," he said approvingly. "My name is Easton. Are you going to tell me your name or do I have to give you a nickname? Cruz calls you Princess, but I think maybe Red. Or maybe—"

"Cat," I interrupted tersely. "Catalina Ryan."

That made him grin even bigger. "Cat. I bet you have claws." Still holding my hand, he ran the pad of his thumb over my palm.

My stupid clit responded by throbbing. He knew

exactly the reaction he was getting from me. I saw it on his face.

"I know how to use them too," I said, trying to threaten rather than entice.

He leaned in closer. "I bet you do. Those claws would feel incredible raking down my back while I fuck the hell out of your pussy. What do you say we get out of here?" He jerked his head towards the door.

I leaned in towards him, almost close enough for our foreheads to touch. "Do you always come on to women you've just met?" I leaned back and frowned. "Actually, the important question here is— Does it ever work?"

He chuckled softly, not even slightly repentant. "Usually. Although, I don't often come on to women. It's usually them coming on to me."

He didn't seem to be bragging, just stating a fact.

I took my hand back and placed it in my lap. "I've noticed that about some hockey players. Women seem to find them appealing. Some women anyway."

"Not you?" He looked at me sideways.

"Nope. I've never seen the appeal myself. Maybe you could explain it to me." I tried to figure out how I could grab my phone back without my fingers accidentally brushing his groin. He didn't need any more encouragement.

He sat back in his seat and placed his hands behind his head. "Aside from the fact we're talented, muscular, fit, strong and know how to handle our stick?"

"You forgot humble and not completely in love with yourself," I said sarcastically.

He grinned. "Those as well. I don't have to be in love with myself, the Ghouls have a growing legion of fans to do that for me. Are you one of them?"

"I've never seen you play," I said bluntly. "In case you haven't noticed, I'm difficult to impress."

He lowered his hands, and held them out in front of himself, palms facing me. His eyes widened in mock horror. "No! I never would have guessed that. You totally don't walk around without an aura of—I don't know—world-weary pessimism."

"I prefer to think of myself as a realist," I said. "I don't see the attraction in chasing a little piece of rubber around the ice with a stick."

"You ice skate and you don't appreciate hockey?" He seemed uncertain as to how to respond to that. "How can that be?"

"You eat, but you don't like all food, do you?" I replied.

His brow crinkled. "I guess, but it's *hockey*. Tell you what, come to a game and let me change your mind. We're playing at the rink on Friday night. Come along and see for yourself. I'll even make you a little bet that you'll enjoy yourself."

"What do I get if I don't enjoy it?" I asked. Since I was going anyway, it didn't hurt to make a little side wager. One I was going to win, because there was no way I was losing to a guy like this. He was a typical, arrogant player, in both senses of the word.

"What do you want?" he countered.

"Not to be interrupted when I'm in my rink time," I said. This might work out all right after all. They could leave me alone and I wouldn't have to go to another game.

"Deal," he replied. "And if I win, you go out with me."

"With you?" I asked. "Why would you want to go out with me?"

He leaned over and brushed stray hair off my cheek with his thumb. "Why wouldn't I? You're cute and feisty. And then there are those claws."

"Which you will never get to feel," I said. "Unless you do something to make me scratch your eyes out."

"You say that now." He looked way too confident.

"Because it's true," I said, just as confident. I glanced at my watch and swore under my breath. "I need to get going. I guess we'll see you on Friday night." I held out my hand again.

This time, he placed my phone on my palm. It was still warm from his groin. For some reason, that was strangely arousing. My device was that close to his cock. That was probably oversized too, like his ego.

I had no intention of finding out. Not with him or any of his friends. I didn't need the distraction, any more than I needed to spend time with guys like that.

My clit throbbed in protest, even after I told her to shut up. She was no help at all.

I took my phone out of his hand, ignoring the way my whole body reacted to the graze of my fingertips over his calloused skin.

Don't be stupid, I told myself. *There's no way you're getting involved with a guy like this.* Even if he was interested, which he wasn't. Men like him were interested in short-term relationships. Nothing more than a night here or there. That wasn't to say I was interested in anything more than that either, but I wasn't going to be some kind of puck bunny. If he wanted someone to bury his cock in, he'd have to find another hole.

"Thanks." I closed my hand over my phone.

"You do have manners, Red," he teased.

"Cat," I corrected.

He snapped his fingers. "Right. Ginger is a better nickname for you then. Ginger Cat."

"If you call me that, I'm going to become a Ginger Snap," I said. "As in, a pissed off redhead."

"That's what I thought you meant." He grinned. "I don't mind if you get pissed off at me. Hate sex is one of my favourite kinds of sex. It's right up there with make up sex."

I suspected he didn't care what kind of sex he had, as long as he had it. I rolled my eyes in response and tucked my phone into my pocket.

"I guess that means I get to call you some ridiculous nickname," I said.

He spread his hands. "Do your worst. I dare you to give me one I haven't heard a million times before." He raised his eyebrows at me.

"I'll think about it," I said. "I'm sure I'll come up with something."

He seemed pleased at the idea. "I can't wait to hear it. I'm sure you're very…creative. You seem like the kind of woman who likes to be unique."

"I am." I rose from my seat. "Now I really have to go. I guess I'll see you on Friday night."

"I'll be counting the days," he said.

"I'm sure you will," I said under my breath. I was counting the days until I won my bet.

5

CATALINA

"Isn't this fun?" Marley asked. She shifted her ass on the seat, trying to get comfortable. In the process, she almost pushed Eden off the side of the bleachers.

"That's exactly why we need an arena." Eden nudged her back over with her hip.

"Or fewer people here," I said. "If you two need more space, I can leave."

Marley grabbed my arm. "No you don't. You're going to stay and enjoy the game with us. Didn't you mention something about making a bet with Easton Grant?"

"I'm starting to regret mentioning that," I said. If I didn't watch, I couldn't say I enjoyed it. Would that mean I won by default? Yeah, okay, of course it didn't. Fine, I'd stick around for a while.

"You regret making a bet with a hot guy who wants to take you out?" Marley asked. "You could have jumped right to going out on a date with him." She fanned herself. Her eyes rolled back like she was swooning.

"Like that would ever happen," I said. "If you want him—"

"Oh no, he asked *you* to go out with him," she said. "Sisters before misters."

"There's no way I'm going out with Easton." I unscrewed the lid of my water and took a sip. "I told you, I hate hockey players. Give me a guy with a regular job any day. Not one who gets treated like a rock star."

"Easton is a carpenter during the day," Eden said helpfully. "Cruz is a car mechanic. Dean Hayes has one of those mobile lawn mowing businesses."

"It's nice to know they have mild-mannered lives outside the rink," I said dryly. "What about the other one, what's his name?" The ridiculously attractive defenceman had given me more sullen looks than the other three combined.

"Shaw Moss," Marley supplied. "I think he's a butcher or something. Something involving sharp knives." She smiled as though somehow that would make him enticing.

"My father works with sharp knives but I don't want to date him either," I said with a grimace.

"He does, doesn't he?" Marley looked thoughtful.

I shoved her with my shoulder. "Marley-Jane Hammond, that's my father we're talking about."

"You brought him into this," she pointed out.

"Let me put him out of it then," I said. The last man I wanted to discuss with my best friends was my father. Especially like *that*.

"What are you going to do if you enjoy the game?" Eden asked. "Are you going to back out of the bet?"

They were both looking at me now, both curious, smiles on their lips. Both absolutely certain how this would end.

"In the unlikely event I enjoy watching a hockey game, I'll follow through," I said. "I'll sit through coffee with him if I have to." No one said I had to go on an actual date, or that I needed to enjoy myself.

"You're welcome to take my place if you want to," I offered. Marley in particular, seemed into him, in spite of what she said.

"Not a chance," Marley said. "But if you have coffee with him, let me know when and where so I can come and sit in the corner and watch."

"I'm starting to think my father needs to find more work for you to do," I told her. "You don't seem to be busy enough."

She sniffed. "I'm definitely busy enough. I'm lucky to get the night off."

"When have you ever worked at night?" Eden asked.

Marley hesitated.

Eden and I laughed.

"That's what I thought," Eden said. "I've never seen

you around Mann Terrace after five o'clock in the afternoon."

Marley crossed her arms over her chest. "Maybe I take my work home."

Before any of us could say anything else, the Ghouls appeared from the locker room and made their way through the crowds, to the ice.

Their competition, the Magpies, followed behind. The Magpies weren't under consideration as an expansion team, but they got a cheer from the crowd regardless.

"The locker room must feel really small with all of those guys in there," Marley said. "Imagine how it will be with the arena. They'll have more than enough space to get ready. And a visitor's locker room. And maybe one for speed skaters." She slid me a sly smile.

I snorted softly. "Even if they did, they'd still think the rink was theirs and not want to share." They'd be worse about that ice than they were about this. On the other hand, if they had their own, they wouldn't need to come here. Maybe I could get behind them after all.

"And maybe you and Easton could have ice skating dates on their fancy new rink." Marley grinned.

"That's as likely as me having a date with Cruz Brewer," I said. "Or any of them." I glanced down to see the left defenceman of the starting line scowling at me. His eyes were narrowed, jaw tight like he was clenching his teeth to keep from leaping up into the stands and wrapping his hands around my throat. Maybe while he fucked me, deep and hard, our bodies sliding against each other…

I shook my head. What was I thinking? Sure, he was hot, but I got the impression he hated me and everything about me, even though he didn't know a thing.

"Especially him," I said firmly. Was I trying to convince them or myself?

I looked back at him and raised my chin as if I wasn't even slightly intimidated. He was a big guy. If he wanted to hurt me, he could. I'd never give him an opportunity.

"He seems to have some unresolved issues," Eden remarked.

I glanced over at her. "Yeah, just a bit." When I looked back at him, he was glaring even harder, clearly aware we were talking about him.

Easton clapped him on the shoulder and grinned up at me. He raised his arm and pointed at me, leaving no one in any doubt who he was looking at.

I felt like everyone in the arena was staring at me. I smirked at him and gave him a small wave.

That made him grin even bigger.

I shook my head at him and caught the look on Cruz's face. The winger was glaring at Easton the same way Shaw glared at me. Like somehow he didn't approve of Easton even *looking* at me. We had that in common, I supposed. Easton was hot, but he should save his glances for the women in the rink who wanted them.

"Isn't that interesting?" Marley said.

"What's that?" I asked.

"It looks like you're on the receiving end of a testosterone bomb." She grinned. "You know, where a bunch of guys fight for your fair affection." She placed a hand under her chin and fluttered her eyelashes. Before pushing her glasses back up her nose.

"I wasn't aware we stepped into a Jane Austen novel," I said dryly. I cleared my throat. "It's a truth universally acknowledged, that a single hockey player in possession of a good fortune, and a cock, must be in want of a willing pussy."

When we all stopped laughing, I said, "None of them are interested in me. Especially Cruz. He's probably annoyed that Easton is talking to me because he hates my guts. He's wondering why he'd want to waste his time with me. That's all there is to it."

"That's not what it looks like to me," Marley said. She glanced over to Eden for backup.

Eden raised her hands. "I'm staying right out of it, but it does look like there's some tension there between them. Whether that has anything to do with Cat or not, is another thing. It could be an underlying situation between them and it could be pressure from this game and the whole expansion thing. With everything going on, I'd expect them to be on edge."

"What she said," I said. "It has nothing to do with me. I'm just an innocent bystander. Someone they had a brief interaction with. The sooner we all forget about it, the better."

I was starting to regret coming here tonight. And making the bet with Easton in the first place. I could have practised earlier in the morning or after work, when they might not be there.

I sighed and looked back towards the ice. Before the goalie, Dean, pulled his mask down over his face, I noticed him watching me too, his eyes intent on my face.

Maybe I was being paranoid. He might be looking at anyone else in the stands. Chances were, that was exactly what was going on. I was jumping to conclusions because of the other guy's glares and my friend's teasing.

"So, we're going for the Magpies, right?" I asked teasingly.

That earned me twin looks of mock outrage.

"Only if you want to be kicked out of Opal Springs," Marley said with a smile.

"And subjected to years of therapy to cure you of your traitorous behaviour," Eden teased.

I threw my hand up in surrender, narrowly missing knocking Marley's drink out of her hand.

"Fine, I'll cheer on the Ghouls if I have to. Or at least, I won't boo them too loudly." I ducked to the side to avoid Marley's shoulder when she tried to shove hers into mine.

"If you boo them, I don't think I can be seen with

you in public again," she teased. "In fact, maybe I shouldn't anyway, just in case."

"Whatever happened to sisters before misters?" I asked with a laugh.

"They're not misters, they're a hockey team," Eden pointed out. "You know what they say, hockey before... something." She shrugged.

I laughed again. "I don't think there's any saying that hockey is more important than anything else."

In Melbourne, I met plenty of people who thought that way. Although, just as many who considered the various codes of football, or sports like cricket, to be more important than breathing. Sports had a way of drawing enthusiastic fans, who followed them for life, more obsessive and passionate than any rock band. Even ones as popular as Wolf Venom and Ice Blue Roses. Not to mention my personal favourites, Blazing Violet.

"Besides, it's not as exciting as ice racing." Not that I was biased at all. I adored everything about my sport. The speed, the rush, the feeling of ice under my skates, the surge of adrenaline at every bend. There was nothing else like it.

"That's what you say now, but wait until you've watched a full game," Marley said. "You might be convinced to swap your speed skates for a pair of ice hockey skates."

"Not a chance," I said. "And before you say it, I'm not going to bet on it." I'd already learned my lesson about betting on my enjoyment of things. I had a feeling the bet with Easton was going to come back and bite me on the ass.

"There's no reason why you can't enjoy both," Eden said easily. "Why choose one sport when you can enjoy a bunch of them?"

"You're not going to try to talk me into playing lawn bowls or darts, are you?" I asked.

She smiled. "Both of those are great fun. Very relaxing. You might enjoy them as a way to unwind."

"I don't think Cat knows how to unwind," Marley said. "Can you imagine her playing a relaxing sport?"

Eden leaned forward and looked over at me. "You have a point. But everyone should have a relaxing hobby or pastime. Something to unwind at the end of a long day."

"That's what reading is for," I said. "But I know you two are going to drag me out to the pub after the game, so I may try darts just for shits and giggles." I might pretend the dartboard was Shaw or Cruz, and that the bull's-eye was the space between their eyes.

Maybe Eden had a point about hobbies. That sounded both relaxing and cathartic. I could print out a picture of one of them and pin it up over the board, just for fun. They'd probably do the same with a picture of me.

An air horn sounded the start of the game.

6
CATALINA

"I told you that wouldn't suck," Marley said. "Don't try saying you didn't enjoy yourself. I saw you bouncing up and down and cheering along with the rest of us."

"I was *not* bouncing up and down," I protested. "I was…moving around to get comfortable."

My friends turned back to grin at me before they stepped through the doorway into O'Reilly's. I shrugged and followed them in.

The most popular pub in town, the owners modelled the exterior and interior on a classic Irish pub. The tables were all sturdy timber, the upholstery on the seats a deep green. Several bar attendants hurried up and down the long bar, serving the quickly growing crowd.

We grabbed our drinks and slipped into a booth to the side of the pub.

"Okay, it wasn't that bad," I admitted. "I might have enjoyed myself."

Marley grinned triumphantly. "See, I knew it. It's exciting, isn't it? The Ghouls played so well. Especially Easton and Cruz." She gave me a knowing look over her vodka and orange.

"I guess they did." I reluctantly appreciated the way the two forwards worked together. As far as I could tell, their alternates were exceptional players, but when the pair was on the ice, everyone was on the edge of their seats. By the end of the first period, I was starting to look forward to the shift change. My opinion about them was no different after watching them play, but I couldn't deny their skill.

"You guess so," Eden teased lightly. "That last goal that Cruz got on Easton's assist was unreal. The Magpies' goalie was so sure they weren't getting past him."

"Right." Marley was the one bouncing up and down in her seat now. "Then bam, biscuit in the basket."

I grinned at her enthusiasm. "Fine, it was exciting." I might have held my breath, watching the way they moved on the ice, their stick control, the way they were always aware of each other and the puck.

Speed skating was an individual sport, but I always had to be aware of my competitors around me. A momentary lapse in concentration could cause a collision. That could lead to injury, like the one to my knee.

"So, why do you really hate hockey players?" Eden

asked. "You don't have to answer if you don't want to, but I'm sensing it's more than interacting with them in the rink." She always was too perceptive for her own good.

I sighed into my cola. "I went out with one for a while, back in Melbourne. I thought things were going well until I hurt my knee."

I glanced down at the worn, scratched tabletop. "He went from burning hot to ice cold overnight. Like, I don't know, somehow he thought I'd be a burden because I was injured."

I looked back up. "He claimed he got busy. He *was* busy, too busy to bother with me." I shrugged one shoulder. Dealing with the injury, surgery and rehab, I could have used Jason's support. By the time I was wheeled out of the operating theatre, he'd moved on to someone else.

"Oh, Cat, I'm so sorry," Marley said, her eyes full of sympathy. "What an asshole. You're so much better than him, and you deserve better." She nodded decisively, like only a best friend can.

"Anyone who can't offer support to their partner at a time of need, sucks ass," Eden agreed. "It's not surprising you'd be reluctant to jump into another relationship. That kind of situation can be difficult to recover from, especially when you're dealing with your own obstacles, like your knee."

"Has anyone told you sound like a shrink?" Marley teased.

Eden grinned, her eyes sparkling. "Only every day. I look like an emo, and sound like Freud." She seemed absolutely content with that. She knew who she was better than anyone I ever met. She'd say it was a façade, but if anyone had their shit together better than Eden, I didn't know who they were. I loved her for it. I'd like to be like her when I grew up.

"You're adorable," I assured her. "You both are. I don't know what I'd do without you." I sucked in a breath and plunged on. "I was worried about coming back here to Opal Springs. What would people think? What would they say? But you two have been nothing but supportive and amazing." I blinked away the prickle in my eyes before they became full-blown waterworks.

"If anyone says anything bad about you, I'll stab them in the eye with a toothpick," Marley declared. "Or better yet, a scalpel. I'm sure your dad wouldn't mind if I borrowed one for that. It's a good cause." She raised her hand and made a stabbing motion. The kind that also looked like a guy jacking off.

I smiled. "Please don't go stabbing people in the eyeball for me. I'm a big girl, I can deal with people saying whatever. Let them. I'll prove them wrong when I'm standing on the blocks at the Winter Olympics, waiting to accept my gold medal."

A quiver passed through me. I pictured myself standing there, the cheers of the crowds, the officials ready to drape that ribbon around my neck. It was so real I could almost feel it, almost taste it. I wanted it so badly it hurt.

"You'll get there," Eden said. "No one will be cheering you on louder than Marley and me. We'll cheer louder than we did for the Ghouls tonight."

"Yes, we will," Marley said. "We can practice right now if you like." She put down her drink and placed her hands on the table like she was about to stand.

I grabbed her arm to keep her down. "Please don't. I appreciate the sentiment, but I get the idea. Save it for that day. Or at least when things get busier and louder in here." I gestured around the pub with a swirl of my finger. "No one will notice when they're all drunk."

Marley flopped back with a huff of air. "Fine. When everyone is drunk, they'll join in. That'll make it more fun anyway." She picked her drink up and toasted me with it. "So when are we getting to the elephant in the room?"

I was wondering that myself, but hoping they'd forgotten. "There's an elephant in O'Reilly's?" I asked innocently. "Is it pink?"

"Ha ha," Marley replied. "I'm talking about you and Easton. You made a bet, are you going to follow through with it? I mean, I hate to remind you, but I think we can all agree you lost. "

"I don't think you hate to remind me at all," I said. "In fact, I think you're enjoying yourself." I rolled my eyes playfully towards the ceiling beam above our booth. It was made of the same timber as the bar, and added to the atmosphere.

She laughed. "You know me too well. "I'm absolutely enjoying myself, but only because you enjoyed yourself. If you were bored out of your mind, I would have felt bad for dragging you along to the game."

"Evading the question won't stop you from having to answer it," Eden said. "Are you going out with him?" After what I told them about Jason, she seemed a lot more understanding of why I might decide to back out. If I did, she wouldn't judge me.

Of course, I'd judge myself. One of the things my father ingrained in me was the importance of sportsmanship. Never be a poor winner or a bad loser. Whatever happens, stay classy. I had every intention of doing just that. After all, what could one little date hurt? It wasn't like we were getting married or even sleeping with each other. Just a couple of friends having a drink together, that was all.

"I said I would," I said. "And I will. If he still wants to, that is. He might have decided not to." Why did that bother me so much? Easton was as cocky and arrogant as they came. He reminded me of Jason.

Now the comparison was in my mind, I realised there were significant differences between them. Easton was more sure of himself. Jason was arrogant, but at the same time he was insecure. It wasn't something I'd realised until after we broke up. I suspected my injury reminded him of his own vulnerability. If I could hurt my knee, then he could do something to himself that would end his hockey career. He wasn't naïve to the possibility, but I guessed that brought it home to him somehow.

Ironically, I wouldn't even wish injury on him. Not on anyone else either. Nothing sucked more than having your own body get in the way of your dreams. In spite of the way we ended, I wanted him to succeed. Although, if the Ghouls went professional and kicked his team's ass, I wouldn't cry too hard. I might cheer a little too loud though. Yeah, that was petty, but the asshole did break my heart.

"I don't think you're going to get out of it that easily," Eden said. "We saw the way he looked at you before and after the game."

After his assist and the winning goal, he'd found me in the audience and grinned. He even gave me a small salute. I might have smiled back at him. A smile which faded when both Cruz and Shaw glared at him and me. Shaw in particular looked like he wanted to use his stick on me. His hockey stick, that was.

I'd returned their glares until all three players turned away. Their momentary lapse in concentration didn't stop them from winning with a score of five goals to two.

I shrugged. "He could have been looking at anyone."

"We all know who he was looking at," Marley said. "Easton Grant has the hots for you. And I've decided I have the hots for Cole Davies, the right defenceman.

He has the most grabable ass I've ever seen." She sighed.

"They're hockey players, they all have grabable asses," Eden said. "It comes with the territory." She nodded over to the pool tables off to the side of the pub. Jagger Sanderson, the Ghouls centre, and his alternate, Mitch Ward, were playing a friendly game of pool. Jagger was leaning over the table, cue in hand, ass facing the room.

"I see your point," I said. "We won't mind if you go and talk to either of them."

"I was thinking both of them," Eden said lightly. "A girl has to have some ambition." She sipped her rum and cola and wiggled her eyebrows.

"Good for you, girl," Marley said approvingly. "Why stick to one when you can have two? Or three. Or four. Five. Or—"

"We get the idea," I said. "Lots and lots of men."

"Exactly," she said. "Look at you, for example. That would stop all of those guys fighting over you. Who says you have to choose just one?"

"I don't plan on choosing any of them," I reminded her. What would it be like to be with guys like that? I couldn't say I wasn't curious, but no doubt it would be complicated, a lot of work and need a shit ton of careful communication. Although, if it worked out, the support system would be amazing. I'd never be alone to wallow, if my knee ultimately put me out of contention for the Olympic team.

I shouldn't be thinking like this. I should be thinking positively. I *would* make the team. What was it they said? Failure was not an option.

A shadow loomed over the table, breaking my thoughts.

"Hey."

I looked up as Easton slid into the seat next to me.

7
CATALINA

I turned to Easton and nodded a greeting, keeping my expression neutral. "My phone is safe in my pocket." Just in case he tried to take it from me again.

He grinned. "Good to know." He leaned in to whisper in my ear. "I don't mind touching your ass to get at it."

His close proximity sent a shiver through me. Warm, smooth breath brushed my earlobe. His voice sent a pulse of heat straight to my clit, reminding me she was a traitor and couldn't be trusted.

"I bet you wouldn't," I said knowingly.

He leaned back and grinned again. A dimple popped in his left cheek, and for the first time I noticed one in his chin. It was completely unfair for a guy to be as good-looking as he was.

I reminded myself that he was also obnoxious, and

took a cooling sip of cola that did almost nothing to slow the rush of blood around my body.

"I came over here to work out the details of our date." He rested his elbow on the table and supported his cheek with his fist. "I'm sure you've filled your friends in on our bet."

"They know about it." I glanced at Eden and Marley, who were both trying to look like they weren't invested in the conversation. "You seem very confident that you won."

"Sweetheart, I *know* I won," he said. "I saw you watching the game, enjoying every minute. And looking super cute the whole time."

My face heated.

"It was okay," I said as easily as I could manage. "I can think of worse ways to spend a Friday night." Like sitting at home alone watching romcoms and feeling very single.

Easton's brow crinkled in a slight but playful frown. "It seems like we need some independent adjudication here." He turned to Eden and Marley. "Would you lovely ladies say Cat had a good time? Be honest now." He gestured at them to go ahead and take the proverbial floor.

"I'd have to say, after careful consideration, Cat did indeed have a good time," Marley said slowly. "I'd go as far as to say she'd watch another game. With some time and effort, she may count herself as a fan of ice hockey."

"Let's not go crazy here," I said.

Easton gestured to Eden. "What do you think? Would you agree with this assessment?" A smile tugged at the corners of his lips at the pretend formality.

Eden looked at me, then back at him before she nodded. "I have to admit Marley's assessment is accurate. Catalina did indeed enjoy watching you play hockey."

"Watching me?" Easton looked smugly pleased at her wording.

"Watching your *team*," I said. "You're just a part of it."

"An important part of it," he said. "However, the conclusion from our independent panel is that you liked what you saw and therefore, I won the bet. So all there is left to do is fix a time and place."

"Eden, I need to go to the toilet. Come with me." Marley grabbed Eden's hand and all but pulled her out of their side of the booth.

Eden glanced back at me to make sure I was all right, before letting herself get tugged away.

"They seem nice," Easton said.

"Are you saying that because you think it, or because they agreed with you?" I asked. They were about as subtle as a falling boulder.

"Both." He shrugged one shoulder. "A person can never have too many honest friends who have their back."

"I'm sure you have lots of friends who have your back," I said. "Which makes me wonder why you want to see this bet through. If you want to walk away right now, I won't mind." He couldn't say I hadn't given him an out.

"Why would I want to?" He seemed genuinely curious.

"I saw the looks you got from your teammates," I said. "Cruz and Shaw, in particular. I know Cruz hates my guts and Shaw seems to, too. I wouldn't want to cause any trouble with you and them. I know how important it is to you that the Ghouls become an expansion team for the league."

"Don't worry about them," Easton said lightly. "They just need to get over themselves. When they get to know you, they'll realise you're actually nice, and not a stuck up, snobby bitch."

I winced. "Ouch." I didn't care if they didn't like me, or even what they said about me, but the idea anyone might think I was like that stung. I was intense when it came to my sport, but I tried to be laid-back outside of that. I certainly wasn't a snob.

"Like I said, they'll get over themselves. I love that you're aware of the importance of the Ghouls to Opal Springs. You've been talking about me." His gaze lingered on my face, dropping to my lips before returning to my eyes.

"My friends filled me in after my…conversation with Cruz at the rink the other day," I said. "In fact, I think it would be fair to say we were talking about him, not you."

Easton grinned. "Ouch. I don't get the impression

you were saying anything nice about him, so in this case, I'll let it slide. For what it's worth, he's driven and committed to the team. To the exclusion of pretty much everyone and everything else."

"I can relate to that," I admitted. "I feel that way when I'm training. Nothing else exists in the whole world. Just me and the ice and…" I trailed off. I was probably over sharing.

"And the ice and?" he prompted. "Go on." His attention was focused completely on me, like I was the only person in the room with him.

When was the last time a guy looked at me like that? Long enough. It was compelling, and difficult not to look back at him in the same way.

"I was going to say, 'and my ambition to skate in the Winter Olympics,'" I admitted.

"Why would you not own an ambition like that?" he asked. "I mean, ice hockey player here." He gestured to himself. "I'd be lying to myself if I didn't say I also wanted to make the Winter Olympics. Standing up there, getting a gold medal in front of the world." He smiled, a dreamy look with slightly glazed eyes.

"Exactly," I said softly. "I want that. I want all of that." I wasn't used to talking about this with people I didn't know well. Not unless they were other speed skaters. Most people didn't understand the sport, or weren't interested. That was their loss, as far as I was concerned.

"Figure skating?" he asked. That was always everyone's first guess when the topic arose.

"Short track speed skating," I replied. I'd tried figure skating, a long time ago, but I didn't have the finesse for it. It didn't get my blood racing the way speed skating did.

His eyes widened. "Ice racing?" He seemed genuinely impressed. "That's fucking cool. I used to do a bit of that when I was a kid, but I preferred to chase the puck around with a stick. It's full on, but I fucking love it."

"You get a break every minute or so," I said lightly. They were on again and off again so quickly and so often it was challenging to keep track.

He snorted a laugh. "Your races aren't much longer than that. We have to get back on after that next minute is over. It's hectic."

"It looks like it," I admitted. "You must not know if you're coming or going sometimes."

He grinned. "Sweetheart, I always know when I'm coming."

I groaned. I should have known how he'd respond to that. Of course, now I was picturing him lying over me, thrusting into my body, eyes half closed as he orgasmed.

"Let me guess, you have to let the whole world know?" I raised an eyebrow at him.

"Just the person I'm with," he said. "But I like to make a woman scream." The meaningful look he gave me made my panties wet. He definitely looked like the sort of guy who knew how to make a girl feel good.

I reminded myself that I wasn't getting involved with him or any of his friends, no matter what happened. Just one date, that was it. We could be friends after, but nothing else.

"I'm sure you do," I said, suddenly awkward.

"So, about our date." His eyes dropped, gaze lingering on my cleavage for a moment before returning to my face.

"I was thinking we could meet at the café for morning tea," I said.

"No way," he replied. "We're having a proper date. Dinner and a movie. I'll even let you pick the movie. And if you're lucky, breakfast the next morning."

I rolled my eyes. "If I'm lucky?"

Once again, he was grinning. "You're right, if we're both lucky." He leaned in. "I'm always lucky. By the time we walk out of the cinema, you'll be ready to jump my bones."

"You're a cocky prick, aren't you?" I asked. It wasn't an accusation, just a statement of fact. One I suspected he'd happily admit to.

"Yes. Yes I am," he said with absolutely no hint of shame. "Don't tell me you think there's something wrong with being confident. Because there isn't. I'm attracted to you. I know you're attracted to me. We already have things in common. Skating, and the fact we both want me to give you orgasms. Lots and lots of orgasms."

If I wasn't wet before, I was now. Yeah, he knew exactly the effect he had on me. That made him dangerous. Maybe I'd let myself go and sleep with him, but I couldn't fall for him or any of his teammates. That was nothing more than a recipe for heartache. I wasn't letting myself go through that again. I had to guard my heart like it was a vault full of gold medals.

"Give me your phone." He held out his hand.

"What for?" I asked. What was it with this guy and my phone? I hadn't pulled it out of my pocket since before the game.

"So I can put my number in there and text you what time I'm picking you up. And so you can text me your address." He wiggled his fingers for me to hurry up.

"I can meet you there," I protested. "Just tell me where or when."

"Like I said, this is a real date," he said. "I'm going to pick you up and give you the royal treatment. Everything a princess deserves."

"I'm not a princess." I grimaced, remembering Cruz and the way he called me that, trying to taunt me. It was only slightly better than Ginger.

"Maybe not, but you'll feel like one by the time I'm done with you." He took my phone when I handed it to him and programmed in his number. He even took a selfie to go with it. Instead of giving it back, he started to tap the screen, a slight frown on his forehead.

"What are you doing?" I asked.

"Setting a ringtone, so when I call you, you'll know it's me," he said. He finally handed my phone back and pulled out his own. He tapped on the screen to put my number in his phone, then pressed again.

The phone rang in my hand, playing *We Are the Champions* at high volume.

I laughed. "That's a very hopeful ringtone." Not to mention being one of the inspirational songs I played when I worked out. That and *Champion* by Carrie Underwood.

"I thought it was more subtle than something about having a big dick." He tapped his phone screen to end the call.

"I'm surprised you can do subtle," I said.

"I can sometimes," he said. "When you ring me, it's going to play *Ride Me*, by Blazing Violet."

"Who says I'm going to call you?" I asked.

His only response was to smile.

8

EASTON

"What the fuck?" Shaw snapped. "What are you doing?"

He stood in the doorway of my room, hands in fists at his sides, glaring at me. I'd heard him turn up at the front door to the house Cruz and I shared, to talk to Cruz about something. I figured if it was something to do with the team, Cruz would fill me in later.

I shrugged and turned back to the mirror. "What does it look like? I'm getting ready for my date with Cat."

"Why are you going out with her?" He stepped into the room, broad shoulders tense. "Is it that stupid bet?"

I started to button down my dark blue shirt. "What else would it be about? I'm looking forward to taking everyone's money."

"You're going to fuck her," he stated.

I turned back to him and grinned. "That's the idea. Get laid, get money. What more is there to life?" I looked back at my reflection and pushed the last three buttons into their holes.

"You don't like her." Shaw stalked in and flopped down on my bed. As teammates went, he wasn't bad, but he was wound up hard so much of the time.

"What's 'like' got to do with it?" I ran my fingers through my hair to give it a more 'just fucked' look. "We're going to eat dinner, watch a movie and then get naked and sweaty together. I don't have to like her for any of that to happen."

For some reason, my words seemed to make him angrier. His teeth were gritted, eyes like chips of stone.

"Are you sure you don't want in on the bet?" I asked. "I'm sure Cruz—"

"I don't want in on your stupid fucking bet," Shaw snapped. "I don't give a shit what you do with your dick, but why her?"

"Why not her?" I asked.

"Her who?" Cruz stopped in the doorway and peered inside. "You got a date, bro?"

"With Catalina Ryan," Shaw said.

Cruz narrowed his eyes. "The fuck? Why?"

"That's what I want to know," Shaw said. "Last week it was Courtney. The week before it was Chenay. Or was it Melissah?" His brow creased in thought. "Any of them are better than Princess bitch."

"What he said," Cruz agreed. "Just because we made a bet doesn't mean you're expected to date the woman."

"That right there is everything that's wrong with

your love life." I smirked. "You just want to get laid, you don't want to get to know a woman first."

They barked matching laughs.

"Since when do you want to get to know a woman?" Cruz asked. "You're all about fuck them and leave them too."

"A guy can change," I argued.

"You do like her," Shaw accused. "Otherwise, why would you bother?" He gestured towards my outfit as if I was wearing a tuxedo or some shit.

"Jealousy is a curse," I told him. "You wish you could look as good as this." I flexed dramatically, hoping to lighten the mood. No way in hell was I going to admit I liked Cat.

Whether I did or not didn't matter. This was a one time thing. Dinner, movie, fuck. I'd win the bet and go on ignoring her like the rest of the guys did.

Although, there seemed to be a lot more glaring than ignoring. They all needed to admit they wanted her bouncing on their cocks as much as I did. There was something about her. She could easily get under my skin. Not that I'd let her. Screwing her would help to get her out of my system.

The trials for the Winter Olympics were in a couple of months. She'd be gone before then and none of us would see her again except on TV.

Why did that thought piss me off? I didn't know, but it did. I'd think about that more later.

"Fuck off," Shaw said. "I look better than that when I get out of bed in the morning."

"Alone," I said.

Cruz chuckled. "He's got you there, bro."

"What the hell?" Shaw turned to him. "Don't you start, asshole."

Cruz held up his hands to either side. "Just stating a fact. When was the last time you got laid?"

"None of your business." Shaw shoved himself up off the bed and stalked towards the doorway.

"Hey," Cruz said before he left. "Save your aggression for the ice. That's where we need it, not here."

Shaw flipped him off over his shoulder and stomped away.

"Maybe you should go a bit easier on him," I suggested. "He clearly has shit going on."

"He's had shit going on since we met," Cruz said. He flopped down where Shaw was just sitting. "We all have. I'm fucked if I'm letting it get in the way of our future. If he or anyone else screws it up for the Ghouls, they're gonna answer to my fists."

"Mine too," I agreed.

I sat beside him. "Are you really that pissed off I'm going on a date with Cat?"

"Are you going to call it off if I am?" he asked.

I grinned. "No. You might as well open your wallet now and hand your money over. I've good as won. You haven't even started."

He smirked. "Not that you know of. You think

you're all over this, but I guarantee she's thinking about me."

"And hating your guts," I said.

"There's a fine line between hate and lust." He leaned back on his elbows. "Last chance to change your mind and stay home instead." His gaze lingered on me.

I swallowed.

His eyes dipped to my throat, watching while my Adam's apple bobbed.

"I don't know if…" I started slowly.

"Yeah." He shook his head and sat back up before he rose to his feet. "Let me know if you figure it out."

"Yeah," I echoed. "You'll be the second to know, after me."

He stood in the doorway, his back to me for a few long moments before turning around. His usual smug-as-fuck hockey god expression was back on his face.

"Enjoy your date, Easty-boy. If she lets you get into her pants, remember one thing. She'll be thinking about me the whole time. No doubt wishing you were me." He grinned.

I grinned back, relieved the mood was lighter again. "Keep telling yourself that, my friend. When I'm the one balls deep inside her, the only person she's going to be thinking about is me."

I pulled my ute up in front of Cat's house and killed the engine. The vehicle was a bit of a shit heap, but Cruz kept her running for now. Until the day we could all afford something better. By then, I wouldn't need a vehicle to keep tools and wood. I might buy another big ute anyway, I liked the way they drove.

In summer, I'd settle for a car with working airconditioning. No one said being a chippie was glamorous. It was a good workout when I couldn't get to the gym or onto the ice, but I wouldn't miss it.

I slipped out of the cab and strode to the front door. At this point, I have to admit I looked up to check she gave me the right address. She seemed like the kind of girl who'd do something like that. Or give a guy the wrong phone number just to get him to go away.

Of course, it was the right address, and the ego boost didn't hurt.

I tapped on the door and stood back. The doorframe was a little worn, sections coming away from the brick beside it. If they were lucky, I might offer to fix it for them. It wouldn't take long and it would make the house more secure.

Although, this was the nicer part of Opal Springs. Where I grew up, the door would have been kicked in long ago, the house ransacked and covered in graffiti.

I did my best to push the shit thoughts away. That wasn't me anymore. It never would be again. That was one thing Cruz and I agreed on. We'd worked our way up from nothing, and we'd do everything we could to make sure no kid had to live like that in this town.

The door swung open slowly. "You're here to pick up my daughter?" Doctor Ryan looked me up and down, scrutinising carefully.

I smiled warmly. "That's right. We have a date." I was not going to be intimidated by Cat's father. I sure as hell wasn't going to remind myself he had skills and sharp implements at his disposable if I did anything to his daughter. So did I. I always kept a hammer in my ute, for one thing. Not to mention a bunch of other tools and nails. I was also around half his age and fit.

"Easton Grant, isn't it?" He made no move to invite me inside.

"The one and only." His scrutiny was starting to make me uneasy.

"I probably delivered you." With a grunt he finally stepped aside to let me in.

What was I supposed to say to that? "Thanks. I appreciate it."

He snorted a laugh. Apparently he was amused at making me visibly uncomfortable. That must be where Cat got it from.

"Good game the other night," he said.

Now that was a subject I could talk about all day. My smile was more genuine now. "Thanks. The season is feeling really good. No reason the AIHL won't choose us as an expansion team."

"They better," he said. "I have money riding on you. The team, not you in particular."

"We're a safe bet," I said. Gambling on various things was somewhat of a pastime in Opal Springs. Okay, in Australia in general, but here in particular. What would he think if he knew I made a bet on his daughter? I suspected he wouldn't be particularly impressed if he found out, which he wouldn't.

I wasn't going to be deterred either way. This wasn't about him. This was about Cat and my cock. He'd probably made similar bets in his day. Maybe he still did. He was popular in town, almost as popular as the Ghouls. I'd seen women swoon over him.

"That's what the whole town is hoping," he said. To my surprise he added, "Don't fuck it up."

I grinned. "We won't. You'll kick our asses if we do."

"Definitely," he said. He stepped towards the door leading out of the room. Before he left he said, "Don't do anything I wouldn't do. And do it safely."

I had a sneaking suspicion nothing got past him. Of course, I was a guy and Cat was a babe. Why wouldn't I want to screw her?

"Always," I assured him.

He grunted and left the room.

Left alone for a few moments, I glanced around. Unlike the exterior of the house, the furniture was relatively new and modern. Each piece looked like it came from an inner city Melbourne townhouse which it probably had. Everything was a bit too big and a bit too fancy for the space. Comfortable, but without looking permanent. Of course, they probably intended to return to Melbourne some time soon.

I picked up a photo from a side table. It was of Doctor Ryan and Cat. A woman stood behind him, and a younger girl beside her. Her mother and her sister, I presumed. The family resemblance was strong. Her mother was a babe too.

"She died a few months after that," Cat said softly.

I hadn't heard her enter the room, but she stood a few metres away from me now. She wore a black dress that fell to just above her knees. Her hair was tied back in a ponytail. She only wore a slight touch of make-up, which enhanced her eyes and cheekbones. If her father wasn't close by, I'd take her over to the couch and fuck her there and then.

"You look beautiful," I said. "I'm sorry about your mother."

"It was a long time ago," she said. "I still miss her, but it's not as raw as it used to be. You know?"

I didn't really know, but I placed the photo back on the table, and said, "Yeah. My mother is still alive, but I never knew my father. Seems like another thing we have in common."

Her eyes lingered on the photo for a moment before looking up at me. "You look nice."

"Just nice?" I asked. I snapped my fingers. "I knew I should have worn a suit."

"Next time," she teased. At least, I thought she was teasing.

"Next time?" I raised my eyebrows. "We haven't had this date and you're already planning a next time?" I gave her my best cocky grin. Maybe I shouldn't rush too fast with her. Cats like to play with their prey. Maybe I could play with her. It would be fun for shits and giggles.

I offered her my arm. "Let's go."

9
CATALINA

"When you said 'restaurant,' this wasn't what I was picturing," I admitted.

"You were expecting fish and chips?" Easton teased.

"Well..." I shot him a cagey look across the table.

He laughed. "I would never take a woman to a fish and chip shop on a first date."

I smiled. "That's definitely third or fourth date stuff."

"At least." He looked uneasy for a moment. "Is this okay? You're probably used to fancier than Penny's."

"Not really," I said. "I don't go out to eat that often. I've always liked this place though. It's very Opal Springs."

I thought he'd be pleased at my response, but he seemed irritated for some reason. It only lasted for half a moment, before he was smiling again.

"It definitely is. When the Ghouls go pro, I'll be able to afford better than this place."

"I'm paying for myself," I said firmly. I got the feeling this was about more than where he brought me. "You seem uncomfortable here. Would you prefer to go to O'Reilly's?"

His jaw clenched and he chewed on his thoughts for a moment. "When I was a kid, this place seemed like… Like luxury. Only rich people could afford to eat here." He exhaled half a breath. "I thought only rich people could eat at Penny's."

He let out the other half of his breath and looked like he expected me to laugh at him, but I nodded.

"It's all relative," I said. "My parents were both doctors, but they had me and my sister not long after leaving uni. We didn't have much when I was little. My mother used to refuse to buy food, even from a café. She used to say we have plenty of ingredients at home and could go and eat there. I thought she was being mean. It wasn't until years later I realised we couldn't afford it. So yeah, I get it."

He stared at me, then seemed to shove away his dark mood. His usual smile was back on his lips if not in his eyes.

"That's something else we have in common. I guess that's why we're both so determined to succeed. We have those memories of missing out on things and won't ever let ourselves go back to that again."

"No we won't," I agreed. I picked up my menu and started to read.

"Can I ask you something?" He also held his menu, but lowered it to raise his eyebrows at me.

"That depends," I said. "On what you want to ask."

"Is it true you're a qualified vet?"

I shrugged one shoulder. "Yeah. After I finish my clinical hours and final exams. Why? Do you have an animal that needs treatment?"

He grinned. "I know a few of them. Cruz, Shaw, Dean, Jagger…"

I laughed. "They're more my father's kinds of animals."

Easton laughed too. "The reason I'm asking is because I'm wondering why you skate? Why not stick to taking care of animals?"

"Why not stick to hammering nails?" I asked back. "Why play ice hockey?"

He frowned briefly. "Because hockey can take me places being a chippie can't. Carpentry got me out of the hole I grew up in, but it can't do for me what hockey can. It can't do for the community what the Ghouls can. But being a vet is better for the community than ice racing."

A prickle of annoyance travelled through me. "I won't be skating forever. Not on the world stage anyway. You know how it feels to get out on the ice and compete, it's addictive. So is caring for animals, but dogs and cats don't make my blood race. I'm passionate about animals, but racing is like nothing else. I want the hit I get from it, for as long as I can."

"I can think of one cat that makes my blood race," he said smoothly. "How long will you keep racing?"

"Until I can't anymore," I said. "Then I'd like to open my own clinic and work for myself. Maybe skate for fun on the weekends." My face was warm and probably pink from his words. He was making my heart race faster than I expected he could. He was right when he said I was attracted to him. How could I not be? He was a good looking, athletic, charming guy. One who knew all the right things to say.

I glanced down at the menu. "You won the bet. I guess that means you won't ask the team to stay out of my way when I'm practising."

"I'll still do that," he said. "Even though you lost, it seems like the right thing to do."

Did he really mean that? Either way, I was going to accept.

"If you can do that, I'll appreciate it," I said. "I only ask for the time I paid for. Nothing unreasonable."

"Right." Something passed over his face, but once again he quickly rallied back to his smile.

"Are you getting shit from your teammates for this?" I nodded down to the menu. I had it narrowed down to the quiche, but couldn't decide between the spinach or the bacon. They both sounded delicious.

"Nothing I can't handle," he said lightly. "Just a bit of petty jealousy, that's all."

"Jealous of me or you?" I teased. "Are you guys close?"

There it was again, a hint of unease or something I couldn't put my finger on.

"Sometimes," he said. "When they're not being assholes."

"So, rarely," I said dryly.

He chuckled. "Basically. You have them pegged pretty quickly, don't you?" He didn't seem annoyed by that. Did I imagine a slight emphasis on the word pegged?

"I like to keep an open mind, but when you get glared at for long enough, you have to come to some kind of conclusion. I don't want to get between you and them, but I'm not going to let them worry me either." I had no time in my day to deal with assholes and people who caused trouble. I liked Easton, but I didn't want to complicate either of our lives.

"Definitely don't be worried about them," he said. "Sooner or later, they'll pull their heads out of their asses. And don't worry about me. Like I said, it's nothing I can't handle."

The server came to take our orders and the menus, and leave a jug of water and two glasses on the table.

"I didn't figure you for a quiche person," I remarked.

"After you ordered it, I thought that sounded good so I'd have some too." He shrugged. "I would have preferred the bacon version. But—" he patted his flat stomach, "I have to keep my figure."

I hummed. "Curious. If you asked me, I would have thought you were the kind of guy who enjoyed another half hour in the gym to make up for eating bacon."

"Because that's what you do?" he asked. "Rather than denying yourself something yummy, that maybe you couldn't have as a kid?" He raised an eyebrow at me.

"Now who has who pegged?" I used the word deliberately to see his reaction.

He swallowed hard. "I'm a good judge of character." His voice was slightly higher on the first couple of words. "You might not agree, given some of the characters I fraternise with."

I laughed. "You said it, not me."

He shook his finger at me. "I'm starting to think I need to be careful what I say around you. I might end up with them biting me in the ass."

He lowered his hand to the table. "For the record, I don't mind if you want to bite my ass. Or lick or suck. I am down for pretty much anything. In fact, if you want to go under the table while we wait for our food and—" He stopped in the middle of his sentence, his lips apart, smiling slightly and side eyed a server as they walked past the table.

I held back a laugh until the server was safely away, in the back of the restaurant. "Polish your shoes?" I asked sweetly.

He laughed too and leaned forward. "I'd prefer you to polish my cock with your mouth."

"I had a feeling that's what you meant," I whispered.

Our faces were close together, breath mingled, sending tingles up and down my spine. "You really are forward."

"Sweetheart, you were the one who pointed out I go after what I want and deal with the consequences later. Life is too short not to live every minute of it as hard and fast and messy as possible." His voice was a low, husky growl.

I couldn't ignore the effect he had on me and my clit certainly couldn't. I looked him right in the eye and said, "I'm not bacon."

"I bet you taste even better," he whispered. "That's what I'm going to be thinking about through the rest of dinner and the movie. How delicious your pussy is going to taste."

It was my turn to swallow hard.

Before I could say anything further, the server appeared with our meals. We jumped apart like a pair of guilty teenagers and let him place plates in front of us.

We both shared a smile before thanking the server and starting to eat.

10
CATALINA

"That was nice." We stepped out the front door of the restaurant, back onto the street. The evening air was cold, carrying a hint of winter. Just the way I liked it. Give me snow and mountains over beaches and heat any day.

"It was." Easton slipped his hand into mine. "Are you sure you want to see a movie?"

His fingers were warm around mine, large and calloused. The kind you'd expect from a guy who works with his hands.

"You said it wasn't a real date without a movie," I reminded him.

He shrugged and said "I did say that, but I'm flexible. We could do something else if you want?"

"I don't know, what do you have in mind?" I should probably know better than to ask, but he had me curious.

"If you trust me, I know a place." He led me over to his ute and unlocked the doors. He opened mine and helped me inside before walking around and climbing into the driver's seat.

"I don't know if I know you well enough to trust you, but I'm game," I said.

He glanced over at me and grinned. "Of course you are. Don't worry, I'm not going to take you out into the forest and throw you into a shallow grave."

"I wasn't thinking that until you brought it up." I made a face at him. "Now I'm wondering if I should get out." I put my hand on the door handle as if I was about to push it open.

He started the engine and peeled the vehicle away from the curb. "Looks like you're going to have to trust me."

I moved my hand from the door to the handle above it, holding on as he took the corner a bit too fast. "I think you missed your calling. You should have been a race car driver."

He laughed. "I like things fast."

"I figured that out about you," I said. Fast cars, fast ice skates, fast women. He might be in trouble when the Ghouls went professional. Guys like that with money and fame were too often on a collision course with disaster.

"Don't tell me you're not the same," he said. "I saw you speeding around the rink before you were rudely interrupted. You love it as much as I do."

"Speed, yes. Smashing into something and dying a fiery death, not so much." I hung on around another corner.

"We're not going to run into anything. Admit it, you're enjoying this too." He glanced over at me.

I looked back. His grin was infectious, as was his obvious excitement.

"Fine, I am, but if the police pull you over, don't claim I was encouraging you."

His eyes were back on the road as we headed out of the downtown part of Opal Springs.

"I'm absolutely telling them that," he said. "I'll tell them you were egging me on, insisting I go even faster. I told you we should slow down, but you wouldn't let me." He pouted playfully.

"You realise there's no way you'd get away with it, right?" I asked.

"I'm an almost famous, professional hockey player the whole town is invested in. I'll get away with it all right." There was no bragging, just stating a fact.

And my friends wondered why I tried to avoid hockey players. He was right, he'd probably get off with a warning. At least the first several times.

"Why does that make me think you've done a bunch of things and gotten away with them?" I asked.

"I might have done a bunch of things, but I didn't get caught. Too smart for that." He slowed at a roundabout before pulling the car onto the highway.

"Like what?" I lowered my hand to my lap.

"A bit of this and a bit of that. Mostly drag racing and hanging off the back of trains. Some graffiti here and there. The usual stuff a bored, dumbass kid gets up to. What about you? You have that innocent look, like you never put a toe out of place. I know from experience, they tend to be the ones who got up to more."

"Always the quiet ones?" I suggested. "Marley and I once got busted smoking weed out the back of school."

He glanced over in surprise, before quickly looking back at the road. "Okay, I didn't expect you'd do weed."

"I don't, we were experimenting. It was something different to the usual bottle of vodka out near the lake until we passed out." We'd tell our parents we were at each other's houses and go out and get shitfaced.

Easton laughed. "So you were a bad girl after all? How old were you?"

"I was a normal girl," I protested. "I was about fifteen or sixteen. The age where you tend to experiment with all sorts of shit and try to figure out where you stand in the world."

"Sex, drugs and rock 'n' roll?" he suggested. "We went to different high schools, or I would have hung out with you back then."

"You probably wouldn't," I said. "I put on a façade of being a huge nerd. Actually, not much of a façade. I was a nerd. But I was rebellious where only Marley and I could see. I'm guessing you were rebellious out in the open."

"Basically," he agreed. "How old were you when you lost your virginity?"

"That's a very personal question," I said.

"Yeah, it is. I was sixteen. So was she. We were at a party, just hanging out. The next thing I knew we were making out and then we did it. It was quick and messy, I don't mind admitting. I had no fucking idea what I was doing."

"Who does at sixteen?" I asked. "I was nineteen. A guy from uni. I thought we were in love. A week later we broke up."

"He was an idiot," Easton declared. "If I took your virginity and you had feelings for me, I'd never let you go. I would have done everything I had to do to keep you."

"I'm glad he didn't. Looking back, he wasn't my type anyway. It never would have worked out." At the time I was heartbroken, but now I wondered why I went out with him in the first place.

"Let me guess, he went into accounting?" Easton grinned. "He wears cardigans and reads non-fiction books. And listens to non-fiction podcasts. Between playing the latest computer games. If that's the case, you dodged a bullet."

"Actually, he runs one of the fastest growing cyber-security companies in the world," I said. "So the accountant part is wrong, but the rest of it…"

Easton snorted a laugh. "You didn't just dodge a bullet, you dodged a full blown nuclear bomb. Your type is much more the hot, confident hockey player who does a bit of carpentry on the side."

"It is?" I opened my eyes wider. "Do you happen to know anyone like that? Can you introduce me?"

"I might just do." He slowed the ute and turned onto the road that led to Opal Lake. "He's a great guy. Good with his hands and his dick."

I sighed heavily out my nose. "Shame. I was hoping for a guy who was good with his tongue."

"I have it on good authority he's that too," he said. "He's never had any complaints. The opposite, if I'm honest. But he tends to only give repeat performances to special women."

"So he's the love them and leave them type?" I asked.

"For the right woman, he wouldn't leave." He drove into a parking space beside the water and killed the engine.

My lips slid over my tongue. "How would he know if she was the right woman?" He wasn't referring to me, and if he was it didn't matter. I reminded myself this was one date. That was all. Nothing more could come of this.

"He'd just know." His gaze locked on me and I thought he might lean over and kiss me. Instead of moving towards me, he moved away, taking the keys out of the ignition and pushing the door open. He came around to my side and helped me out.

Usually, I'd protest that I could get myself out of the

vehicle, but his ute was high off the ground and climbing out with heels was precarious at best.

"Thanks." I managed not to fall on my ass, and closed the car door behind me. It shut with a satisfying thunk. The vehicle was old, but it was solid.

He laced his fingers in mine, and we crunched over the gravel car park, to the expanse of grass that led down to the lake.

The water was almost perfectly still except where it lapped softly against the shore. The sound was rhythmic, soothing. Overhead, the sky was completely clear, the stars on full display. I could have stood there and counted them, one by one. The sky in Melbourne never looked like this.

"I love it down here," I said softly. "It's one of my favourite places."

"Mine too," he said. "My only regret is that it doesn't freeze over in winter so we can skate on it."

"That's true." My breath misted the air. "But it's beautiful anyway." Especially when no one else was here like tonight. It was too cold out for most people.

We stopped on the water's edge. He pulled me to him so my breasts were pressed against his chest. "Beautiful is the word." He tucked a few strands of hair behind my ear. "I meant what I said about not letting you go. That guy was an idiot, but it's his loss."

His hand slid around to the back of my neck. He grabbed a fistful of hair.

The spike of pain sent a jolt of need through me.

I'd always enjoyed being handled rough. It was another side of the 'it's always the quiet ones,' equation. I'd never been into boring sex, never minded if a partner left a few bruises here or there.

"You're so fucking gorgeous." His lips were right near my ear. His breath brushed my cheek. I shivered lightly.

He grazed his mouth over my skin, light and slow until his lips reached mine. He brushed over them once, twice then slammed his mouth down onto mine, kissing me with fierce desperation. He pushed my lips apart with his tongue and plundered my mouth.

My arms went around his neck, pulling him closer, until our bodies were so hard against each other I wasn't sure where I finished and he began.

His growing erection pressed into me, eager and needy.

Finally, breathlessly, we broke apart, fingers still tangled in each other's hair.

"So fucking gorgeous," he said again. "Your mouth tastes like heaven."

"So does yours," I said softly. He tasted sweet and salty at the same time, along with his own unique flavour. I wanted more. My clit throbbed like crazy. I wanted to feel his tongue on my pussy. I wanted to feel his cock slide inside me.

My panties were already ruined. I was wet as hell from one kiss. I needed him to fuck me, hard and fast.

Judging by the size of the bulge in his pants, he'd fill me perfectly.

Fucking yes please.

"Easton…" I whispered.

He was silent for a moment, then said, "I should get you home. It's getting late and I have training in the morning."

I blinked. I wanted to protest, but I pushed away my disappointment. He was right, it was getting late. I had practice and work in a handful of hours.

"Right. Me too." I drew in a couple of breaths and blinked again, to clear my thoughts so I could think with my head, not my clit. "We should get going."

Just one date, I reminded myself. It was definitely better to end it before things went too far. Before we did something I'd regret.

Still, my vibrator was getting a workout when I got home.

11

CATALINA

I skidded to a stop, ice spraying up behind me. I turned around, my long plait flying out behind me. I flicked it back over my shoulder and grinned.

"How was that?"

"Not bad." Dad scribbled my time down on his clipboard.

"Not bad?" I scoffed. "That has to have been one of my fastest times since I've been back in Opal Springs." It felt good. Every bend was almost effortless. If I was in form like that, or better, for the trials, I'd be on the Olympic team in a heartbeat. I'd leave my competition in my wake.

"There's always room for improvement." He looked up from his clipboard before tucking it under his arm. "You need to bend your right elbow less when you come out of the band."

"Why have an A+ when you can have an A+ +," I said dryly.

"Anything less won't get you where you want to go," he said steadily. "But that was definitely better than you've done in a while. You're more confident than I've seen you. More so than before you hurt your knee. Does this have anything to do with a certain hockey player who took you out the other night?"

"Is this where you swap your coach hat for your dad hat?" He'd always worry about me, no matter what I did or who I went out with. I loved him for it, but I was too old to be fussed over.

"After Jason—" he started.

"Easton isn't Jason," I said. In response to Dad's raised eyebrows, I continued, "He's nicer. Much more…"

"If you're about to say humble, I'll laugh now and get it over with. He seems all right, but at the end of the day he's ambitious. He'll do anything to get ahead. Just like Jason."

I couldn't help bristling. "You don't even know him."

"Neither do you," Dad pointed out. "One date doesn't make you an expert on him and his motives."

"His motives?" I raised my gloved hands and dropped them to my sides with a slap. "Are you concerned about my virtue now? I didn't realise we stepped back into the nineteen fifties." What was it with people in this town? The assumption I couldn't take care of myself was starting to grate on my nerves.

"I care about you," Dad said firmly. He ran a hand over the back of his neck. "Let's talk about this later, at home. We have twenty minutes left, let's not waste it."

"You could save yourself some time and get off the ice now." I hadn't seen Cruz and Shaw approach, but they both stood at the side of the rink, dressed for training.

I narrowed my eyes at Cruz. "What the fuck are you talking about?"

He clicked his tongue condescendingly and gestured over to my father. "What language is that in front of your coach?"

"None of your fucking business," I retorted. "If you have something to say, come out and say it."

He shrugged. "Fine. You're wasting your time skating around like that. Go and empty some anal glands and leave the ice to the experts."

I was tempted to kick him in the anal glands with the blade of my skate. Instead, I stood my ground and glared at him and Shaw, who seemed to agree with everything he said.

"Mind your own business," I snapped. I turned to Dad and rolled my eyes.

He helpfully gave me an 'I told you so' glance and smirked at both players.

I shook my head. He was just as bad as they were. It must be a man thing.

"Let's go again," I said. Hands behind my back, I

skated back to the starting cone. I couldn't let Cruz get to me. I had to keep my focus.

"What happens on our ice is our business," Cruz called out. "Right, Shaw?"

"She shouldn't be here," Shaw said, his tone dark. Even darker than Cruz's.

I turned back to look at him.

Shaw's jaw clenched. The expression on his face sent chills down my spine. Every nerve in my body told me to move away from him as far and as fast as I could. And stay as far away from him as possible. I could almost see him thinking he wanted to wrap his hands around my throat and squeeze hard enough to crush my windpipe. I pictured his face looking down at me while I struggled for breath. Squeezing. Squeezing. Only letting go when there was no life left in me.

I swallowed and looked away. I'd like to think I wasn't easily scared, but he freaked me the fuck out.

"What are you dickheads waiting for?" Easton shouted out cheerfully. Dean was right behind him.

"Princess bitch is still occupying the ice," Cruz replied. "Shaw and I were just about to—"

"Shut the fuck up!" Dad snapped. "Catalina is training. She's just as entitled to her time as you are yours."

Cruz muttered something that sounded like, 'entitled sounds about right,' but he didn't say anything further.

I shot Dad a grateful look, which he responded to with a grunt and a grimace.

I leaned forward, ready to start another lap.

"Sorry about that, Doctor Ryan," Easton shouted. "Cruz doesn't know when to shut up sometimes."

I straightened up, frustrated by the distraction. Why had Easton spoken right then? I glanced around to see him grinning and accepting a high-five from Cruz. The asshole did it on purpose? Of course he did. Dinner last night was all about him winning a bet, he didn't give a shit about me. Thank fuck I hadn't slept with him when I wanted to.

I reminded myself that was only because he stopped it before we went too far. If he hadn't, I would have fucked him.

You need to make some better life choices, I told myself.

Easton caught my eye and smiled. He even had the nerve to wink.

I gave him a filthy look and flipped him off.

By now, most of the team was standing on the edge of the rink, watching. All of them laughed, except Shaw and Dean. Shaw's expression hadn't changed, and Dean looked bothered. I couldn't tell whether it was by my presence or the way his team was treating me.

Either way, I looked away and gathered up every bit of focus I had left. I shut out all of the assholes and waited for the word from Dad.

"Go," he said with more urgency and meaning than usual. He was as pissed off as I was and wanted me to show those assholes what I was made of.

I started to skate, flying across the ice until the rest

of the world washed away. Nothing was left but me and the air rushing past my ears, the power of my legs, the slice of my skates and the joy of doing something I loved more than just about anything.

I slid into the first corner, taking it effortlessly. The fingertips of my gloves grazed the surface of the ice, but I barely needed the contact to stay up on my skates. My left knee bent almost double before I came up out of the bend. Even that was almost effortless. My knee felt stronger today. With any luck it would stay that way.

I skated hard, leaning forward, arms back, hands tucked away to make me more aerodynamic. I flew into the second bend.

I knew the moment I hit it that my angle was off. Nothing I couldn't fix. I'd corrected myself a million times before. I did so again, but a twinge in my knee forced me to drop to the ice. I landed on my side and slid until I crashed into the boards at the side of the rink.

I hit and bounced with a jolt of pain through my shoulder and hip, but the impact wasn't enough to break any bones. This time.

I slid to a stop and got to my feet to howls of laughter from the watching hockey players.

I turned to glare in time to see Easton start a sarcastic clap which was taken by the rest of them one by one.

Cruz was grinning like he'd never seen something so amusing in his life. He held his phone in one hand

and was clapping his thigh with the other. Recording my fall, like the asshole he was.

Dean was clapping, but looked uncertain, uneasy. He glanced around at his teammates, his lips pressed hard together.

I saw no sign of Shaw. No doubt he could watch Cruz's video over and over and have a good laugh later. If he knew how to laugh.

"You okay, Cat?" Dad called out.

"I'm fine," I said as lightly as I could. I glanced at the clock on the wall. It read a minute before eight. Time to get off the ice. I nodded to Dad, and followed him through the gate and passed the players who were ready to file on for their training.

"Nice display," Cruz said as I stepped past him. "Very elegant."

I stopped to look up at him. "I thought so. Maybe we could practice some synchronised board smashing some time. I'm pretty sure you'd be good at it. You seemed to spend enough time being slammed into them during the game the other night."

He smirked. "That's supposed to happen when you play hockey, not when you ice race. Or was that ice slip?" He exchanged glances and grins with Easton.

"You're both ice holes," I told them. I couldn't help but give Easton a particularly bitter, dirty look. I thought we had a nice time last night, but clearly I was wrong. He was laughing behind my back along with the rest of them.

"Yeah, she's hot for you," Cruz said to him. "I see what you mean when you said she was panting for your cock."

Easton said that? He was a bigger asshole than I suspected. The only thing I didn't understand was why he didn't sleep with me. That was the point, wasn't it? To get laid. Especially knowing he could come back and tell the team all about it and have another good laugh at my expense. Apparently he did that anyway. He probably told them I sucked him off or something. The stupid thing was, I would have and, for that, I felt like shit. Not as bad as I would have if I'd done it.

Dad stopped, turned around and came back to stand beside me. "That's my daughter you're talking about. May I remind you I am a fully qualified medical doctor. I know at least a hundred ways to end your careers without anyone suspecting me." He smiled unpleasantly.

"I can fight my own battles," I said under my breath.

He patted my shoulder. "Of course you can, I thought they might need a reminder. I'm sure they already know a vet knows more than a hundred ways to get back at them if she wants to. And dispose of the evidence inside one of her patients."

"I don't want to get back at them," I eyed Cruz and Easton in particular. "I just want them to stay the fuck away from me."

"That's all we want too," Cruz said. "Not to have

some princess hanging around distracting us and fucking with our team unity."

In the corner of my eye, I saw Dean watching Cruz. He looked as though he had something to say, but was holding back. Once again, I wasn't sure if he agreed with Cruz or wanted him to lay off me.

I didn't care, he could stay away from me too.

I shook my head, turned and walked away. I didn't give a shit what any of them said, I wasn't going to stop practising. I wasn't going to let them distract me either.

12
CATALINA

"If you ask me, they all sound like douchecanoes." Marley crossed her legs at her knees and chewed her gum a little faster.

I glanced up from the senior Labrador whose teeth I was checking, and hummed my agreement. "That's a good word for them."

"Leonard, on the other hand, is such a good boy." She leaned forward and scratched the dog behind the ears.

"He's the best boy," I agreed. "If the average hockey player was as well-behaved as this, the rink would be a better place." I let him close his mouth, and stepped away to take off my gloves and wash my hands.

"The whole world would be a better place if people were like dogs," she said. "Especially goodest boys like this one."

I offered Leonard a liver treat, which he happily

accepted and chewed on. His tail thumped a couple of times.

"Do you think Cruz has a point?" I asked softly. "I love doing this. Caring for animals. Do I really need to keep pushing myself the way I have been? I could be focusing on this, worrying about getting my clinic hours up."

"Are you asking that because you want to give up racing, or because Cruz is getting to you?" She glanced up at me, a frown etched on her brow.

"I don't want to give it up," I said quickly. "I don't want to deal with those assholes anymore." I exhaled out my nose and grabbed Leonard's collar to help him down the steps and off the examining table. "Everyone keeps telling me how important the arena is to Opal Springs. It would be so easy for them to paint me as the bad guy and make everyone in town hate me."

Before she could respond, I led Leonard out the door to reunite with his human. This was the last appointment for the day, so I locked the door behind them and returned to the examining room.

"First of all, there's no way everyone in town is going to hate you," Marley said. "You're way too awesome for that. Most people know what the guys are like."

"That won't matter if they suggest I'm getting in the way of them becoming an expansion team," I said. "They can be the biggest assholes on the face of the planet and I'd still be the big bad wolf. I'd hate me too if I was getting in the way of something like that."

Marley pushed herself to her feet. She fixed me with her stern best friend expression that she mastered early on in high school. The one that was somewhere between, 'or else,' and needing to fart. It never failed to make me smile.

"Catalina Joanna Ryan. You're not getting in the way of anything. You know that as well as I do. If they go around spreading shit like that, they don't deserve to go pro."

"It's not about what they deserve, it's about what Opal Springs deserves," I argued.

I scratched my forehead and sighed. "If there was somewhere else to practice, I'd use it. Even if I have to drive a long way to do it." There was nowhere else though. Nowhere closer than two or three hours each way. I couldn't do that and get my clinic hours in at the same time. The team wouldn't drive that far either. I was starting to wish the arena was built already. I wouldn't have met any of them then.

"Maybe it's time to go back to Melbourne," I concluded. "That might be the best thing for everyone." Including my bruised hip from where I hit the boards. A padded training rink wasn't such a bad thing.

"No!" Marley insisted. "I mean, if that's what you have to do, but I'd miss you so much." Her puppy dog eyes could have competed with any of the actual puppies I'd treated today. Including Leonard.

"I'd miss you too Marley-Jane," I said. "I'm not ready to go back yet, but I don't know what choice I have." I'd have to work with a new coach if I went back to Victoria. I wasn't going to uproot my father again to come with me. Even if he insisted. His life was here now.

I thought mine was too, but I couldn't have everything. If I stayed here, I was going to have to choose to forget about racing, or find a way to get those assholes off my back. Maybe I should train at midnight.

"For what it's worth, I think you should ignore them," she said. "There's no reason why you can't keep working here and train. Whatever those guys' deal is, it's their problem. You don't have to make it yours."

"It became mine when Cruz posted the video online of me crashing out the other day." Of course it went viral. People always enjoyed watching other people get hurt. Or at least, have accidents.

"We should go to the game on Saturday night," she said. "If we're lucky, we can video one of the guys getting a puck to the nuts." She looked as though she'd thoroughly enjoy that happening. Admittedly, that was something the Internet would love to see too. Videos of men being hit in the balls never seemed to get old.

I snorted. "That would be funny, but they wear padding and cups. They wouldn't feel anything." A puck to the part of their face that wasn't covered by a mask, on the other hand, would hurt like hell. I couldn't even bring myself to wish that on them. In spite of everything, I didn't want to be that petty. If I did, that would be a victory for them somehow. Like I lowered myself to their level.

Let them act like a pack of high school boys. I wasn't going to do it. Someone had to be the adult in the room.

"They might not feel it, but the footage would still be gold," Marley said with a grin.

She adjusted her glasses and exhaled softly. "I guess that would be juvenile. I just really hate to see you sad about all of this, and thinking about giving up your biggest dream."

I took some bandages off the corner of the examining table and put them away. "That's the thing though. Shouldn't I be grateful to be doing this? Maybe I'm being greedy."

"All of those guys did apprenticeships to become fully qualified at their trades," Marley said. "And they still want to give it up to play hockey."

"Those trades might not be their dream job," I said. Maybe they were, but I suspected hockey was where their hearts lay. Assuming they actually had hearts.

"No, but they can make a good living out of it. No offence, but there's not too much money to be made from speed skating."

"Yeah, none." Winter Olympians didn't get paid. At best, I might get endorsements if I won.

"Right, you're doing it for the love, not for the money. They could give up hockey today and still pay the bills. You skate because it's a passion. It's part of who you are. Just like working with animals is. You're not greedy for having a dream."

"I suppose so," I said reluctantly. "But I won't even have this if they create trouble for me. People might stop bringing their pets here."

Opal Springs had grown significantly since we were kids, but even in a town of this size, if someone got a reputation, word got around quickly. If people didn't want me to treat their pets, the clinic would have no choice but to let me go. I'd never be able to start my own. Not here. Maybe in Melbourne or somewhere like Dusk Bay.

"The animals and their humans love you," she insisted. "No one is going to stop bringing them here. We see how you are with them. If the guys start something, we'll deal with it. Like we always have."

"With too much vodka?" I grinned.

"Exactly," she agreed. "So tell me about your date with Easton."

I didn't want to talk about it, but at least she wasn't suggesting starting rumours about Cruz's ability as a mechanic, or Easton's as a carpenter. I refused to be the vindictive one in the story. Besides, ruining their reputations would do nothing to restore mine. They'd probably find a way to make things even worse.

I leaned my back against the bench that ran along the side of the room. "I thought we had a nice time. He seemed sweet and we have a lot in common."

"But then the next day, he was a dickhead along

with the rest of his team?" She blew a bubble and popped it, narrowly missing gum sticking to her glasses.

"Basically," I said. "He was laughing along with them."

"Ugh," she groaned. "Men. What about Dean and Shaw?"

I told her about the way they looked at me, and their teammates. And about the way Shaw gave me the creeps. "Did you say he was a butcher?" I asked. "I felt like he wanted to put me up on the block and cut me into slices."

"Sounds like Dean likes you," she said. "For all you know, he's growling at the rest of them when you're not around. He seems like the shy kind."

All I could say to that was, "Maybe. He's still one of them. Plan A is to stay out of the way of all of them."

"But you don't want to?" She cocked her head at me. "You enjoyed yourself with Easton."

"I could have had the best date ever, but he still acted like a dickhead the next day," I said. "Clearly he's not as nice as he lets on, and I was right in the first place when I told myself it would only be one date because I lost the bet."

"If you could do it all over again, would you skip going out with him?" she asked.

"I… I don't know," I admitted. The date was fun and the quiche was fantastic. The kiss almost convinced me there could be something between us. I wasn't sure if

I'd miss all of that to avoid the frustration of the day after.

"I'm going to give you some advice and I hope you don't get angry with me," she said tentatively. "I think you should talk to him. Tell him what you're thinking and make sure he understands that it's not okay to behave like a douchepotato."

My first instinct was to dismiss her words out of hand. After a few moments of thought, I nodded slowly.

"I suppose it couldn't hurt to try to clear the air." I wasn't going to let them think they could walk all over me with no consequences.

"He might even get the rest of the team to back the fuck off," she said.

"Doubtful. I'm not even sure my father's threats made much impact."

Her eyes widened. "Oliver threatened them?"

My eyebrows twitched upwards. "Since when are you on first name terms?"

Her face turned slightly pink. "It's a recent thing. He suggested since we worked together, we should be a bit more casual with each other."

For some reason, her response made my skin itch. "You're not interested in my father, are you?"

"What? No," she replied immediately. She wouldn't meet my gaze.

"Good. Don't go there." I grimaced. "That would be

weird. I don't need one of my best friends as my stepmother."

"Yeah, weird," she said vaguely. "Anyway, are you going to talk to Easton?"

"I might," I said. "I'll make sure he's not wearing any padding over his groin, just in case." I smiled faintly.

Marley giggled. "If you knee him in the groin, I have no doubt he deserved it."

"I'd only do it as a last resort," I said. I had a feeling she might be right.

13

CRUZ

"What's your fucking deal, bro?" I sat on the bench that ran the length of the locker room and adjusted the laces on my skates.

"You might need to elaborate," Easton said. "I have a bunch of deals going on at any given time."

He gave me a look like he didn't know exactly what I was talking about.

"Cat, dickhead," I snapped. "You went out with her, but then you were acting like you hate her guts as much as the rest of us."

"Nothing's changed." He shrugged. "All I'm thinking about is the bet." He didn't look all that convincing to me.

"You're not claiming you won," I pointed out. "You're the one who said she was panting for you." The look on her face when I'd said that. I wanted to laugh and punch myself in the face at the same time. Yeah, that was a stupid reaction. It made no sense to me either. She was a pain in the ass, but my cock wanted to climb out of my pants whenever I saw her. I needed to fuck her and get her out of my head.

"She was." He went on taping up his stick.

"Then, that brings us back to what's your deal? Why didn't you fuck her?" I was glad he hadn't, but only because I wanted to win his money. That was what I told myself. If he wanted to throw away his chance to win, that was his problem.

Easton glanced up and grinned. "I figured I'd play with her for a while. See how wound up I could get her before I have her on her knees, those pretty lips around my cock."

He glanced away before I could wipe the smile off his face with my fist.

What the fuck was my deal? This woman was screwing with my brain.

"Maybe you don't want to win," I suggested. "Are you giving up?"

"Not a chance." He tore off the edge of the tape and set it aside. "I'm still in if you are. Maybe Dean should join us. I saw how he was looking at her."

I saw it too. I looked over to where Dean was pulling on his padding. So far, he played his cards close to his chest. Maybe giving Easton and I enough rope to hang ourselves with before he made his move.

"Not a chance." Dean glanced up briefly. He looked

like he was going to say something else, but ducked his face back down again.

I stood up in my skates and walked over to him. "You good?"

"Yeah." He still averted his gaze. "I'm good. I just… I dunno."

"You think we're being too harsh on her?" I asked.

"I guess so," he said. "She seemed kinda upset. I feel like we're all on edge because of this shit."

"You going to go and kiss her better?" Easton teased.

Dean looked over at him, his lips pressed in a tight line. "That's what I'm talking about. There's too much on the line for this kind of friction."

"It's not the kind of friction I like." I pictured her lying on my bed, on her back, that look of anger on her face, her legs apart while I drove into her. Hating me, but at the same time letting me use all of her gorgeous body. Her pussy nice and wet for me, waiting for me to come inside her.

Dean grunted and went back to fixing his padding into place.

"I'll meet you clowns out on the ice," I said. For once, Cat wasn't training before us. Glaring at us like she owned the rink. That fuckable mouth all pouty and angry. Ready to wrap around my dick.

I stepped out of the locker room with a smirk on my face, that only deepened when I saw her standing at the edge of the rink.

"This is our rink time." I strode over to her like I owned the place.

She turned to me and glared. Fuck, she was hot when she did that.

"I know that, I'm here to talk to Easton."

No way, he had his chance. Whatever was going through his head, it was time for me to get into hers. And under her skin.

"He's not here today," I lied. "Want me to pass on a message?"

Her lips pressed tighter together. "No, I'll see him some other time." She started to turn away.

Without thinking I reached out and grabbed her upper arm, nice and firm. Even with a shirt and jacket on, the contact sent a jolt of heat to my cock. I wanted to touch her bare skin.

"Maybe we can talk." I pushed her towards the women's locker room, knowing no one would be in there right now.

"What the fuck would we ever have to talk about?" She jerked her arm away, but let me guide her anyway.

I let the door swing closed behind us. "Let's start with how much you want me."

She stepped away from me, until her back hit the wall.

I stood in front of her, my hands to either side of her head, caging her in.

"You're delusional," she said. "You've been nothing but an asshole to me since we met. Not to mention that fucking video you posted online. Why would I want you?"

Her breath was coming a little faster, increasing the rise and fall of her breasts. Her eyes darkened. She was so angry, she was aroused.

"That video made a lot of people happy," I said. "You don't want people to think you're a perfect little princess, do you?"

"I'm definitely not perfect, but posting that proves how much of an asshole you are." She lifted her chin at me defiantly.

I wasn't going to apologise for the video, because I wasn't sorry. I'd seen enough skaters to know she'd hit the wall because she was showing off, trying to prove to us that she was better than us. The video was a reminder that she wasn't.

"And yet, you still want me. Do you know why?" I smirked. "Because you're only human." I leaned in and ran the tip of my tongue from her chin, the side of her jaw.

She quivered under my touch. Yeah, that was what I thought. She felt the electricity between us too. That burning ember, ready to become a full blown fire.

"The question is, are you going to fight it?" I ran my tongue across her neck, down to her throat. She smelled like lavender body wash and some kind of soft, floral perfume. Her skin was perfectly smooth. She made no attempt to pull away. If anything, she leaned into my touch slightly. Instinctively wanting more.

"There's no way anything is going to happen between us." Her voice was soft and low, husky with need.

Another pulse of heat and my cock was diamond hard.

"You say that, but your body is giving me different signals." I captured her mouth with mine, kissing her warm, soft lips and sliding my tongue between them. Her mouth tasted of mint and some kind of tea. A hint of vanilla or something. Ironic, because there was nothing vanilla about this woman.

She moaned.

Holy shit, if she did again, I was going to lose my load in my pants.

I broke off our kiss. "Admit you want me."

"I hate you," she whispered.

I chuckled. "Yeah, but you want me." I kissed her again. She kissed me back, her tongue probing inside my mouth.

I broke off again. "Say it. Say the word and I'll give you what you want."

The anger in her eyes was just what I imagined and hoped for. That flash of fury that carried a world of lava hot heat and promise.

"I fucking hate you, but I want you," she said. Her voice was a deep, frustrated growl, reminding me of Easton for a moment. I pushed him out of my head for now. He was a whole other complication. Right now, I wanted to focus everything on Cat.

"There, that wasn't so difficult was it?" I taunted. The angrier I made her, the better this would be for both of us. I wanted her stone cold furious, ready to use those cat's claws of hers to scratch the hell out of me. That would come. She could leave scars on me if she wanted to. Every time she looked at me, she'd know they were there. That she'd marked me because she couldn't resist what my body could give her.

I kissed her again while undoing the front of her jeans and tugging them down far enough to get my hand inside. I ran the tips of my fingers over the front of her black lace panties.

"You're so fucking wet." Of course she was. Her body was aching for me to touch her.

I slid my hand up and down her seam and under the edge of her panties. I broke off our kiss and looked her right in the eyes while I pressed two of my fingers straight inside her saturated pussy.

I pumped my fingers in and out of her a few times before adding a third. Her pussy was a tight fit. So fucking perfect. She'd feel incredible around my cock.

She didn't look like a princess now. She looked like a fucking goddess. Her eyes were wide and dark. Some of her hair had come out of her ponytail and now floated around the sides of her face.

With my spare hand, I pulled the hairband out of her hair, letting all of it tumble down past her shoulders. I wanted her to look messy, so everyone could see what we'd done here. They'd know she surrendered herself to me. I wanted her to look completely destroyed. I wanted to see her come around my fingers. I wanted her to feel good because of me, my touch. Because she gave herself to me this way. She couldn't resist the animal attraction between us.

I hooked my fingers around to rub her G spot, while the heel of my hand massaged her clit.

Rougher and rougher, taking all my hate out on her, I fucked her with my hand, right there up against the wall. And she let me, taking everything I gave her with no restraint. If she was panting for Easton, she was downright melting for me. I was going to make sure she enjoyed every minute of it as much as I did.

She rolled her hips, bucking and grinding against my hand. She dropped her head back, half closed her eyes and moaned.

"Mmm, just like that, don't stop." She'd hate herself for those words later, but I loved every syllable. I wished I recorded it on my phone, but it was seared into my brain. I'd relive it over and over.

There was no way I was stopping now. If I did it would piss her off, but making her come would piss her off even more. Later on, when she thought back to the way I made her feel, she'd be so fucking conflicted. Yeah, she hated me, but she was going to want more. She'd need more until she let me make her body mine. And I would. I'd claim every centimetre of her. I'd teach this princess who her king was. Who owned her.

"Come for me, princess. Come around my hand." I

worked her harder and harder, playing her body like she was my personal guitar.

She groaned. "I'm so close. So… Ahhh." She rocked harder as her orgasm claimed her. She cried out my name and went on grinding herself against my hand. Coming and coming and coming. If my fingers weren't wet before, they were drenched now.

She came because of me. I gave her that orgasm. The first of many. My cock ached to be deep inside her, but that would have to wait.

Easton had a point. Fucking her wasn't enough. I needed her shattered into a thousand pieces until all there was left was for her to turn to me.

Then I'd break her.

14

CATALINA

What the fuck was I thinking?

I stood against the wall for a long time after Cruz left, trying to get my head around what just happened. I let him touch me. I let him get me off. Had I completely lost my fucking mind?

Yeah, I wanted him, but the last person I should have even been alone with was Cruz Brewer. The man was the definition of alphahole. Sex on legs, or in this case skates.

"It was just an orgasm," I whispered to myself. It was purely physical. Just two people giving in to lust.

I walked over to the sink and splashed water on my face. I looked up at my reflection as droplets slid down my skin and back into the sink.

It was more than two people giving in to lust. It was me giving in to him and his oversized ego.

"Fuck." I watched my lips move as I said the word.

Still red from kissing him. What little mascara I wore would have made tracks down my face if it wasn't waterproof. I suspected he would have enjoyed that.

He'd pulled the hairband out of my hair and made it messy. That was exactly what he wanted. He wanted people to know what happened here, even if it meant thinking we fucked.

I searched around for my hairband, but couldn't see it anywhere. It wasn't lying on the tiles, or scrunched up in the corner. Had he taken it with him as some kind of trophy? He was fucked up enough to think it gave him some kind of victory over me.

He'd think that about getting me off, but I had to show him that wasn't the case.

I carefully rinsed my face and patted it dry with a piece of paper towel. My hairbrush was in my car, along with my bag, so I combed out my hair with my fingers and patted it back into place. By the time I was finished, I looked more or less put back together. My clothes were neat and the red had faded from my cheeks and mouth.

Back straight, I pulled the locker room door open and stepped out into the rink.

The rest of the team had appeared from the men's locker room and were getting ready to go out onto the ice.

Cruz stood with Easton and Dean, looking smug as fuck.

He caught my eye as I went to walk past. He slipped

a couple of fingers into his mouth, sucked on them for a few moments, then pulled his glove on over his hand.

My face immediately heated, making him chuckle.

Easton grimaced at him. He clearly knew what went down, or had a fair idea.

Dean glanced at them both like he didn't approve of either of them. Was he envious he wasn't the one who got me off? If he was the lesser of several evils, maybe I should have let him.

I lifted my chin and walked past them. Past Shaw, whose eyes followed me all the way, expression heavy with judgement.

I was busy judging myself too.

Whispers and gazes followed me all the way out the door. I felt as though they clung to me while I got into my car and tied my hair back in a ponytail with a fresh hairband.

I had a late shift at the clinic today, so I started the car and drove to the other side of town.

I pulled into a parking spot ten or fifteen minutes later. Grabbing my bag off the seat, I headed into Eden's florist shop.

I found my purple-haired friend standing at the kitchenette, making herself coffee. She took one look at me and grabbed another mug to make me tea.

I stepped into a chair and sat and waited.

She handed me my drink and sat beside me.

We sipped in silence for a minute or two.

"I let Cruz Brewer give me an orgasm," I said finally.

Her eyes widened. She nodded, making no judgement of me. Yet. "How do you feel about that?"

"I don't know," I admitted. "If he wasn't such a prick…"

"What would you do if he wasn't?" she asked.

"That's like asking if I'd live on the sun if it wasn't so hot," I said. "I mean, it is, so it's not even a question."

She set her coffee aside. "You're attracted to him, right?

"Like a moth to a flame," I said bitterly. "Same with Easton. Dean seems nice enough, but he's probably an asshole too. I know Shaw hates my guts. The rest of the team too, probably. At the end of the day, it comes back to the fact I should stay away from any hockey players. They seem to be bad for me."

"The lure of forbidden fruit?" she suggested.

"More like a flower that looks pretty, but will kill you if you touch its petals," I said. "Why am I attracted to guys who are bad for me?"

She smiled. "Isn't that the age-old question? There's something about bad boys that girls like us can't seem to resist. But you know, there's nothing wrong with having a physical relationship with anyone as long as it's consensual. So what if you sleep together? If you have boundaries and stay in them, then where's the harm?"

"Are you saying I should let Cruz keep giving me orgasms? Even if we hate each other?"

"I'm saying you shouldn't feel guilty for fucking

anyone if that's what you and your body want to do," Eden said.

"I guess so," I said slowly.

She picked up her coffee and took another sip. "I can't condone his behaviour, or that of Easton Grant, but I wouldn't be much of a friend if I told you you did the wrong thing on the spur of the moment."

"But you think I did," I said. "You wouldn't touch either of them with a forty foot bargepole?"

"Yes I would," she replied. "That would be just long enough to smack some sense into both of them at the same time."

I laughed.

"Do you want me to tell you to stay as far away from them as you can?" she asked. "Because I can totally do that."

"You're not surprised by what happened?" I asked.

"I've seen the attraction between you and those guys," she said slowly. "If I was you, I'd fuck their brains out and enjoy every minute of it. But be careful."

"When am I not careful?" I asked. "Apart from approximately an hour ago. And making that bet with Easton. And following through with it."

I groaned and rubbed my temples with my thumb and fingertips. "I'm starting to think I should ask you to insist I stay away from them. Those guys are good at clouding my judgement." And making me think with my clit.

"If you ever feel like you're about to do something

you shouldn't, you know you can always call me and I'll talk you out of it," she said. "Or Marley will."

"Marley is more likely to talk me *into* it," I said.

Eden laughed. "You're right, yes she is. She likes to live spontaneously."

"She'd definitely fuck their brains out. While they were insulting her," I said. Which brought me back to something else. "Cruz wasn't sorry about posting the video online."

The expression on his face when he talked about it, he'd shown no remorse at all. I didn't mind making people laugh, but having everyone see me crash out when I was trying to prove myself to the whole team? That was embarrassing. I shouldn't have tried so hard. Maybe I deserved to have him post that video.

"Would you be sorry if you posted a video of him online?" Eden asked.

"I wouldn't do it in the first place," I said. "He really is the last guy I should be getting involved with."

"But you still want to screw him?" Eden asked.

"How fucked up that is?" I grimaced. I'd like to say I made good choices, but I was starting to develop a pattern of being attracted to the wrong kind of guy. First Jason, and now them. Was I some kind of asshole magnet? That would be just my luck.

"He's done some shitty things, but I think deep down, he's a decent guy," she said. "What did Easton say about all of this?"

"I didn't get a chance to talk to him," I admitted. "I

got caught up with Cruz." My face heated again. "You really think there's a good side to Cruz Brewer?" If there was, I hadn't seen it. Not really. His loyalty to his team and his teammates was obvious, but loyalty was only one positive trait. It wasn't enough to balance out the rest. Not even that orgasm was enough to do that.

"I think you wouldn't have let him touch you if you didn't see something in him," Eden said. "Just like you wouldn't have gone out with Easton. We all say and do stupid things from time to time. The guys are very passionate about their team and that makes them territorial."

"And they think I'm trying to muscle in on their territory," I concluded. "I'm not going to back off." Even if I could, my pride and stubbornness wouldn't let me. I didn't need to beat the guys, just stand up to them. I wouldn't let them snap me like one of Eden's flower stems. I couldn't let them get under my skin any more than they already had.

"I wouldn't ask you to," she said. "Once they realise you're not competition, they might stop being assholes." She looked at me sideways. "What happens then?"

"I have no idea," I said. "I'm not going to try to change any man, but if they decide to stop flexing their muscles and being pricks…" I couldn't finish that. It was a fine line between hate and lust, but as far as I was concerned, it was a very solid, high wall between hate and love. Or even between hate and like.

"I might hate them less," I said finally.

She smiled. "That might be the best anyone can hope for."

I finished the last of my tea and placed my empty cup on the table. "Thank you for letting me get that off my chest." I would have driven myself crazy dwelling on it all day. I didn't even feel bad telling her about it. Not when it was obvious Cruz did the same thing. And Easton too. At least I wasn't bragging. Looking back, I should have walked out of the rink with my hair and clothes a mess and owned every moment of it. I had nothing to be ashamed of.

She leaned over to hug me. "Was it a good orgasm?"

I exhaled. "It was incredible. He definitely knows what he's doing with his hands."

Even now, my body ached for more. I wanted to feel his cock inside me, pounding as hard as his hips could thrust. Filling me all the way until I felt so good I forgot my own name.

"I love that for you," she said. "Should we stop glaring at him every time we see him?"

"Oh no, keep glaring," I said with a laugh. "He can take it."

She laughed too. "I noticed that about him. He can dish out shit, but he can take it too. That's more than I can say for a lot of people."

"Yeah." I hated him slightly less than I had. I was definitely going to have to be careful around him. The last thing I needed was to fall for Cruz Brewer.

15

EASTON

"You're a sneaky prick." I sat beside Cruz and started to undo my laces.

He glanced over at me and grinned, no apology or shame. "Don't tell me you wouldn't have done it. Oh wait, you could have and didn't. Your bad." He shrugged and tugged off his skate.

I narrowed my eyes at him. "You're not claiming you won the bet. How far did you go?" And why did I want to rip his fucking arms off? I knew something happened between them when he stepped out of the women's locker room. The smirk on his face said it all. Her following him out a couple of minutes later, looking deliberately put back together, chin raised, said the rest.

I'd never wanted to punch anyone more than I wanted to punch him then and there.

He wiggled his fingers in front of my face. "Ask my fingers how wet and warm her pussy was."

I batted his hand away. "Get that thing away from me."

He lowered his hand. A flash of something crossed his eyes, before his bravado reasserted itself.

I knew he was interested in me, but I was uncertain for so many reasons. We'd known each other since we were kids, and we were teammates. If we crossed that line, there'd be no going back. We could screw up everything between us. I wasn't afraid of much, but I was afraid of losing the best friend I ever had. Although, this thing with Cat was already starting to get between us.

"In case you haven't heard it recently, jealousy is a curse, bro," he said lightly. "Sometimes you just have to grab the opportunities when they open themselves up to you."

"And yet, you didn't fuck her," I pointed out. "Otherwise you'd be waving your cock around instead."

Before he could respond, Dean sat down opposite us and started pulling off his padding. "Who didn't fuck who?"

"Cruz didn't fuck Catalina," I supplied. "Just with his fingers."

"That was more than you did," Cruz snapped.

"Because I told you, I wanted to mess around with her," I said. "I still do. I saw the expression on her face when she walked out of here. She's confused as fuck."

"Keep telling yourself that," Cruz said. "She didn't

seem too confused when she was screaming my name. I think it might be you who's confused."

"Maybe you should call off your bet," Dean suggested. "If you two are going to fight over her, she's not worth it."

"We're not calling it off," I said. "We can handle it. We can handle her."

"Dean is right," Shaw said. I hadn't noticed him listening until he sat down beside the goalie. "You should forget all about it and her. I don't see the point of fighting over a woman neither of you really want."

"Who says we don't really want her?" Cruz asked.

"You did," Dean said. "And Easton did just now."

"Are you trying to get us to back off so you can step in?" I asked him.

Shaw turned and narrowed his eyes at Dean. "It's a good question. Are you?"

"No." Dean tossed his padding down on the bench beside him.

"Are you backing out of the wager?" I asked Cruz. "No one will mind if you need to admit defeat."

"I could say the same to you." He smirked at me.

"Fuck off," I snapped. "I'm not backing down. I'll take her out again and next time I'll fuck her until she can't skate for a week."

"Unless you're going to keep messing with her," Cruz taunted.

"If you're going to—" Dean started.

"You four, stop your pissing match," Coach Foster

snapped. Kage Foster was a Canadian who played professional hockey before coming to Australia to help us nab the expansion spot. He'd been to the Stanley Cup play-offs twice, winning the second time. If he told us to do something, we did it.

Not without glares aimed at each other.

"Sorry, Coach," I called back. "Just a bit of friendly rivalry."

"Save the rivalry for the opposition." Kage gave us all a long look before he turned away.

Dean grunted his agreement. "He's right. We all need to lighten up a bit. Especially you two." He looked toward me and Cruz.

"I still think you're trying to convince us to get out of your way," Cruz said with a grin.

"What if he is?" I asked rhetorically. "Dean and Cat sitting in a tree, f-u-c-k-i-n-g."

"What are you, three years old?" Cruz asked.

I laughed. "Just having a bit of fun. What do you say Dean?"

"I say Cruz is right, you're a three-year-old," he said.

I flipped them both off.

"I think you're all as bad as each other," Shaw said. His tone was scathing, hazel eyes boring into us like he hoped to make our heads explode or some shit.

"Speaking of people who need to lighten up," I said. "Are you sure you don't want in on our bet? Or maybe you could find some willing pussy, because you, my friend, need to get laid."

"It's none of your fucking business," he snarled. He picked up his skates in one hand, pushed himself up off the bench with the other and stalked away.

"At least he didn't hit us in the head with his skates," I said offhandedly. "I thought, for a minute there, he might."

Cruz laughed. "He only would have hit you anyway. He wouldn't have caused too much damage if he clocked you in the head with them."

"Yeah, keep trying to convince yourself I'm not smarter than you," I told him. "I am, and I'll tell you why. I plan to take things slow with Cat until I get so deep under her skin she can't get me out." I had some regrets about laughing along with the other guys the morning after our date. I enjoyed spending time with her and I wanted to do more of it. A lot more. I wanted to get in so deep that, when I backed away, I'd rip her heart right out of her chest. She'd think twice about fucking with guys like us ever again.

"Like a rash?" Cruz grinned.

"Just as encompassing but less itchy," I said. "She'll become part of me. Her whole life will centre around me and the things I do to her and with her. She won't be able to think without my permission. And when I cut her loose, she's going to feel it."

"You're a brutal asshole," Cruz told me.

I responded with a smile to match his words. "Of course I am. Watch and learn." I nodded to Dean to include him.

"You're a delusional, brutal asshole," Cruz said. "It's you who will be watching and learning while I take her down all the pegs she needs to go down to end up on her knees, my cock down her throat."

The mental image made me curl my hands into fists. "It's my cock—"

I stopped when Kage turned back to glare at us again. I forced my posture to loosen and smiled. We totally weren't arguing, no way.

He pressed his lips together and stepped away.

I wrapped the towel around my waist and stepped out of the shower cubicle.

My dumb ass was still fuming over the mental image of Cruz and Cat. The stupid bet was my idea, but Dean was right, it was getting out of hand. I shouldn't have let either of them anywhere near her.

At first, it was just a bit of fun, messing around with a random woman none of us gave a shit about. It wasn't the first time we'd done it. We often bet on which women we'd take home from O'Reilly's after a game.

Of course, it was easier when they were hanging all over us. The more I got to know her, the more I realised there was more to her. I wasn't the kind of guy to commit to a woman, so it would never last, but I wanted to enjoy every minute of the ride. I wanted to know what made her tick. What did she like and not like? What would she let me do to her? I wanted to tie her to my bed and fuck her harder than she'd ever been fucked before. I'd ruin her for every other guy that came after me.

Whoever it was she settled down and had babies with, she'd always think of me and wish he was me when he thrust into her. She'd cry out my name when she came. She'd get herself off thinking of me.

Part of me wanted to get her pregnant so she'd be tied to me forever. She'd have other children, but whenever she looked at ours, she'd see my face. A permanent, constant reminder of my existence.

I glanced at Cruz as he stepped out of his own shower cubicle. My thoughts were conflicted. In him, I saw so many things. My childhood friend. My teammate. A man with an undeniably perfect, sculpted body. One that, if I was honest with myself, I wanted to touch. How would it feel to have him on his knees in front of me, sucking my cock? How tight would his ass be if I fucked him? Tight as hell. As far as I knew, he'd never been with another guy.

He'd only shown interest in me. That was one of the few things I wasn't arrogant about. Cruz didn't trust easily. He opened up to very few people. I was probably the only one, apart from himself, who knew about that preference.

Even if he was curious as fuck, he'd hold back in spite of himself to protect himself from condemnation.

I'd give him shit about a lot of things, but never that. Not when my body responded to his too.

Sometimes, I thought it would be easier to be a woman, so I could hide my arousal. Not that I was ashamed of my response, or my cock, but a guy couldn't be private when his dick was standing to attention.

I turned away so he wouldn't see my half-erect cock when I slipped off my towel and started to get dressed. I pulled on my bright red boxers, and my track pants over those before I turned back.

Cruz was watching me, like he knew all the things I thought about him, but reminding me of what we were right now.

Rivals.

He didn't nod or smile, and his customary smirk was nowhere to be seen. Instead, he turned his back and finished getting dressed.

I caught Dean watching us both, taking in the tension between us. I smiled, but it was a forced one that didn't reach my eyes.

He didn't smile back either. He seemed to be thinking something, but fuck only knew what. He was difficult to read at the best of times. Was he planning how he was going to get to Cat to win the bet before Cruz and me?

If he was, I'd figure out how to get in his way, or beat him to it. I wasn't beyond playing dirty to win. Not when there was so much at stake.

I grabbed my hi-vis work shirt and pulled it on over my head. I didn't bother to tuck it in. I sat on the bench to pull on my socks and work boots. I was fucking looking forward to never having to do this again. Train at what I loved, then hammering fucking nails for the rest of the day. The sooner the AIHL chose us, the better. I was ready to claim my prizes.

A professional hockey contract and Cat's pussy.

16
CATALINA

"I should be there with you." Dad's regretful voice came down the line.

I adjusted the phone against my ear. "I'd be lying if I said I don't wish you were, but I can handle this. You're needed up there in Opal Springs for your patients."

"As your father, and as your coach, I should be there," he said. "But I'm there in spirit. I know you'll keep me posted every step of the way."

"Of course I will," I said. "I'll call you again in a few hours."

"I'll be here, waiting impatiently." He chuckled. "I love you, honey."

"I love you too, Dad." I hung up and sent him a GIF of a hug before sliding the phone into my pocket. I wheeled my suitcase out of Melbourne airport and over to the waiting car I'd booked ahead.

The morning air was colder here than in Opal Springs. Brisk, with a cutting breeze. Judging by the people around me, wrapped in jackets and scarves, I was the only one who enjoyed the refreshing, biting cold. Still, I was happy to climb into the warmth of a car and sit back for the drive to Docklands.

I asked the driver to drop me off near the stadium, and walked the rest of the way to the training centre.

Pulling my suitcase through the door felt like coming home. I'd spent hours practising on the rink in here, racing against other skaters and learning how to be the best.

At the same time, this homecoming was bittersweet. It was here I injured my knee. For a while, I thought I'd never race again, but here I was. Determined to prove to the coaches that I was well enough and strong enough to qualify for the Olympics.

The actual qualifiers were in a few weeks, but they wanted to see me back here to test me out in person.

I was more than happy to prove myself.

"Hey!" Footsteps caught up to me and I found myself enveloped in a hug. "It's about time you showed up here!"

I laughed. "I missed you too, Eiko." A good friend of mine for years, she was tiny compared to me, but made up for it in enthusiasm.

I waited for her to let me go so I could turn around and hug her back.

"I told them you'd return," she said. "I said, *Cat loves us too much to stay away*."

"I do. I was never here for the skating. I just wanted to hang out with you and the others."

She laughed. "You suck at lying, but thank you. My ego could always use the boost."

I didn't think there was too much wrong with her ego, but compared to the Ghouls, she was as humble as they came. As refreshing as the winter breeze.

"Is Felicia around?" As far as I could tell, nothing had changed. It was like I hadn't left at all. People bustled past here and there, but through a set of glass doors, the rink was empty and in darkness.

To some, it might have looked ominous, but a thrill of excitement passed through me. I'd worked hard for this moment and it was finally here. Once I got through this, the trials would be the final hurdle.

My dream was so close I could almost reach out and touch it. I wanted to curl my fingers around it, grab hold of it, and never let it go.

"She's waiting in her office for you. Do you remember the way?" Eiko grinned teasingly.

"I think I might," I replied. "I'll shout for you if I get lost." I could find my way to the coaches' office in my sleep. Or anywhere else in the building.

"You do that, but you better shout loud, because I have to get to work." Another hug followed a cheeky grin before she was hurrying away toward the front doors.

I shook my head at her back and wheeled my suitcase towards the offices at the other end of the building.

Felicia's door was open, but I tapped anyway, not wanting to startle her or be rude. Getting on the wrong side of the short haired woman was always a bad idea.

She glanced up from her desk. "Catalina. You're looking well. How's the knee?" Her eyes dipped to my leg. Of course that would be the first thing she'd ask. That was a priority and my reason for being here today. She'd want to be sure I wasn't going to waste her time.

"Back to strength," I said. "I'm ready to show you." At the same time, I was trying really hard to keep myself from throwing up the meal I ate on the plane.

"Excellent." She looked up at my face, her brown eyes shrewd, assessing. She missed nothing that went on around her. She nodded. "Go and get changed and I'll meet you on the ice."

"Yes, Coach." I backed out the door and hurried to do as she asked. A shiver of nerves passed through me, but I pushed it away. I had to focus on what I was here to do. If I screwed this up, then I'd come all the way to Melbourne for nothing.

Don't fuck it up, I told myself.

The ice felt good under my skates. Right. I could have slid across the surface for hours, enjoying the way I moved across it faster, then slow, taking the bends gently while I warmed up.

Yeah, it was also nice to skate somewhere I didn't have a hostile audience. The rivalries here were mostly friendly ones. No one trying to tear me down or make my body respond to them. No one videoing me, ready to post it online if I failed. No eyes following like they wanted to eat me up. No temptation for me to let them.

"Looking good so far," Felicia said.

I wasn't sure if her scrutiny had risen any higher than my knee. Fair enough. It was easy for me to claim I was fine and another thing for her to see for herself. I couldn't come back and train if I wasn't in shape. I'd already had to undergo an intensive physical from a doctor who wasn't related to me. If at any point they decided I wasn't up to it, that would be that.

"Are you ready to show me what you've got?" She pulled out a stopwatch and held it in her hand. "Three laps."

"More than ready," I agreed. I was itching to get up to speed, like the ice was calling my name. Telling me to go faster, faster, *faster*.

I skated over to the starting line. An actual line here, not a traffic cone. For some reason, I almost missed our makeshift racetrack. Dad and I did the best we could, but it wasn't much in comparison to the real thing. Everything suddenly felt so much more real and serious.

I leaned forward, head down, arms by my side,

ready. I rolled my shoulders to loosen my muscles. Too much tension wasn't a good thing. So was too little.

"Go," Felicia said. She didn't need to shout. That one word was enough to reach to the far side of the rink, much less to me who stood a few metres away.

Smooth, like I'd done a million times before, I started to skate. Like always, the rest of the world disappeared and all that was left was me, the ice and the wind that brushed past my face.

I smiled to myself as I dipped into the first bend, the knuckles of my glove brushing across the cold, hard surface. I straightened up and flew faster, maybe faster than I'd ever gone before. In the back of my mind, I remembered crashing out in front of the whole hockey team. Even though they weren't here to see it, I took the second bend with practised ease. I wasn't going to hit the padded edge of the rink, not today.

Felicia was a blur as I passed her to finish the first lap and the second. On the third, she called out, "Time."

I gradually slowed before skating in a wide circle, and skidded to a stop beside her. I'd barely broken a sweat.

Until I looked at her face.

She was one of those people who were almost impossible to read. Her expression made my heart race faster. Sweat sprung up under my arms and under my gloves.

Was she about to tell me she didn't think I was up to competing in the trials? I could go back to Opal

Springs and settle down to life as a vet, but the whole hockey team was going to have a good laugh at my expense.

Fuck.

Finally, she nodded. "It's good to see you back to where you were. I wish there was enough money to lure your father back here to coach. He clearly knows what he's doing."

"Thank you," I said tentatively. "I guess it doesn't hurt that he's a doctor. He knows my limits better than I do."

She chuckled. "That wouldn't surprise me one bit. People as competitive as us tend to like pushing those limits as hard as possible."

"We like to win," I said unapologetically. "It's in our blood."

"That it is," she agreed. "You recorded a passable time. I noticed no tightness or weakness in your knee. According to the doctor, you passed the physical. I need to consult with the committee, but I see no reason why you can't compete in the trials. We'd welcome you back here to resume training." She dropped the stopwatch into the pocket of her hoodie.

A pile of weight was immediately lifted from my chest. I could breathe again.

"I'd like that," I said. "I have a few things I need to sort out in Opal Springs, like time off, but I look forward to getting back to things here."

"I have to speak to the committee first," she warned.

"I'll put in a good word. They usually have the sense to listen to me."

I grinned. "I'm sure they will this time too."

"When I tell them I think you're our best hope for a women's short track medal, they will," she said. "Things like that tend to sway people's minds."

I could happily have skated a hundred laps around the rink after her words. Coming back from injury was difficult, but to hear she believed in me like that... It meant everything. I would have given her a hug but I knew she didn't like them. Not even a handshake. I respected that and I respected her.

She wasn't the easiest person in the world to deal with, but she was honest. If she told you something, you could take it as gospel.

Sometimes her words came across as harsh, but there was no malice in them. I doubted she had a mean bone in her body. Still, a person had to have thick skin around her. Some people didn't want to hear her blunt honesty. Personally, I preferred it to bullshit and pretence. What was the point of sugarcoating something if doing so led to damage in the long run? If a skater wasn't good enough, that was something they should be told. How else would they get better?

"I appreciate your faith in me," I said instead. "I'll do my best not to let you down."

She snorted slightly. "Be more concerned about letting yourself down. We are, after all, our own worst enemies."

I couldn't argue with that, although I could think of a couple of guys who were almost as shitty to me as I was to myself.

"Yeah, we are," I said softly. I'd miss my father while I was back in Melbourne, but I was already finding it difficult to get those guys out of my head.

17
CATALINA

Still floating, I changed back into my street clothes and headed towards the exit. Felicia assured me I'd hear back from her in a couple of days, but if she was confident, I'd be confident too.

I wheeled my suitcase out the door and off to one side. I pulled out my phone and unlocked the screen. With any luck, I'd catch Dad between patients.

"Cat, I heard you might be heading back to town," a familiar voice drawled.

I whirled around, immediately on edge. "Jason."

All six feet of him, dark hair, blue-green eyes. Body like a Greek god. I used to think he had a beautiful mouth, but looking at him now, I just saw the petulant set of his jaw beneath his crooked nose. Too many pucks to the face.

He looked me up and down. "You're looking good.

Better than good." He stepped towards me. "I've missed you."

I took a step back until my calves touched the wall. "Thanks. I'm feeling good."

He smiled slowly. "You always did." His eyes lingered on my cleavage.

I groaned to myself. I'd walked straight into that one. On the other hand, he could have left it alone. Just like he did me.

"Did you want something?" I tilted my chin up and met his gaze evenly. I wasn't going to give him a centimetre.

"If you're coming back to Melbourne, we can pick up where we left off," he said as though I was the one who ended it by leaving town. Worse, he seemed to be suggesting we somehow put our relationship on pause.

I looked at him like maybe he'd lost his mind.

"Let me think about that for a moment." I scrunched up my brow in thought. "How about fuck no?"

"Cat, babe—" He pressed the palm of his hand to the wall beside my shoulder.

"Don't 'babe' me," I snapped. "Let's think about this for a moment. Where we left off was with you ignoring me after I hurt my knee. You didn't answer my calls or my texts. Nothing."

He dipped his head, his mouth uncomfortably close to my collarbone. "I admit it. When you got hurt, I freaked out. I was busy with the team and didn't know how to deal with what you were going through. So I backed off when I should have been there for you. I was a fucking idiot back then, but that's in the past. Seeing you like this, I'm reminded of all the good times we had. I know you remember them too." He ran the back of his knuckles down my cheek.

I jerked my face away from him. "I remember we always did what you wanted to do. I remember supporting your dreams and you switching off whenever I talked about mine. In fact, you did me a favour by not responding to me. Thank you for that." I started to move away.

He grabbed my arm in a bruising grip.

"I fucked up," he said in a tight voice. "We had something special. Don't pretend we didn't. I'll prove to you that we belong together."

I tried to shake off his hand, but his hold was too tight. "There's no way in hell I'm getting back together with you," I snapped. "If you don't let go of me, I'm going to scream."

"You heard her," a voice growled behind him. His hand slipped from my arm as he was hauled backwards.

Jason was a big guy, but Easton was bigger. And angrier. He held a fistful of Jason's shirt and twisted it, making the fabric dig into his throat.

"What the fuck?" Jason hooked his fingers into the neck of his shirt and tried to pull it away from his skin. "This is between me and my girlfriend."

"Ex-girlfriend," I said. "Heavy emphasis on the ex."

Easton eyed me past Jason's shoulder. "You went out with this douchebag?"

"A long time ago," I said. I ignored the irony in his question. That was a conversation for later.

"We were just talking about it," Jason said. "Back off motherfucker."

"Funny." Easton twisted the fabric a little more. "I'm sure she said the same thing to you, *motherfucker*. She doesn't want anything to do with you. Right, Cat?"

Jason gave me a last hopeful look, but it wasn't about us getting back together. He was scared of Easton and wanted me to save his ass.

"Let him go," I said after a few moments. "He's not worth it."

"If you're sure," Easton said lightly.

"I'm sure," I said.

"Huh. Okay then." Easton gave Jason a shove at the same time as he untangled his hands from his shirt. "I strongly suggest you fuck off and stay the hell away from her. I have no trouble kicking your ass if you don't."

Jason muttered something that sounded like 'fucking psycho' before he walked away quickly.

"Thanks," I said grudgingly. "He's always been…"

"A giant dickhead?" Easton suggested.

"Yeah." Apparently I had a type. I wrapped my arms around myself. "What the hell are you doing here anyway? It's a long way from Opal Springs."

"I'd suggest I'm stalking you, but the truth is I had a

meeting," he said. "Coach Foster and I came down to talk to the AIHL. We meet with them every now and again to talk about the expansion and keep them updated on everything."

"They trust you to do that?" I couldn't resist the dig. It was nothing he didn't deserve.

He grinned. "Believe it or not, they think I'm one of the more fine, upstanding members of the team. Which is exactly why you don't see Cruz here." Something crossed his eyes, and his gaze dropped towards my pussy before he looked back up again.

"I'd suggest you're a good actor, but we both know that already," I said. I grabbed the handle of my suitcase and started to wheel it away. I'd call Dad when I was in my hotel room.

"The only people I act around are my team," he called out after me. "That date, that wasn't an act. Everything I said to you, I meant it. Including that kiss."

I stopped walking but didn't turn around. Part of me wanted to believe him, but the run in with Jason, on top of everything else, had me rattled.

It only took Easton a couple of strides to catch up to me. He stood in front of me, expression intense. "You had fun, didn't you? You feel that electricity between us. You don't have to say anything. I see it in your eyes right now. You felt it when we kissed. I didn't want to go too far, too fast, but I want to see where we could go. Have lunch with me. I'll show you I don't bite. Unless you ask nicely." He grinned.

I tried, but I couldn't ignore the way my pussy throbbed and my heart flipped. I *did* feel electricity between us, but I also didn't want to get my heart broken into a thousand pieces. Between him and Cruz, I hardly knew which way was up.

I sighed. "Fine. Lunch. I could eat, I guess."

He grinned. "Of course you could." He took the handle of my suitcase. "Where are you staying?"

"It's a good thing I don't live in Melbourne." Easton leaned his shoulder against the wall beside the door and patted his stomach. "I'd eat so much I'd explode."

"Sam's is one of the better restaurants around." I swiped my card over the lock and pushed the door open. "Thanks for the company."

While I still stood in the half-open door, he hooked his hand around the back of my neck and slammed his mouth down to mine.

Before I could think about it too much, I found myself kissing him back. He slid his tongue between my lips and thrust into my mouth like he was pounding his cock into my pussy.

He guided me deeper into the room until the door closed behind us.

I didn't fight him as he led me over to the bed and pressed me down onto my back. I didn't want to fight him. I wanted him to touch me. I wanted him to learn every part of my body and make me his.

Without breaking off our kiss, he supported himself on his knees and elbows while he lay over me. Only the lightest pressure from his weight held me in place. Having him on top of me like that made me as aroused as hell.

I groaned against his mouth and wrapped my legs around his hips so his already erect cock was nestled between my thighs. He ground himself against me slowly, putting pressure on my clit through all the layers of clothes. I was wetter than hell in a handful of heartbeats.

Finally, he broke off our kiss and worked his way down so he could undo my jeans and tug them down my hips.

"Black lace. You must have known you'd see me today." He glanced up at me and grinned.

I rolled my eyes at him.

He chuckled and pulled off my shoes so he could work my leggings the rest of the way off. He bent my knees and ran the back of his hand over the gusset of my panties.

"You're so wet." He cocked his head. "Why is that?" He slipped a finger under the fabric and over the seam of my pussy. "This isn't for that douchebag, is it?"

He raised an eyebrow at me, but looked like he'd rip Jason's head off if I said it was. I should have been disturbed by that, but instead I found it hot. I suspected he might have come close to strangling Jason earlier. It might be the underlying current of violence that attracted me to hockey players. The aggression they worked out on the ice, which still bubbled just under the surface. Ready to be used with a fist or an elbow. Or even with barbed words.

"Fuck no," I replied.

"Then who?" He was toying with me. "Tell me who made you this wet, Cat." He ran his fingers back the other way.

"You did," I said, my voice husky. "You made me that wet."

He smiled. "Of course I did." He hooked his fingers into the waistband of my panties and tore them in two before shoving them into his pocket. He lay down with his head between my legs and replaced his fingers with his tongue, teasing my clit and entrance.

"You taste better than anything I've ever eaten," he groaned.

He went on licking and sucking me, nipping my clit every so often. At the same time, he slid a finger into my pussy, then another. He hooked his hand around until he was working me from the inside and out. His touch was firm, rough at times. Obviously practised. He knew just what to do to make me feel good.

I grabbed handfuls of bed covers and gripped them hard while I rocked my hips, grinding myself against his mouth. The stubble on his cheeks and chin grazed the tender skin inside my thighs, but I loved the way it felt. Rough and masculine.

He lifted his shining mouth. "Come for me, Pussy Cat." He lowered his mouth again and grazed his teeth over my clit.

I groaned, arching my back and closing my eyes. Letting everything melt away but his touch on my most sensitive places.

"Easton," I moaned. "I'm so close." Every touch felt so good. Every lick and suck drove me closer and closer to the edge. Finally, I pitched over, into an orgasm that swamped my entire body, from the tips of my toes to the top of my head.

I arched my back and cried out his name, while he went on working me long after I came down from the peak of bliss. He only stopped when I melted into a puddle on the mattress.

18
CATALINA

I grimaced to myself and pulled my bag up to my shoulder. I'd managed to avoid the team since I got back to Opal Springs. After Easton ate me out, he hurried off to his meeting. Since then, I'd been skating at night, after the kids' classes were finished. So far, I hadn't seen them training once and I hadn't bumped into any of them around town.

Until now.

Shaw pushed into the rink as I was just about to head out. A bag over his shoulder suggested he was here to skate too.

He stopped to give me a glare.

Not that I owed him anything, but I pushed my bag further up my shoulder and said, "Don't worry, I'm moving back to Melbourne at the end of the week." That might head off any argument before it began. No doubt the rest of the team would know within the hour. Whatever, I didn't care if they did.

His jaw clenched. "That's for the best." He looked me up and down, but his expression didn't change; it still suggested he wished I'd never been born. Honestly, the feeling was mutual right now. As far as I was concerned, he could go fuck himself.

I was tempted to ask why he hated me so much, but what did it matter now? In a few days, I'd be gone and focusing on training and the trials. With any luck, by the time I returned to Opal Springs, the Ghouls would have their own arena and I could have this place to myself. I wouldn't have to see them again, unless they had a pet that needed treatment. If that was the case, they could take the animal to another vet if they had a problem with me. I would never refuse an animal treatment, no matter who their human was. The clinic would side with me if any of them decided to make any trouble. At least, I hoped they would.

"Right," I said instead. I stepped around him and headed out the door. I sensed his eyes on me until the glass door closed behind me. I resisted the urge to look back.

I walked across the darkened car park to my car. When I arrived a few hours ago, it was full of family vehicles. I'd had to park in the back corner furthest from the rink, and the lights. I didn't mind the walk or how cold the night was. I was warmed up from training. So much so, it was refreshing out here.

I unlocked my car and opened the back door to toss my bag in before closing it again with a thud.

I took a step to the driver's side door. I'd just reached for the handle when I was slammed face first into the side of my car.

Pain lanced through my cheekbone, forcing a cry from between my lips. My eyes filled with tears of pain and surprise. I hadn't even heard anyone come up behind me.

Rough fingers grabbed my hair, pulled me back and turned me around. He pushed me against the side of the car.

"What the—" I struggled and tried to pull away but I was held hard.

All I could make out was a long, lean figure, dressed in black. Male, judging by the height and physique. His face was covered, but it was too dark to make out what with. It could have been a ski mask, or a scarf wrapped several times around his head, leaving his eyes exposed.

That was all I registered before he drove his fist into my face.

I cried out again. My head spun. I crumpled to the hard ground beside my rear tyre. The knees of my leggings tore, gravel grazing my skin.

He dropped to his knees beside me and pounded his fist into my face again.

I threw up my arms to protect my head, and curled up as small as I could make myself. I tried to cry out for help, but I couldn't manage a sound other than grunts of pain as he punched me over and over.

My whole existence consisted of pain and terror. Every strike was harder and more agonising than the one before.

I was going to die. He was going to kill me right here beside my car, outside the ice rink. My father and my sister were going to be devastated. And my cat. Poor Lucifer wouldn't understand where I went. I hoped Dad gave her lots of tuna. Why that was what went through my mind, I didn't know, but it did.

Finally, the punches stopped. I kept my arms firmly over my head, my eyes screwed shut. Had he left? I didn't think so. I sensed him close before I heard his ragged breathing. Puffing lightly from beating me.

"You shouldn't have come here," he growled softly. His voice was low, barely more than a harsh whisper. "You should have stayed away. Everyone would have been better off."

The gravel crunched under his shoes as he got to his feet. He kicked me a couple of times in the side before he stepped away.

I started to register relief that I was still alive, he was gone.

His footsteps returned.

Please no. No more. I curled up in a tighter ball.

"I'm going to make sure you never get in the way again."

Terror became blind panic. He was going to kill me. Murder me in cold blood right here, right now.

No, I couldn't let that happen. I had to do something. Fight back, run, *something*. I'd never given up on anything before, I wasn't going to start now.

I scrambled to my knees and started to crawl.

He leaned over and grabbed my ankle.

I kicked out, my shoe connecting with his leg.

"Fucking bitch." He let go of my ankle. I must have kicked him harder than I realised. Good. Next time I'd aim higher. Right in his balls.

I crawled faster, trying to reach the front of the car where I could lever myself to my feet. I considered rolling under the car, but he could find me there. I cursed myself for putting my phone in my bag instead of keeping it on me. I could have lain under the car and called the police.

"*Now* you want to leave." He struck something against the palm of his hand. It made a dull slap, again and again, deliberately ominous and threatening.

Don't let it get to you, I told myself. *That's what he wants. For you to feel helpless. Cat Ryan is not helpless.* If I ever needed to be strong in my life, I needed it now. If I was going to get out of this alive, I had to fight.

I glanced back to see him tapping the handle of a hammer against his opposite hand.

Shit.

I lunged around the side of the car and sat for a

moment, trying to gather myself. He was playing with me now. Certain he had me. It was only a matter of time before he caught me and killed me.

I needed to get the hell out of here. Back to the rink or... Somewhere.

I turned around and knelt in front of the car, gripping on as best I could with shaking hands. Teeth gritted, I forced myself up.

Everything hurt. Blood trickled down my face. I thought my cheekbone might be broken. A couple of ribs too.

If I was going to get out of here alive, I needed to work through the pain. My options were to give in and die, or ignore the agony until I could get to help. Working through the pain from training was one thing, this was another. Harder, but not impossible. I reminded myself of all the things I'd gone through in the last couple of years. I hadn't let any of it defeat me and I wasn't going to let him do it either.

Be strong, I told myself.

I stood at the front of the car, my palms pressed against the cold metal. My legs trembled, weak as a newborn horse. I forced them to keep supporting my weight. They had to. I had no other choice.

He moved closer.

I took a step, but my vision went dark. I shook my head. If I couldn't run, then maybe help could come to me in time. I'd have to yell loud to be heard inside the rink. If anyone was left to hear me. I couldn't turn my head to see if the light was still on. I just had to hope like hell.

I tipped my head back and started to shout, "Fire!" That would get people's attention faster than calling for help. If there really was a fire, people would come running.

I barely got out the F when he lunged towards me and slammed his fist into my face. I cried out. Once again, I crumpled to the ground. I barely felt myself fall, until my hand grazed over the gravel and my shoulder hit with sharp agony.

My vision went darker still. The pain was starting to get the better of me. Despair took the place of determination, slowly, but steadily.

These would be my final moments.

I hadn't thought much about my own death, but I never would have guessed it would come like this. Not in a fit of violent, angry darkness. Not with my blood seeping into the ground.

My cheek was pressed against the cold gravel, my shallow breath faintly misting the air in front of me. A visual reminder that I wasn't dead yet, but I soon would be.

I never should have returned to Opal Springs. Not after my injury, and not after seeing Felicia. I should have stayed in Melbourne. I was scared the Ghouls would take the rink away from me. That I wouldn't be able to skate here and get my fitness back for the trials.

And now, they were going to take a lot more than that away from me. My life. My future. I didn't know which one of them this was, but I had no doubt it was a member of the team.

I tried to think, to put the voice together with a name, but the only thought that ran through my head over and over was, "I'm so sorry, Dad. I'm so sorry." Nothing else was coherent, or made any sense. Just this one thought.

I wanted nothing more than my father's arms around me right now. If he was here, he'd make things right. Somehow. He always made things right, no matter how bad I thought they were. No one could kiss my bumps and bruises better, or chase away nightmares like he could. It was a long time since he'd done either of those things, but if he was here, he'd do them now.

He wasn't here. He was at home, probably watching some kind of reality TV beside the fire. Was Lucifer on his lap, purring her head off? He loved it when she did that. Loved to stroke her fur while she curled up, sharing his warmth.

"I'm sorry, Daddy." Did I say that out loud, or just in my head? I didn't know. I didn't think it passed my lips. The only sounds coming out of my mouth were groans of pain and the occasional agonised breath.

I didn't know how many times I thought that before my attacker knelt down beside me again.

"Now you can stay out of our way." That was the

last thing I heard before he slammed the hammer down onto my leg.

    I screamed in pain and the whole world went black.

19

SHAW

I tried to focus on skating. All I could think about was Cat and the feeling of unease that crept up my spine the moment she walked out the door. I could have ignored it, but I'd learned in the past that ignoring my instincts led to regret. If there was anything in life I didn't have time for, it was regret. Make a choice and live with it, that was how I did things.

That didn't stop me from grunting with annoyance as I changed my skates back to sneakers and threw them into my bag. I swung the strap onto my shoulder and flicked off the lights before I stepped out, locking the door behind me.

I peered across the dark car park. A flash of movement caught my eye. I swivelled my head to look down to that back corner. I saw nothing but darkness and a car still parked in the lot.

Why was Cat's car still here? The back of my neck prickled.

I stepped closer. A faint groan broke the silence. Soft enough for me to wonder if I'd heard it at all.

I hesitated for a moment. If she wasn't alone…

I squashed down the rising anger. There wasn't time for that now. I needed to be in control, like always.

Another groan, fainter this time. That was not a sound of pleasure.

Fuck.

I dug into my pocket for my phone and turned on the light.

Fucking hell.

"Cat?" I ran the few steps to her and dropped to my knees beside her. My bag slid down my arm and hit the gravel. I jerked my wrist out of the strap.

Cat lay on the ground, hair fanned out behind her. Her face was a mess of blood and bruises. Her hoodie was covered in blood. One of her legs lay at an angle, the fabric of her leggings torn. What I could see of her leg looked smashed up. At first, I thought she was dead. A tiny whimper slipped out from between her lips, but her chest barely rose and fell.

Fuck.

Fuck.

Fuck.

"Cat," I whispered. "What the hell? We need to get you to a hospital." I smoothed the hair off her face while holding the phone in the other hand to make the call.

Every strand was wet with blood. So much fucking blood. Too much.

"They won't be long." I shoved my phone back into my pocket and sat down beside her. Every instinct told me to gather her up and hold her close, but common sense prevailed. I couldn't tell how injured she was. If I moved her, even a little bit, I could kill her. All I could do right now was whisper soothing things and stroke her temple.

"Please don't die," I said softly. "Why would anyone do this to you?" Why hadn't I listened to my instincts sooner? I might have been able to stop this from happening. I remembered the flicker of movement. Was that who did this to her? I must have just missed them. A couple of minutes earlier…

"I'm so fucking sorry." My voice was a harsh sound in the quiet night. The only sound apart from the occasional passing car. Otherwise, we could have been alone in the world. I wanted that, but not like this. Not when she might…

I swallowed. "Don't fucking die. Hang on for a bit longer. The ambulance is coming."

The sirens were audible in the distance, quickly getting closer. I willed them to hurry up. It felt like an eternity passing by for every second that ticked over.

I thought about looking for whoever beat the shit out of her, but even if I could tear myself away from her, they'd be long gone by now. They ran when they saw me. If I'd come out of the rink any later, they might have used whatever they used on her leg on another part of her. They might have killed her. They might have raped her.

As far as I could tell, her clothes were still more or less intact. That was a small fucking mercy.

I was still going to rip them apart when I found out who they were, and caught up with them. It was bad enough, Cruz and Easton were always hovering around, trying to screw her or screw with her. The things they said about her made me want to punch them both in the face. Her returning to Melbourne would have gotten her away from them.

That was best for her, even if it meant she was away from me too. I could only stand to lose her if she was also away from those assholes.

Or so I thought. Now, I didn't know what to think. If she died…

"This is bullshit," I told her. Nothing about this was random. I wasn't sure who did this to her, but it was one of the guys on the team. My team. I wasn't close to any of them, not really, but we were supposed to work together. None of them were supposed to do shit like this.

Before I could contemplate any further, the ambulance pulled into the car park and headed over to us. I raised my hand in front of my face to keep from being blinded by the headlights. And to wave, to show them where we were.

"Help is here. They're going to make this better."

It was a flat-out lie. They could take her to the hospital and make her physically well, but nothing was going to make any of this *better*. Someone targeted her and beat her. That would fuck anyone up. She was going to be scarred from this forever, even if she made a full physical recovery. Memories of the attack would always linger in her mind.

I stood and moved out of the way as the ambulance crew got to work.

"Shit, is this—" One wheeled over a gurney. Her badge read Kendall.

"Yeah." Her partner was assessing Cat's injuries. "We'll need to let Doctor Ryan know." He glanced up at me. He obviously thought I had something to do with this. I didn't give a shit. I just wanted him to do his job and stop her from dying right here, on the cold fucking ground.

"I'm not finding anything life-threatening," he said finally. "Let's get her on the gurney and get her to the ER."

"I'm coming too," I said. I didn't give a crap if my car got stolen out of the parking lot while I was away. A piece of metal wasn't important compared to her.

When they loaded her into the back of the ambulance, I climbed in and sat beside her.

"Are you related?" Kendall asked.

"I'm her boyfriend," I said. Let them think whatever they wanted to, they weren't getting me out of here without dragging me. None of us had time for that.

The only thing that mattered right now was getting Cat to the hospital. She was so pale and still. They'd wiped enough of the blood off her face for me to see scrapes and bruises, mostly over the left side of her face. The asshole who beat her was probably right-handed. That only ruled out a couple of guys on the team. As far as I was concerned, the rest were under suspicion until proven otherwise.

Kendall climbed in and sat on the other side of the ambulance before the door was closed behind us with a thud.

"I found her like this," I said softly. "But it's my fault. I had a feeling something was wrong and I didn't act on it sooner." I didn't know why it mattered, but for some reason it did. I didn't want anyone to think I'd do this to her. I'd sooner beat Cruz, Dean and Easton to a pulp to keep them away from her than hurt a hair on her head.

"You'd be surprised how often I hear that," she said. "But it's not your fault. You found her in time to call us. If she lay there all night in the cold, this might have had a very different outcome."

I nodded. My stomach turned at that thought. If I hadn't skated tonight, I might have arrived at the rink in the morning to find her cold, dead body. No one deserved to die alone like that, especially her.

Correction, whoever did this to her deserved to die alone, and in agony. After I broke every bone in their body.

"I just wish…" A couple of minutes could have made all the difference.

Although, should I have seen this coming before tonight? Most of the team, Cruz in particular, were pissed at having to share the rink with her. He, Easton and Dean wanted to take her down however many pegs they thought she needed to go. I couldn't put this past any of them.

"What she needs right now is your positive thoughts," Kendall said. "Focus on her getting better. Let the police deal with the rest of it."

"Yeah." I'd never felt so powerless in my life. I'd do whatever I had to do to help her heal, but I'd never shake the thought that I could have stopped this before it happened. I should have been meaner. If I had, maybe she would have stayed in Melbourne. Then this wouldn't have happened.

I sighed to myself. Yes it would. She was stubborn. She would have returned just to piss me off. There was nothing I could have said or done. Nothing but listen to my instincts sooner. That was going to live with me and her for the rest of our lives.

"Have you known her for long?" Kendall asked.

"No," I said honestly. "A few weeks. It feels like I've known her for years. She's that kind of person, you know? She's like a magnet."

Kendall smiled softly. "I only know her through her father. She seems lovely, but he might be slightly biased."

"Nope, not biased," I said. "She *is* lovely." That wasn't a word I used often. Or at all. Fucking gorgeous was more accurate. Smart, beautiful, sexy as hell. But lovely would do.

"I can see you care about her a lot," Kendall said.

"I do," I said. "The moment I saw her." I didn't believe in love at first sight until I lay eyes on Catalina Ryan. My heart wanted to leap out of my chest and my cock out of my pants. Fucking Cruz spoke to her first. I stood back and listened, wanting to punch him in the face. Instead, I glared at her, wanting to make her uncomfortable enough to stay away. For her own good.

Warning Cruz would have had the opposite effect. He would have gone after her harder. Bad enough that I had to hear about him touching her, making her come. Then Easton, tracking her down in Melbourne. He told us all the details and had a good laugh.

Asshole.

He also told us about her run-in with her ex. I could get behind Easton warning him off her. Ironic though that was. None of them should have been anywhere near her. Not even in the same room. Not the same city. They didn't deserve to breathe the same air as her.

"That's so sweet," Kendall said.

I blinked a couple of times, trying to remember what I last said. My thoughts certainly weren't sweet. Right, I'd said something about the first time I saw her.

I shrugged. "When you know, you know."

"I can tell you care about her very much." She

smiled. "Don't worry, we'll do all we can to help her to a full recovery. Our main concern is concussion and the state of her leg. It looks pretty smashed up."

"Yeah, it does." My gaze drifted to her leg, even though it was covered with a sheet and a splint. I didn't want to think about the implications of that injury. I'd see her through it. Whatever it took, I'd be by her side. Then I would destroy the person who did this to her.

They should enjoy breathing while they could.

20
CATALINA

A low voice broke through the haze of semi consciousness.

"Yes it's not…" They spoke so low I couldn't hear the next bit.

Another voice responded. "It's badly broken. The x-rays showed…"

"The surgeon said she'd need pins…"

I drifted off again.

The next time I woke, someone was holding both of my hands. No, there was tape around one, holding a needle in place. My eyes open long enough to see a tube leading to an IV bag hanging from a pole.

"Kitty Cat?"

I groaned softly. "Daddy?" I rolled my head the other way and blinked at his worried face. "You're here."

He smiled and brushed hair off my face. "Where else would I be? How are you feeling?"

"Like I've been run over by a truck." My face felt stiff and a little sore. The IV was probably keeping the worst of the pain at bay.

With a rush, I remembered what happened. The attack, the hammer. Panic started to worm its way through me.

"It's okay, try to relax.," Dad said quickly. "You remember what happened? Did you see who it was?"

I frowned. Stopped when it hurt my cheek. "No. They had something over their face. They were tall… strong. I tried to fight back. I tried." Tears prickled my eyes.

"Of course you did, Kitty Cat," he said gently. "We'll find who did this to you, I promise." He glanced over his shoulder.

I followed his line of sight and my whole body stiffened. "What is *he* doing here?"

"Shaw has been here the entire time. He refused to leave, even to get something to eat."

Shaw rose from the chair beside the door. "Hey." He didn't smile, but his expression wasn't his usual disdain. He looked exhausted. "When I found you next to your car, I thought—" He lowered his gaze to the floor.

The increased confusion hurt my head.

"He was the one who called the ambulance," Dad said. "He saw your attacker leave, but not who it was. If it wasn't for him…" He swallowed hard. "I'll leave you two to talk. I'll be back in a couple of minutes." He nodded to Shaw and slipped out the door.

Shaw lowered himself into the seat my father just vacated. He massaged the back of his neck with his hand. His clothes were wrinkled, chin covered in at least a couple of days' growth of stubble.

I should have been wary, but for some reason I wasn't. That didn't stop me from speaking bluntly.

"He seems certain you didn't do this to me." What could he do that was worse than what was already done?

Shaw didn't seem surprised by the thinly veiled accusation. "Because I didn't. I'm going to find out who did and make them drown in their own blood." He winced and worked out a knot before lowering his hand.

"Why?" I asked. "You hate my guts more than the rest of them do."

He leaned forward and rested his elbows on the side of the bed beside my shoulder. "I never hated your guts," he said in a whisper. "I hated the way those assholes treated you."

"You wanted me gone," I said evenly. As evenly as I could with him so close. He smelled faintly of sweat, and coffee, the scent warring with the sterile hospital smell.

"I wanted you away from them," he said. "I wanted their bullshit locker room talk about you to stop. I wanted you to be mine, but I was furious you gave any of them the time of day. I couldn't understand why you'd do that. It was easier to tell myself I hated you than to think about you with them."

"You had me convinced." I narrowed my eyes at him. I wasn't completely certain he wasn't about to grab a pillow and smother me with it. I was sure Dad was close if Shaw tried anything. "Why haven't you left?"

"Because we both know this wasn't random." He traced the line of my jaw with his fingertip, manoeuvring around bruises. "I wasn't going to leave you vulnerable to them again." He exhaled out his nose. "I already did that too many times. Last night in particular. I should have been there to stop him."

I shook my head slightly. "I don't understand. Why do you give a shit?" Why should I trust him when the rest of his team treated me the way they did? What made him any different?

"I give a shit because I've been in love with you since the first moment I saw you," he said. "Cruz, Easton; they were already in the way. Them and their bet." He sounded bitter.

"Their bet?" I had one with Easton about me enjoying hockey and then going out on the first date together. I didn't think Shaw was referring to that.

He looked angry, but it wasn't aimed at me. "The two of them made a bet on who would fuck you first.

Which of them would get the cock into your pussy before the others. Then Cruz and Easton bragged that they were toying with you, making you fall for them. Dean seemed to be biding his time, waiting for them to piss you off. He seems nice, but he's a sly son of a bitch. For some reason, he seems to idolise those two. The three of them are as bad as each other."

Tears threatened again. "It was all just a bet?" I should have guessed. Why else would they show any interest in me? I could easily have fallen for them, and they would have ripped my heart out.

"I'm sorry," Shaw whispered. "I should have done something sooner. I could have told you but I wasn't sure if you'd believe me. They can be charming when they want to. Especially Easton."

"Yeah, he can." I got him so wrong. At least now my hate for Cruz was fully justified. Easton, who seemed to save me from Jason, was as much of an asshole as my ex. "Thank fuck none of them won the bet."

Shaw looked relieved at that, but it only lasted for a few moments. "Your leg, did you happen to see what he used?"

I didn't want to think about it, but I nodded. "It was a —" The breath left my body. "He had a hammer." I thought back, but the details still weren't clear in my mind. "You think it's possible *Easton* did this to me? My attacker said he wanted me to go away. That sounds more like Cruz."

Shaw shrugged. "I wouldn't put it past either of

them. They might have worked together on it. They're both driven to make sure the Ghouls succeed, at any cost. If that means doing something like this, they'd do it. When I figure out which one of them it is, I'll break their fucking legs."

I believed him, but then his words made my blood run cold. "That was the point of this, wasn't it? They were never going to kill me, they just wanted me out of their way. Off the ice."

"They could have killed you," he said tersely. "If I hadn't found you when I did…" His jaw worked, back and forth in agitation and frustration.

"One of them might have turned up to rescue me," I said bitterly. "They would have let me be grateful to them." I might have let them win the bet because of it.

"They might have," Shaw agreed. "I wouldn't put that past them either." He gritted his teeth. "For the record, you don't owe me any gratitude. You don't owe me anything. I'm just grateful I could tell you how I felt."

I wasn't sure what to say to that. I couldn't deny the physical attraction I felt the moment I first saw him. He saved my life and stayed with me when he could have left and got on with his life. He might not need gratitude, but he had mine.

"Thank you," I said softly. "You could have walked away and left me there."

"The other guys might have done that, but I

wouldn't," he said, his tone gentler this time. "I'm just sorry I didn't get to you before I did."

"Unless you were in on this, then it wasn't your fault," I said. "I just don't understand why they'd do this. I was leaving at the end of the week."

"Did any of them know that?" he asked.

I frowned. "No. You were the first one I told. I guess that's proof you didn't do this. Unless you didn't want me to leave."

"I didn't, but I would have let you go, to get you away from them," he said. "None of this should have happened, not like this. It might not have if they knew you were leaving. They would have tried harder to win the bet before you left town. Then they would have bragged about it for the rest of the season."

"So it's my fault," I whispered. "I should have made sure they knew."

His expression and voice were firm. "None of this is your fault. They were acting like entitled pricks from the start. Toddlers who couldn't share a toy. And now, here you are, in the hospital. Because of them."

I pushed myself up into my elbows and looked down at my sheet covered body. I wriggled my toes. Those on my right feet moved easily, but the left were a little stiff. My leg was encased in what felt like a bandage.

Tentatively, I lifted the edge of the sheet and looked down. I hadn't let myself think this far, not yet. In the back of my mind I knew I'd have to face it. I'd heard my father speaking when I was half asleep. Something about a bad break and pins.

"It's not good is it?" I lowered the sheet and sat back against the pillows Shaw placed behind me.

"You should wait for your father." He pulled the chair closer.

"If you care about me the way you say you do—" I started.

"I do and I'd only give you a vague, uneducated answer," he said. "But I'm a butcher by trade and I'd say it looked tenderised." He wasn't pulling any punches. "They did x-rays while you were asleep. For what it's worth, they said your face is bruised but not broken. Neither are your ribs."

I lightly touched my face with my fingertips. "It feels like a mess."

"You still look fucking gorgeous to me," he said.

I snorted. "Do you have a mirror?"

"I have a phone." He pulled his out of his pocket and turned the screen on. He turned around to face me. "See? Hot as hell."

The left side of my face was covered in bruises, black, blue and yellow. "It looks like my face was tenderised."

He turned off his phone and shoved it back into his pocket. He pushed himself up off the chair and sat down beside me on the edge of the bed.

"You're beautiful," he said softly. "I'm going to make you a promise right now. Nothing like this will happen to you ever again. I'll personally make sure of it. Even if I have to follow you around and never sleep again." He leaned in and lightly brushed his lips over mine.

"I may never sleep again if you're going to stalk me," I said. I liked the way his lips felt on mine, but I was wary. Of him. Of any other guy. Of myself.

"Not stalk," he said. "Think of it more as following you around like a bodyguard or a puppy."

"I never would have thought of you as being like a puppy," I said. "Bodyguard works better. Except that puts you in a bad position with the rest of your team, doesn't it? They all hate my guts."

"They don't all hate you," he said. "A couple of them are all right. Jagger, Mitch and the other guys. And Coach Foster. And me."

"You would say that," I said. "Why should I trust you?"

"I know I haven't given you any reason to, but I'll prove myself to you," he said. "Whatever it takes. If I have to give up hockey, I'll do it. I don't give a shit about that. I need to make it up to you, for not getting to you in time. And letting those guys do all that shit to you. This is their fault, but it's mine too."

He shook his head. "I fucked up bad, but I'm going to do what I can to fix it. I don't want you to keep doubting me forever."

"I want to believe you," I said. "My track record sucks. I can't just—"

He cut me off. "I know you can't. I don't expect you

to. I have a shit load of work to do. I'll make you another promise. I'll never lie to you. If I do, I have a nice sharp cleaver at work. You can use it on me if you want to."

"I'd rather use it on whoever did this to me," I said.

"Me too," he said, his voice low and angry. "Me too."

21
CATALINA

Dad came back a short time later, one of those big x-ray envelopes in his hand. His expression was grim.

"Go home and get some rest," he said to Shaw, leaving no room for argument. "You're no use to yourself or anyone if you're exhausted."

Shaw looked like he wanted to argue anyway, but eventually he nodded and leaned over to kiss my cheek. "I'll be back later."

I watched him leave, not sure what to think. He did have a cute ass, I'd give him that. Believing everything else— That was a different story.

Dad closed the door and sat on the edge of the bed, right where the player just vacated. "He seems nice."

"There's a few of them who do," I said dryly. I nodded to the envelope. "Do I want to know?"

"Cat…" He exhaled heavily.

"It's not good, is it?" I asked.

He looked like he wanted to tell me everything would be fine and kiss my leg better, but he couldn't lie to me. Not about this.

"No," he said finally. "It's not good. You're going to need surgery. I've spoken to the surgeon and he's fitting you in as soon as he's able to."

That was no surprise. It wasn't the first time I'd had surgery. I'd had it when I first injured my knee. I expected that might be the case this time too.

"Okay," I said lightly. "I have surgery and then work on recovering." I was trying very hard not to think about the very next thing on my mind. I had no choice when Dad went there first.

"You'll miss the trials. The Olympics." He set down the envelope beside me.

I swallowed back a ball of emotion. "I know, but there's another one in four years."

"Cat." His eyes were full of regret.

"No," I said firmly. "I'll miss this one, but I won't be too old the next. I'll just keep working hard and… And…" My emotions were getting the better of me.

"The surgeon said it's unlikely there will be a next," he said. "He said you'll walk again. Eventually, you'll be able to skate, but the damage is too extensive. Your leg won't take the pressure of intensive training."

Tears were pouring freely down my face. "He says that *now*." A sob escaped from between my lips.

"Sweetheart, he's an expert," Dad said. "I wouldn't

let just anyone treat my baby girl. If he says you'll never compete again, chances are you won't."

"No no no no." I shook my head and dissolved into more tears and silent sobbing. "It can't be forever. They took that away from me."

I remembered thinking my attacker was going to take my life, but he might as well have. He'd stolen my dream. The thing I'd spent my whole life working towards. The first thing I thought about when I woke in the morning and the last when I went to sleep. And for what? Because they were, like Shaw said, a spoilt toddler who couldn't share.

Dad wrapped his arms around me and pulled me to the comfort of his broad chest. He rubbed a hand up and down my back, speaking soothing words in my ear.

I didn't know how long I cried for. It didn't help to wash away the pain or the anger. All it did was leave me feeling exhausted and wrung out, like a limp dishrag. Not even having my father's arms around me helped. I'd never, in my entire life, felt as defeated as I did right then. Or as furious.

I let them touch me when I should have been kicking them in the balls. Whether it was Cruz or Easton, or one of the other players, I didn't give a shit. They knew what was going on and did nothing to stop it. As far as I was concerned, they could all get fucked.

Finally, the sobs subsided and Dad wiped my eyes with a tissue. "Selfishly, I'm glad you won't be leaving Opal Springs."

It was fortunate I'd just blown my nose, or my snort would have been messy. "I'm so glad there's an upside to this."

"The upside is that you have a good job you can still do. If ice racing was your career, your whole life would be in limbo."

"It was my passion," I said softly.

"Animals are your passion too," he reminded me. "You're in a much better position to train a cat army to chew on your attacker."

I wiped my eyes again. "I can't tell if you're trying to cheer me up or if you're serious about that." A cat army sounded perfect right about now. Maybe with a few puppies thrown in. And Leonard. The old Labrador could lick the crap out of them. No, he deserved better than that.

"A bit of both," Dad said. "The point is, it's not the end of the world. It's not even the end of *your* world. There's nothing stopping you from skating again when you've recovered. You could coach."

I heard the catch in his voice and looked at him steadily. "I'm sorry. Sometimes I forget you had to stop doing what you loved too."

"Under the circumstances, you're forgiven for forgetting about me," he said. "Yes, I did have to give up speed skating too. But I wouldn't change a thing. I love treating patients and I love being a father to you and your sister. I wouldn't have missed any of that. And you won't regret having to focus on your career. Skating is only one thing about my beautiful daughter. Not the whole picture."

"Yeah," I said on an exhale. "I just have to take time to accept what I've lost." What I had stolen from me.

If Cruz or Easton were in front of me right now, I'd punch them both. They deserved to be dragged down to earth with a painful thud. For the bet, as well as for the attack. What sort of asshole bets on fucking someone? Who makes a game of getting someone to fall for them? Did working full-time jobs and playing hockey leave them with so much time to be petty fucking asshole pricks from hell?

Evidently, it did. They'd regret all of this, I'd make sure of that. If I could get them both kicked off the team, that would be the sweetest revenge. Dean too.

I never hated anyone before, not like I hated them now. I wanted to ruin their lives. With or without an army of cats and puppies.

If I could trust Shaw, he could help me.

"It will take time," Dad agreed. "The police will want to talk to you too. Think about everything you saw and commit it to memory. Even the smallest detail could help find this asshole. He better hope the police find him before I do." His smile was brutal.

To protect me, there was nothing he wouldn't do. I wasn't sure if that extended to killing, but the look in his eyes suggested he was ready to do it.

"Is this where I tell you not to do anything rash?" I asked.

"I never do anything rash," he said. "I do things deliberately, carefully and with precision."

"I'm glad you're my father and not my enemy," I told him. "Because you're suddenly as scary as hell."

He gave me a squeeze. "No one hurts a woman I love and gets away with it. Especially my Kitty Cat."

I squeezed him back. "Thank you."

He leaned back and looked at me. "For what?"

"For being my dad." I kissed his stubbled cheek. "I couldn't have asked for better."

"I don't know." He looked regretful. "I could have tried to stop this before it happened. I could have kept you in Melbourne. If I had, this wouldn't have happened."

"It's not your fault," I said firmly. "They didn't have to do any of this. We shouldn't have to live somewhere we don't want to because of some assholes. Our lives are here in Opal Springs. You're a vital part of the community, everyone knows that. The town is lucky to have you. If they had to decide between you and a hockey team, I know which one they'd choose."

"The one that will contribute to the growth of the economy?" Dad said, looking accepting of that reality.

"The economy isn't important if you're dead," I pointed out. "How many lives do you save every week? How many times have you diagnosed an illness before it got too far? How many times have you cured people's constipation?" I couldn't help the slight tease. No one liked to be backed up, after all.

Dad chuckled. "People don't always have their priorities straight." He looked at me intently. "Obviously, or they would have used their time more productively than hurting my baby. When I think of how scared you must have been, I want to tear the whole world apart." He went from amused to an angry growl in a handful of sentences.

I leaned my cheek against his chest. "I was terrified, but I kept thinking of you. Even though you weren't there, you were still taking care of me." I was so convinced I'd never see him again, holding him now felt surreal. I'd have to make more time to spend with him and appreciate him and the things he did for me. Life was too short. The attack was a stark reminder of that.

"That's the best job I ever had," he said. "I'll do my best to do it better from now on. If anyone lays a hand on you without your permission, they'll live to fucking regret it."

"Get in line," I told him. "They have to deal with me first."

"And that Shaw guy," Dad added.

"You think he's genuine?" I asked. "I'm not sure I even know what genuine is any more." I thought I was a good judge of character, but clearly I was wrong. So fucking wrong.

"I don't know, but I saw the way he looked at you and stayed, keeping an eye on you when you slept. I thought he was going to punch the x-ray technician for going anywhere near you."

"That's both scary and sweet," I said. Easton would have done the same to Jason, so it gave me no firm conclusions. Just more questions that had no answers. But if Dad trusted Shaw, maybe I could too. If not, we'd add him to the list of people who'd regret fucking with us.

"The technician wasn't very impressed," Dad said. "You know as well as I do that medical staff don't go to work to get threatened. In the end, Shaw backed off for your sake, but he refused to leave. He might be almost as stubborn as you."

"Is that even possible?" I said jokingly.

"Probably not." He kissed my temple. "I have to speak to the specialist, but I'll be back in a few minutes, okay?" He stood and scooped up the envelope from the bed.

I nodded and leaned back against the pillows. It wasn't until he left that I let the tears overwhelm me again. I turned and curled up against the pillows to sob quietly.

Someday I'd come to terms with all of this, but it sure as fuck wasn't today. Today I just wanted to grieve the death of my dream. Later, I'd harden my heart.

22

CATALINA

"Oh my God, Cat." Marley stepped through the door, eyes wide. Eden was right behind her. "Oliver… Doctor Ryan said you were a bit battered and bruised, but I had no idea."

They both carried a gift basket in one hand and a 'get well soon' balloon in the other. The baskets each contained plush animals and more chocolate than I'd eat in a year.

"I hope you're going to help me with that." I managed a smile.

They stepped inside and noticed Shaw slumped in a chair in the corner surrounded by the same balloons they bought me.

"What is *he* doing here?" Eden asked.

Shaw regarded them both, his hazel eyes unimpressed and unmoved.

"He's appointed himself as my bodyguard," I said.

I fell back to sleep after I cried, and woke to find him sitting there again. He claimed he'd been to training and was due some time off work, so I didn't argue with him. I had no energy for that anyway. Or much of anything else for that matter. Right now, I couldn't even get out of bed without help.

"Did you have anything to do with this?" Marley asked him. She was nothing if not blunt.

"Nope," he replied. "Unless you count calling the ambulance 'involved.' And staying with her to make sure nothing else happened. If you have a problem with that, too fucking bad."

Marley sniffed and sat down in the chair beside the bed so she could hand me her gift basket. "I hope you like teddy bears. That's all they had in the gift shop. I wanted to stop and buy a bottle of tequila, but Eden said no."

Eden shrugged. "I figured alcohol might not go well with pain meds." She leaned past Marley to hand me her basket.

"I'm not sure I care about that right now," I admitted. A bottle of tequila might be exactly what I needed. "This is very sweet of you though. You shouldn't have. Especially you." I gestured toward the huge bunch of flowers Eden already sent.

"It's not enough, considering what you're going through," Eden said. "How are you feeling?"

Once again, my eyes started to glaze with tears.

"If they're upsetting you…" Shaw placed his hands

on the arms of the chair and started to push himself to his feet.

"They're not," I said quickly. The last thing I needed was him trying to toss my friends out on their ears. "Maybe you could give us a few minutes."

He looked like he might object, but he pushed himself up the rest of the way, gave both women a warning glare and stepped out the door.

"He's, um, intense," Marley said. "Didn't you say he hated your guts?"

I opened her gift basket and handed them both chocolate. "I thought he did. Turns out it was his way of trying to encourage me to stay away from the assholes on the team."

Reluctantly, I told them both about the bet the guys made on me.

"What motherfucking Neanderthals," Marley said. "I'm so sorry we dragged you to that game in the first place."

"It started before that," I said. "None of this is your fault. It's them and their bullshit egos."

"With any luck, they'll get kicked off the team before the arena is built," Eden said.

"If they aren't on the team, the AIHL might not choose the Ghouls," I pointed out. "That doesn't mean I'm going to take this…" I grimaced. "I was going to say lying down."

Marley leaned over to give me a hug. "Knowing you, you won't be lying down for long. You'll be back on your feet in no time. And on your skates?" she asked tentatively.

"Only recreationally," I said. I sucked in a deep breath and told them what my father said about not racing again.

"Oh, shit, Cat," Eden said softly. "That's so unfair."

"They won't be on the team when the police arrest them for doing this to you," Marley said.

"What do you think this means for the expansion?" Eden asked. "If the team is under investigation, the AIHL might postpone any decision."

"They might," I said softly. I hadn't thought of that. Why did it seem like no matter what I did, I was the bad guy here?

If the league passed over the Ghouls, people would blame me, even though I did exactly nothing wrong. This was all on my attacker and anyone who worked with them. I only hoped the people in town realised that. If this opportunity was lost, it wasn't through my actions.

Unless you counted my stupid attraction to asshole hockey players. I should have tried harder to stay away from them.

"All the more reason to find out exactly who did this," Marley said. "Then everyone can get on with their lives." She gaped at me. "I'm so sorry, I didn't mean—"

I waved her off. "I'm not going to claim I'm not devastated, because I am, but the last thing I need is for you to walk on eggshells around me. Okay? You've never done it before, don't start now."

"How are you such a badass?" Marley asked. "I'd be falling apart right now."

I snorted softly. "What makes you think I'm not?" On the inside I was an absolute mess. A jumble of dark emotions and unshed tears. And a growing sliver of anger that currently had no direction. I wanted to lash out at the world, but not at my friends. They didn't deserve that anymore than I deserved this.

"Because we know you better than that," Eden said. "You're the strongest woman I know. You'll bounce back from this bigger, badder and stronger than ever."

I wiped a tear off my cheek. "I don't know about that. But I'm lucky to have both of you in my corner. I don't know what I'd do without you."

"You won't need to find out," Marley said. "We have your back, no matter what happens. Would you like Eden and I to go and break some kneecaps? Because we totally would for you."

"I think that's what Shaw is for," I said. "He's ready to go off and hurt someone."

"Are you and he together?" Eden asked.

"That's what he wants," I said.

"What do you want?" Marley opened a piece of chocolate and popped it into her mouth.

I want to go back to that night and stay home instead of going to the rink, I thought.

"I don't know," I said. "I don't think I'm ready for

those kinds of decisions. I barely know what day of the week it is right now."

"It's Tuesday," Eden said. "There's a game on Friday night if they're still playing. As far as I know, they are."

"Most of the team had nothing to do with this," I said. "As far as I know. Shaw said most of them are okay guys."

"And you trust him?" Marley said around her mouthful.

"I don't know about trust just yet, but I believe him," I said. "As much as I can believe anyone with a cock right now." Which wasn't very far.

"What happens now?" Eden asked. "When do you get out of here?"

"Tomorrow," I said. "My father promised the surgeon he'd keep an eye on me. Apparently my leg now has enough pins in it to set off a metal detector."

Not really, but if I didn't make light of it, I might go crazy. "I'll be on crutches for a while. Which will be really handy if I run into any of those guys." I mimed raising a crutch and swinging it around in front of me.

Marley giggled. "You could take up fencing. Crutch versus hockey stick. May the best stick win."

I managed a small snort of laughter. "Maybe I will. We could start a whole new sport. Crutch duelling."

"Winner puts their crutch in an asshole's crotch." Eden grinned.

"That sounds like winning to me," I agreed. I'd like nothing more than to rack those guys in the balls so hard they'd spend the rest of their lives singing and talking in high-pitched voices.

"Who's winning?" Shaw asked as he stepped back through the doorway.

Marley looked over at him and grinned. "We were just talking about hitting guys in the nuts."

He grunted and slumped back in the chair in the corner. "As long as you don't direct that at me, I'm in. I have a better use for my balls." He gave me a glance, his eyes growing darker and more intense.

"You're not on the list right now," Marley told him. "But if you hurt Cat in any way, you'll move right to the top automatically."

He smirked at her. "If I hurt Cat, I'll put myself at the top of that fucking list. You'll all have a free shot." He spread his hands to either side.

"Don't think we won't take it," Eden said. "Because we totally will. Cat has been through enough."

"Yes, she has." His expression softened slightly as he looked back at me. "I'm making it my personal mission to make sure nothing else happens to her."

It was hard not to find that hot, even when I felt so fucking broken. I'd like to think I didn't need anyone to watch out for me, but I felt safer when he was in the room with me.

In the back of my mind, I reminded myself I'd felt safe with Cruz and Easton too. That left me not sure what to think or who to believe. Sooner or later, I'd have to face those guys.

Whatever happened, I wasn't letting them take anything else away from me.

"I appreciate all three of you," I said, fighting back another haze of tears. "You've all helped to get me through the last few days." Shaw with his constant presence, and Eden and Marley texting me non-stop until I was ready to have visitors.

The last couple of days were a blur of surgery, anaesthesia and pain. Days I could barely remember even now. I was aware of little more than my father's presence, and that of the hockey player in the corner. And the constant reminder of the attack.

"None of us are going anywhere," Marley said. "I think Shaw has the right idea. I might camp out here too."

"I've got this," Shaw said. "Just be around when she needs you."

She turned to him, and planted her fists on her hips. "Who died and made you the boss of Cat?"

"She almost did, and me," he said, unflinching. "I'm not the boss of her, but I'm not letting anyone upset her. She needs her rest."

I wanted to remind him that I could make my own decisions, but he was right, I was exhausted. I could happily have closed my eyes and slept for another three days. I might as well. What else did I have to do until I was well enough to get back to work?

Marley looked like she might argue with him, but finally she nodded. "We don't want to wear her out. She might decide to ban us from coming here to see her." She smirked at him, making it clear who she believed was in charge here.

"Let's not fight amongst ourselves," Eden said. "We all want the same thing. For Cat to make a full recovery."

Marley lowered her hands to her lap. "You're right. That's exactly what we all want. Don't think I won't take him up on his offer to hit him in the nuts if he does anything to slow that down."

"Noted." Shaw slumped back in the chair, his hands in his lap. It couldn't be comfortable to sit there for hour after hour. I didn't suggest he leave, even after Marley and Eden did. Whatever I said, he was staying put unless someone else he could trust was here with me.

23
CATALINA

"Don't tell anyone, but this is one of my favourite parts of the job." I pulled off the pink wig and tossed it into my bag.

"Dressing up like a princess?" Cruz gave me the side eye.

"Like you weren't having as much fun as I was." I returned his look, with added smirk. "I saw you singing *Twinkle Little Star* with the kids."

"The things we do for publicity." He brushed purple glitter off the front of his hoodie. "You like it so much, maybe you should have been a clown. Oh, wait, you already are one."

I flipped him off. "You like visiting the sick kids in the hospital as much as I do. You say you don't, but you're full of shit. Right, Dean?"

"Sounds right to me," the goalie said. "I'd rather deal with kids than paparazzi any day."

"When do you deal with paparazzi?" Cruz asked.

Dean shrugged. "I haven't yet, but we will be soon."

I grinned. "True that. You know what they say, when assholes like that follow you around, you know you've made it. And when you get invited to spend time with kids here." I gestured around the hospital corridor.

"Yeah," Dean said with a grunt. "I gotta go. Catch you guys later."

"Boxing training?" Cruz asked. Dean recently took it up as an extra exercise, as if he didn't get enough already.

"Yeah, boxing." Dean glanced at his watch. "I'm gonna be late." He hurried off down the corridor.

"I think he needs to get laid more than I do," I remarked. "Which is saying something." I hadn't been interested in a woman since I met Cat. The taste of her still lingered on my tongue. The sound of her coming echoed in my ears. Hearing her was better than the cheer of the crowds when we won a game, but it did nothing to ease the ache in my balls.

"If you're expecting sympathy, you've come to the wrong fucking place," Cruz said. "The universe keeps giving you opportunities and you don't take them."

"I told you I was taking my time," I said. "Anyway, the universe has been short on opportunities lately."

I hadn't seen Cat at the rink or anywhere in town since I got back from Melbourne. I hadn't had time to hunt her down either. I hoped she'd come to me. She felt the electricity between us, we both knew it. Sooner or later, she'd give in and insist on giving herself to me. That was what I wanted, for her to beg.

"She's learned to stay out of the team's way, I call that a win," Cruz said.

"You giving up on the bet?" I asked. "I accept your gracious defeat if you do."

He gave me the side eye again. "I ain't giving up anything. She can stay away from the team at the same time as wanting my cock. She's probably hiding in her room thinking about me and getting herself off. Come Friday night, she'll be at O'Reilly's, ready for the taking."

"By me," I said. We'd win our game and I'd win the bet. And her.

"Dream on." Cruz smirked.

I glanced into a hospital room as we walked past.

Froze.

"What the fuck?" I turned back around.

"What is it? More purple fucking glitter?"

I shook my head. "No." I walked back to the doorway and stared.

Shaw Moss was slumped in a chair in the corner, beside the window. I barely registered his presence. My attention was all on the gorgeous redhead lying in the hospital bed.

Cat's face was covered in bruises and one of her legs was covered in plaster from her ankle to just above her knee.

"Holy fucking what?" Cruz asked, gaping the same

way I was. "What the hell are you doing here? What the fuck happened?"

Her eyes widened as she registered our presence.

A moment later, Shaw was up in our faces, anger flashing in his hazel eyes.

"What the fuck you doing here? She doesn't want to see you. Either of you." He glanced out into the corridor before glaring at us again.

I shook my head. "Get out of the way, Moss. She can speak for herself." I shoved past him and stalked over to the side of the bed. "Did you get in some kind of accident?"

Where her skin wasn't bruised, was so pale her freckles stood out more than usual. Even like this, she was so fucking cute.

She recoiled from me when I put out a hand to brush hair off her face.

Recoiled.

What the hell?

"As if you don't know," she snapped.

I glanced back at Cruz, who was clearly as confused as I felt. He stood in the doorway beside Shaw, who looked ready to punch both of us.

I looked back at her. "Sweetheart, I have no idea. If I did, I would have been here sooner." What in the ever loving fuck was going on?

"I'll call the cops," Shaw said.

"Wait, what?" I held out a hand before he could pull his phone out of his pocket.

Shaw growled. "Since you're determined to play dumb, I'll tell you. She was attacked in the car park outside the rink. Beaten and her leg smashed. With. A. *Hammer*."

It took almost a full minute for his words to register. When they finally did, I didn't believe them.

I shook my head slowly. "You think I did this?"

"You or Cruz are at the top of our list," Shaw said.

I blinked hard a few times. "What the fuck do you have to do with any of this?"

"I found her," he said coldly. "If I hadn't, she could have died."

Now it was my blood that was cold. I turned back to Cat. I saw fear and accusation in her eyes.

"I didn't do this to you. I would *never* do something like that. I…care about you."

This wasn't how I wanted to tell her, but from the look on her face, I may never get another chance.

"You care about me?" She snorted in disbelief. "That's why you made a bet on who would fuck me first? Why you told your whole team what we did? And you." She nodded to Cruz. "And Dean. He was in on that bet too, wasn't he?"

"It was never meant to—"

She interrupted me. "Never meant to do what? Never meant to humiliate me? Never meant to make me feel like a piece of meat? Never meant to encourage the whole team to treat me like I was a fuck toy? I'm a person with actual fucking feelings. With hopes and dreams. A person who will never race again because of this." She waved towards her leg. "Because you felt the need to treat me like shit to boost your egos. One of you did this to me, directly or indirectly."

"My guess is directly," Shaw said.

"I swear on every hockey stick I've ever owned that I didn't do this," I said. I turned back to Cruz. He was the one who wanted her away from us the most. Away from the team. Away from the ice. Isolated so he could take full advantage. This was a stretch, even for him, but I wouldn't put it past him.

"The fuck, bro?" He raised his hands to either side. "You think I did this? That's bullshit and you know it. I save my aggression for the ice."

"Where were you three nights ago?" Shaw asked. He addressed the question to both of us.

I glanced at Cruz while thinking back. "Watching a movie at home. I got halfway through and went to bed. Remember?"

"Maybe you went to bed and maybe you went out for a while," Cruz said.

"Maybe you went out after I went to bed," I countered.

I turned back to Cat. "I admit we were assholes. That whole bet was a stupid idea. The locker room talk was bullshit. But I promise, we didn't do this, and we sure as fuck didn't ask or encourage anyone to."

The idea of anyone touching her made me want to break their arms. The thought of them hitting her made me want to kill them. The expression of disdain and mistrust on her face made me want to kill them, bring them back to life and kill them again.

Okay, I wasn't innocent, but if she hated me because of this, I was going to find who did it and make them regret ever taking their first breath.

"You might not have told them to do it outright," she said. "But you made me feel like shit." She paused for a moment. "My attacker told me to stay away from the team. That started with you." She looked pointedly at Cruz.

"It didn't end there," Shaw said. "They were both very open about fucking around with you." There was no doubt who he blamed.

"We screwed up," I said softly. "It was meant to be a bit of fun between friends."

Which she was never supposed to know about. Shaw telling her didn't help anyone. Except him. What was his game? He wasn't in on the bet, but he seemed defensive of her now. Was he trying to muscle in on what was mine? If that was what was going on, I wasn't going to let that go without a fight.

"How do we know you didn't do this?" I stared him down. "I didn't hear you telling us to shut up about her."

"As if you would have listened," he scoffed. "Cat knows I didn't hurt her. That's all I need." He gave her a glance that revealed everything. The motherfucker had it bad. I wanted to smash his head in.

"Do you know that?" I asked her. "You believe him when he says he did nothing to you?" I wanted her to say she trusted him as much as she trusted me right now. Not at all.

"Yes, I believe him," she said. "He's been looking out for me. Which is more than I can say for either of you." She glared at me, then at Cruz.

I rubbed a hand over the back of my neck. "What do I have to do to prove I didn't hurt you and never intended to hurt you?"

"Me too," Cruz said. "I might have gotten a bit out of hand with the whole rink thing. It went too far. I'm a big enough guy to admit that. It ends here. The bet too. It's off. Done."

"Too little, too late," Shaw muttered.

I ignored him. "Cruz is right. The bet is off. Locker room talk is off. We fucked up. I fucked up and I'll make it up to you."

Shit, she was supposed to be begging me, not the other way round. Yeah, I made a small mistake, but what happened to her to put her in the hospital and end her racing career, was nothing to do with me. Nothing I was ready to admit to. I was Easton Grant, up-and-coming hockey god. I'd find a way to make her forgive me.

"Stay the hell away from her," Shaw growled. "You can both get out. She doesn't have anything else to say to you."

"You don't get to decide that," Cruz told him.

"Shaw is right," Cat said. "I don't want to see either of you again. Get out of this room and stay away from me."

I glanced at Cruz. He looked angry, but it was directed at Shaw and himself, not her.

I looked back at Cat. "I'll find out who did this to you. When I do, I'm going to tear them apart with my bare hands. If you want, I'll give you his head in a box." That was extreme, but I didn't care. No one touched my woman without facing the consequences.

What if it was Cruz? I'd figure that out later.

I gave Cat a long, intense look before I turned and left the room.

24
CATALINA

"I can manage," I protested.

Ignoring me, Dad and Shaw all but carried me into the house.

Marley and Eden carried my bag and a couple of teddy bears I'd chosen to keep. Most of the plush toys and flowers I donated to the kids who weren't lucky enough to be leaving the hospital today. I couldn't bring myself to give away the ones my best friends gave me. That left at least twenty, given by the vet surgery and the patients there. Apparently the huge floppy rabbit was from Leonard the Labrador. I appreciated his thoughtfulness.

"It's our job to take care of you," Dad said. He helped me down onto the couch and moved a few cushions closer, in case I needed them.

"It's your job to take care of sick people," I corrected. "I'm not sick. I just have a broken bone." I didn't want too much of a fuss made of me. I spent enough time in the hospital wallowing, I wanted to get on with my life now. Including never seeing Easton or Cruz outside watching their team play hockey.

I didn't know what to think about their response to my attack. They'd already proven they were good actors, they might be lying through their teeth about this too. And the bet. I wasn't sure if they were genuinely sorry, or just sorry they got caught. Probably the latter. Guys like them didn't waste time with regret. They were probably making a bet about some other woman as I settled in to get comfortable.

"It's my job as your father to take care of you," Dad said. He leaned over and kissed my temple. "Can we get you anything?"

"I'd like some tea, but I can get it myself." I reached for my crutches.

"I know you need to learn to use them, but let me make you tea," Dad said. "Just this once." He held up a hand before I could argue and headed into the kitchen.

"If anyone is wondering where my stubbornness comes from." I waved in his direction and settled back down again.

"We figured." Eden sat down hard enough to make the couch bounce. "Shit, sorry."

Shaw gave her a look of warning, but didn't say anything. I couldn't kick him out of my hospital room, but I could kick him out of the house if he threatened my friends.

He smirked, but sat carefully on the other side of me.

"I'll go and help Oliver make tea," Marley said. She flashed me a smile and hurried off into the kitchen.

They just work together, I told myself. She'd never go there, and neither would he. I hoped.

"I can't believe those guys," Eden said. "They really had no idea what happened?"

"I didn't tell them," Shaw said.

Eden snapped her fingers. "That's right. You play on the same team. You trained with them a bunch of times and didn't say anything about the attack on Cat?"

"Nope." He sat back and laced his hands behind his head. "It was none of their business. If they wanted to know, they could have tried to find out."

"They wouldn't have known to ask you," I said. He probably wouldn't have told them anyway.

"They would have known to ask at your job. If either of them was interested in you, they could have dropped in to ask you out. They didn't. You know why?" He raised his shaggy eyebrows. "Because they both thought you'd go to them. They're used to women chasing them. They would have sat back and waited for you to fall onto their cock."

"Ugh, that fucking bet," Eden groaned. "That's so icky. I wonder if anyone has ever done that to me behind my back?"

"They better not," I said. "I'd send my kitten army after them." I exchanged glances with Shaw. His eyes showed his amusement, but he didn't smile. Did he ever smile? I hadn't seen him do it yet. If talking about a kitten army didn't do it, I didn't know what would.

"Cat and her kitten army." Eden grinned. "That's so perfect. I can think of a few people I'd like to send them after."

"The list is long," I agreed. "Starting with Jason and ending with my attacker. Cruz and Easton are right in the middle."

"What about Dean?" Eden asked. "Where does he fit into all of this?"

"He doesn't," Shaw said. "He has no reason to come anywhere near Cat."

"I got the impression he liked her," Eden said. "Or was he mouthing off in the locker room too?"

Shaw frowned. "I don't remember him saying anything. Not about Cat. He's the kind of guy who listens more than he speaks. He talks with his stick." He blinked. "Hockey stick. I don't want to think about his other stick. He's a good goalie. One of the best. When he's not training or working, he's working out. Running, lifting weights, boxing, whatever."

"That might explain why he never approached me," I said slowly. "He was too busy exercising." I was as crazy about fitness as the next athlete, but it was good to have a social life too, once in a while. I reminded myself he was in on the bet before I let myself get too sympathetic toward him.

"Maybe," Shaw agreed. "I don't give a shit, to be

honest. As long as he stays away from you, I don't need to break his nose. I fucking wanted to when those two stepped into your hospital room. I was ready to throw them both out the window."

"Since Cat's room was on the second floor, you wouldn't have done too much damage." Dad stepped back into the room, carrying a cup of tea in one hand and a chocolate chip muffin on a plate in the other. He placed them both down on the table in front of me.

"I would have tried," Shaw said. "I could run them over with my car if you'd like."

"I'm going to pretend I didn't hear that." Dad raised his eyebrows at the defenceman before heading back into the kitchen.

"At least we know your father won't tell the cops," Shaw said slightly louder than was necessary.

"If they hurt my daughter, then I know nothing," Dad called out.

"Didn't you take an oath or something?" I asked.

Dad came back out with more muffins and cups of coffee. "Yes, I did. The day you were born, I swore to you I'd take care of you no matter what. I take that oath more seriously than anything else in my life. Besides, it wouldn't be me doing the harm. Not with my own hands."

Shaw rubbed his chin with his thumb and forefinger while picking up a cup of coffee in his opposite hand. "I'm starting to like you, Doctor Ryan."

"Call me Oliver." Dad sat down in the chair beside

Marley. "Since we're clearly on the same side, we should be on first name terms."

Shaw nodded. "Okay with me." He sipped his coffee.

"Have the police found anything?" Marley asked. "Have they figured out who did it yet?"

"They've interviewed the entire team," Shaw said. "And everyone who worked in the rink. So far, they haven't arrested anyone." He looked irritated. "As far as I know, they haven't even found the hammer. They only need to look as far as Easton's ute."

"You're very sure he did it?" I asked.

"You're not?" Eden asked.

I shook my head and tore off a piece of muffin. "I don't know what to think. He seemed genuinely surprised to find me there in the hospital. If he and Cruz knew I was there, why not come and see me sooner? What better way to make it look like you had nothing to do with something?"

"Or they took the time to get their story straight," Marley suggested. "And perfect the art of pretending to be innocent when they were guilty as shit."

"Maybe," I said slowly.

"You really don't think so, do you?" Eden said. "Is it because you want to think the best of them? Because you don't have to be so nice if you don't want to. If they were involved, they don't deserve your goodwill."

"I know," I said quickly. "They just don't seem like the kind of guys who do more than stupid, high school locker room crap. They'd lose their careers if the police could prove they were involved. Their day jobs and their hockey dreams." I was thoughtful for a moment. "My attacker knew about my dream. He knew how to end it and what it would mean to me. Would someone do that if they had big dreams of their own they'd worked their asses off for?"

"If they thought they'd get away with it," Shaw said. "Those assholes think they're above everyone else. Why wouldn't they think they're above the law, or smarter than the cops? They think they're fucking untouchable."

"Why cover his face then?" I reasoned. "If they're untouchable, would they care if I saw them and could identify them?"

"That would have made the situation more complicated," Dad said. "Untouchable or not, they would have known what the consequences were if you pointed your finger directly at them."

"I suppose so." I realised I still had the piece of muffin in my fingers. I popped it in my mouth and groaned in pleasure at the taste. "That's so good."

My groan must have had an effect on Shaw. He gave me a look, his eyes darkened.

My clit throbbed in response. My leg was broken, not the rest of my body. Whether or not I trusted him completely, there was an undeniable attraction. Not to mention there was something particularly attractive about a guy who didn't take part in high school locker room bets.

Not to mention ones who growled at his teammates the way he had yesterday. I believed he would have punched the shit out of them on my behalf, given half a chance.

"What you need to do right now is get some rest," Dad said. "Practice using your crutches but don't overdo it. Do the exercise your physio gave you."

I made a face at him. "Yes, Father. I wasn't planning on curling up on the couch and doing nothing until the cast comes off." Although, now I thought about it, that sounded tempting. Only slightly though. I had to get back to work and life. I had to move as much as I could, especially if I was going to eat chocolate chip muffins as good as these. Getting back to fitness was going to be difficult enough without letting myself wallow for weeks on end.

"We'll all make sure you take care of yourself," Marley said. "Won't we?" She looked around at everyone, but her eyes lingered on my father.

"Yes, we will," he said softly.

I hadn't heard him use that tone of voice for years. Not since my mother. I'd have to talk to both of them at some point. Before anything developed between them. Now might be a good time to look into setting up my own clinic. I could give Marley a job as my receptionist. I'd need one and they'd have no excuse to spend time together.

I knew a couple of older women I could introduce my father to. Anyone but my friend. I wanted both of them to be happy, but that couldn't happen if they were together.

"You have an extra room?" Shaw asked. "Otherwise I'll sleep on the couch."

Dad turned and raised his eyebrows at the defence-man. "You're staying here?"

"You couldn't keep me away." Shaw sipped his coffee, while leaning back on the couch and looking very much at home.

"I guess that's settled then," Dad said.

I wanted to tell Shaw it wasn't necessary for him to stay, but for some reason, I didn't want him to leave. Something that went beyond keeping an eye on me.

25

CATALINA

Everything was dark. His clothes, his face, his voice. He struck out at me. I threw my hands up in front of my face to stop the barrage of blows. They kept on coming. He struck my arms, my hands, my wrists.

I cried out for him to stop, but he didn't. Over and over, his fists pounded into me.

I begged him to stop but he didn't even slow.

I was lying on the ground and he was kicking me again and again. The toe of his heavy boots slamming into my ribs, my stomach, my chest.

I tilted my chin back and screamed.

And screamed.

"Cat," a low, soothing voice spoke in my ear. "Shhh. It's okay."

A strong arm surrounded me, holding me close until I stopped thrashing and screaming.

"Shhh, it's just a dream. Just a bad dream. I've got

you." He rubbed a hand up and down my back, slowly and deliberately.

My eyes popped open. "Shaw?"

"Yeah. You were having a nightmare." He didn't stop soothing my back.

I blinked tears out of my eyes. "It felt so real. He was right there."

"I know it felt real, but it wasn't. You're okay, I've got you." He held me tight, muscular arms chasing away the worst of the shadows. "Did you notice anything you didn't remember before?"

"It wasn't you," I said vaguely.

He made an indeterminate sound in the back of his throat. "I already knew that. But something made you say that. What was it?"

"I heard his voice. I remember thinking it wasn't you. I still can't place who it was."

I closed my eyes and thought back, but couldn't pin it down. His words were too few and in the moment, I was too overpowered with fear.

"At least you can rule me out." He turned me around to face him and kissed my forehead. "I don't want you to have any doubts about me. I'm in this for the long haul. You're it for me."

"Shaw…"

He pressed his finger to my lips. "You don't have to say anything. You're still recovering. When you're ready, I'll be here."

I waited until he lowered his finger. "I want to say something. I need to say thank you."

"What for?" he asked.

"For finding me when you did," I said. "I think he would have killed me if you hadn't. Thank you for being here for me. The last couple of days have been difficult. You've helped me through it, more than I can ever express."

I exhaled softly. "I'd like to go back to work so I can stop thinking about all of this, but I'm not sure it'd help. I can't stop. Those fucking crutches won't let me." Not to mention the cast.

I nestled into him. "Thank you for not giving me pitying looks." Those were the worst. I appreciated that people cared, but I didn't want them feeling sad for me.

"I have a feeling if I looked at you like that, I'd get a crutch to the nuts," he said dryly.

I snorted softly. "Exactly."

He lightly ran his knuckles down my cheek. "When I look at you, I don't see someone who should be pitied. I see a gorgeous, intelligent woman with bigger balls than most guys I know. A woman who won't be held back by what happened. If anything, this will make you even stronger. If I were those pricks, I'd be shaking in my skates."

"I have a feeling not much scares you," I said.

"It doesn't," he agreed. "The only thing I'm scared of right now is that you won't feel the same way I do. If you don't, I'm willing to put in the work to convince you we belong together. I've never been more *sure* of anything in my life." He sounded amused at the subtle pun of rhyming with his own first name.

"I'd be lying if I said I didn't care about you," I said. "Right now, I feel like you're the only one who really gets me. You make me feel the most... I don't know, normal."

He hummed his disappointment. "I'm not doing my job if I make you feel normal. I want you to feel as beautiful as you are." He skated his lips lightly over mine.

The touch sent a jolt of electricity snapping through my core, igniting me from the inside out. I immediately wanted to throw a bucket of water on it. I believed he had feelings for me, but he couldn't be physically attracted to me when I was such a mess.

Could he?

"Shaw," I whispered.

"Cat." He kissed me again and lightly ran a hand over my stomach, under my pyjama shirt. "So fucking gorgeous."

"I'm so broken," I said.

"Just your bone. The rest of you is perfection." He ran a thumb across the underside of my breast. "I want to touch you everywhere."

I shivered. "Promise me."

His hand stopped moving. "Anything."

"Promise me this has nothing to do with any bets." If it was, another part of me might break.

He placed his other hand on my cheek, his fingers

stroking my temple. "I swear on everything I care about, being with you is because I want you and I want to make you feel good. No games. No bullshit. I want you so fucking bad."

"My leg—"

"I'll be careful," he assured me. "If I do anything that makes you uncomfortable, just say the word and I'll stop." He resumed his exploration of the underside of my breast with his thumb, gradually moving it up to circle one of my nipples.

Every movement was slow and careful, every touch, every caress.

He pushed up the front of my pyjama shirt and traced circles around my nipple with his tongue. He drew my sensitive peak between his lips and sucked gently.

At the same time, his hand wandered down the front of my pyjama pants and to my pussy. The tips of a couple of his fingers grazed over my clit, gently at first but then more persistent.

He pressed a finger inside me. "I was hoping you'd be wet. You're even wetter than I imagined." He slid his finger in and out a couple of times before working my pants down over my cast and off onto the floor. He shimmied down and bent my good knee to open me up to him.

He lowered his mouth to my pussy and started to lick and suck my clit and all around my pussy. "You taste incredible." He slid his fingers back inside me and worked me from inside and out.

My body responded to him, but rolling my hips was difficult with the heavy cast. It took a few tries to get the rhythm right. When I did, I forgot all about my broken bone and enjoyed the way he was feasting on me.

"Come for me, Cat," he insisted. "I want to hear you."

With my father in the house, I wasn't going to scream, but I moaned his name as I shattered into more pieces than my leg bone. I arched my back and ground my pussy harder against his stubbled face.

I came back together faster than my bones would heal, but with less anguish and a lot more pleasure.

"You're perfection when you come." He kissed his way down the inside of my thigh to my knee and back the other way. He kissed up my hip, my stomach and over my breasts. He grabbed the hem of my pyjama shirt and pulled it over my head. His T-shirt and track pants were next, leaving him a naked, muscular hockey god.

In the glow of the streetlight that peeked in from the edge of the curtains, I saw all of him. His flat stomach, chiselled abs and the V of his hips. A cock so big I wasn't sure how it fit in his pants. His chest and arms were covered in tattoos, most of which I couldn't make out. I hoped I'd get a chance to see them in daylight.

He lay beside me, angling me carefully so one leg

was bent to give him access without having to lean any of his weight on my cast. Instead, he rested his weight on his knees and elbows and carefully positioned his cock outside my entrance.

"Tell me you want this," he whispered.

"I want this," I said. "I want you inside me. I want you to fuck me." I wanted to feel as beautiful as he kept telling me I was. Wanted and needed. Desirable.

"Good, because I want to fuck you." He slid himself slowly inside me, stopping every few moments to let me get used to his size. "Holy shit, Cat, you feel incredible." He went on pressing until he was all the way inside me.

"So do you," I said breathlessly. I knew I needed this, but it wasn't until he was fully seated inside me that I realised how much. He was right, I wasn't someone to be pitied. I was tough and strong and beautiful. I wasn't going to let anyone or anything hold me back.

He slid out and all the way back in again, always moving slowly and carefully. Always keeping his weight off my leg.

"The first moment I saw you, I wanted to sink into you like this," he said. "But this is even better than I imagined." He palmed my breast, rolling my nipple with the heel of his hand.

"I don't think anyone would have imagined this," I said. "Unless you have a thing for plaster."

He chuckled. "If you're in it, I'm into it. But when I thought about claiming you, claiming your body, a cast *might* not have occurred to me. It doesn't diminish how fucking good you feel. If anything, it gives me something to look forward to. The day you can drape both of your legs over my shoulders. Then, I can fuck you harder."

His words gave me delicious shivers. Maybe I should think it was wrong for him to suggest he was claiming me, but I didn't. Something about it felt very right. I wanted to be his.

I hated a few hockey players, but what I felt for him, it was the opposite. If I wasn't careful, I was going to fall for him. Really fall. Not just the physical attraction I had for Cruz and Easton. I wouldn't let myself think I felt anything more for either of them. I couldn't. That vulnerability all but broke me.

"I better work hard at my rehab then," I said. "So we can do that."

"Good girl," he said softly. "I don't doubt for a minute you'll do that for me. For us. You know I'd do anything for you."

"I do know," I replied. I placed a hand lightly on his abs, closed my eyes and enjoyed the feeling of him thrusting into me. I'd never been called a good girl before. I liked the way it sounded, coming from his lips.

"Shaw," I whispered.

"Yes, beautiful?" he whispered back.

"Come for me," I said. "I want to feel you come inside me." I wanted him to feel as good as he made me feel.

He groaned. "You're such a fucking good girl. Just for you, I'm going to come inside your beautiful body. I'm going to fill your pussy with my cum."

His words drove me over the edge again into a second, more intense orgasm. He was half a heartbeat behind me, thrusting a little faster before he stilled and came, grunting and grinding into my body.

"Fucking… Yes…" He panted. "Good girl. Take every drop of my cum. Such a good fucking girl."

I ground against him, milking myself every drop of pleasure and him for every drop of his own release.

When I came back down, I was warm and wet and satisfied as hell. And fucking glad my cast hadn't gotten in the way too much.

"That was—" I panted lightly.

"Just the start," he said softly. "Just the start."

The start of something incredible.

26
CRUZ

I tapped the puck with my stick, passing it over to Easton. He skated forward and passed it back. We did that a couple of times before he hit it into the empty goal. Usually I enjoyed training, especially the morning before a game, but I found it difficult to give a shit today.

We turned and skated to the other side of the rink, giving the next pair room to practice.

"We shouldn't be feeling this way," Easton said.

I glanced over at him. "Like we fucked up bad? Because I have news for you, bro. We did." I wanted her to turn to me. I wanted to bring her down a bunch of pegs. I didn't want her beaten half to death. I sure as fuck didn't want her to look at me like she hated my guts. That whole fucking bet was a stupid idea. Everything since we met her was a stupid idea. Everything except the part where I met her.

"She shouldn't have found out about the bet," Easton said. "We fucked that up."

"Shaw fucked that up for us," I reminded him. "She never would have known if he hadn't opened his big fucking mouth." I glanced over to where the defenceman was practising his stick skills.

Dean skated over to join us. "Seems to me he's done nothing but cause trouble. Her too. We're better off without her around." His jaw was tight as hell.

I fixed him with a look. "What's with you and her? You didn't want to join in on our wager, but I saw the way you watched her." His gaze was like glue whenever she was around.

He shrugged one shoulder. "I'm not interested in her. I want to be a team player. That's how we win, if we all are."

He kept his gaze on Shaw, as though silently reminding me the defenceman wasn't a team player off the ice. As if I needed reminding. Right now he, Easton and I seemed to be determined to out-glare each other. It was starting to affect our performance in practice. If it had a negative impact during the game, I was going to be pissed off as fuck.

"You're a team player." Easton clapped Dean on the shoulder. "In the interest of team unity, I would have taken your money if you joined in the bet."

Dean gave him a glance.

"The bet is off," I reminded them. "No more fucking stupid bets." I had no doubt I would have won if Cat wasn't attacked. I was giving her some space, but I still intended to win her. I didn't care about the money. She was mine and I'd make her see that. Even if I had to go through Shaw to do it.

"You worried you'll lose?" Easton taunted.

"Hell no." I gave him the side eye. "If there's one thing I'm good at, it's winning. Whether it's on the ice or claiming some pussy."

"You're still into her?" Easton asked.

"You're not?" I asked.

"I am, I was giving her some time before I moved in on her again." He seemed very certain that was all there was to it. "If you think she's—"

"Hasn't there been enough bullshit over her?" Dean asked. "We're supposed to be a team, not arguing over some slut."

I resisted the very strong urge to hit him in the head with my stick.

"Catalina Ryan is no slut," I growled. "She's—"

"Not interested in you," Dean said. "Forget about her, bro. Is she really worth fighting each other over? The minute you fuck her, you'll forget her. You'll move on to someone else. Move on now and save us all the trouble."

He nodded to Easton. "You too. You both said yourselves she's just a bit of fun. You both wanted her out of the way and now she is. This was how you wanted things, you should be happy."

"Yeah," I said. But I didn't believe it. Seeing her lying on the hospital bed like that, battered and broken, I wanted to destroy whoever touched her. I should have been the one to leave bruises on her. She belonged to me. Did they not understand that? I would have considered sharing her with Easton, because I wanted to share myself with him too, but some asshole out in the car park who dared to lay a hand on my woman… I would find out who was, and I would make them pay.

"I'm not forgetting about her," Easton said. "I can have team unity, a professional hockey contract and her."

"Brewer. Grant. You guys asleep out there?" the coach called out. "Get your minds back into practice, or get off my fucking ice."

His words hit a bit too close to the bone, but I turned and nodded, waving my apology. "Sorry, Coach. Just discussing a play." I wasn't wrong, not exactly.

"Hayes, keep them out of the goal," Coach added.

Dean glared at us both. "With pleasure."

"The fuck is his problem?" Easton muttered.

"No idea," I said. Dean was usually the quiet guy we didn't notice until we got on the ice and he stopped the opposition from scoring a goal with skill even someone who knew nothing about hockey could appreciate. "I guess he's on edge about the expansion thing."

Fair enough, it was getting to all of us. If the AIHL didn't choose soon, I was going to go out of my mind.

Now the cops had interviewed us and came to no conclusions, surely we were still on the table? We had to be. Otherwise whoever fucked with my woman and my team was a dead man walking.

I wish I could rule out that he was a dead man *skating*, but I couldn't yet. All I could do right now was keep my eyes and ears open. Eventually, the fucker would make a mistake and we'd be all over him like a puck bunny on a single rookie. Much less enjoyable for him though.

I hit the puck to Easton, harder this time, keeping half an eye on Dean. The goalie's whole body was tense, ready. Like his head was in the game better than mine. No, there was more to it than that. He still looked angry. He wasn't going to let the puck get past him because he had a point to prove to me and Easton. We need to focus better and move past Cat.

Fuck that. I could focus, but I wasn't moving past her. Would she come to the game tonight? I hoped so. I fought harder when she was watching. She made me more competitive, hungrier.

Yeah, I gave her shit when we first met, but she gave it back. She had more guts than most of the guys on the team. When I got going, most people backed down. Not her. She came back twice as hard. Thinking about her made me twice as fucking hard too.

The way her pussy felt around my fingers, clenching me when she came. The breathy little moans she made when she claimed to hate me but was quick to orgasm.

She might not admit who owned her, but her body did. Her body wanted me, my touch. She could glare at me all she wanted, but she wanted me to sink my cock deep inside her.

I knew it. She'd come to know it. She was a smart woman, she'd see the truth soon enough.

I intercepted the puck from Easton and pretended I was going to hit it back. Instead, I drove it toward Dean's left, where he left a space open beside his skate.

He was quick to snap down that way and stop the puck with his glove. He flicked it back in my direction.

He didn't say anything, but his expression said, 'Really? What is this, rookie practice?'

I curled my lip at him. I was no fucking rookie. Prick.

"Nice save," Easton said.

That scored him a faint smile from Dean.

I sighed to myself. I should have said that. Although, Dean was being an asshole at the time.

I turned and skated back to the other end of the rink as the coach and his assistants started to set up traffic cones for us to skate around and through, to practice our puck handling skills.

"Dean is right, we shouldn't be arguing with each other," Easton said.

"Who's arguing?" I asked.

"The look on your face when he stopped the puck," Easton said. "The fact you won't concede defeat over Cat. When you—"

I turned and gave him a shove with my gloved hand.

He slid backwards and hit the boards with a grunt. "What the fuck, bro?

I skated forward and pinned him against them with my body. I didn't know when I dropped my stick, but my hands were pressed to the boards on either side of him, caging him in. My face was a couple of centimetres from his. Close enough to feel his breath and smell his sweat.

He jerked against me, but didn't make more than a token effort to push me away.

"I'll tell you what the fuck," I growled. "You can't even admit there's something between *us*." Being this close to him made my cock start to harden.

He forced himself to meet my gaze. "I never said there wasn't," he said softly. "I just don't know how to…" He shook his head. His stubbled jaw worked back and forth, but no words came out from between his plump lips.

I wanted to kiss him, but I jerked myself away instead. "There is no *how to*. There are no rules. You either do it or you don't do it."

Maybe I shouldn't have given him a choice in the first place. Like I wasn't giving Cat one. I should have made him mine. Then her.

Fuck, they were making my balls ache. That, and I hadn't been with anyone since I met Cat. Her and Easton were the only ones my cock was interested in.

Stupid dick. I could have relieved the tension with any number of women and a handful of men since then. But no, he wanted to torture me instead.

I gave Easton a long look, to which he responded by dropping his gaze to the ice beside my feet.

If I was ever going to make a bet again, I'd bet on his dick being hard behind his cup. He just needed to have the balls to admit it. Then I'd have him on his knees, sucking my cock. Him and Cat, side-by-side, taking turns.

If I kept thinking like that, I was going to blow my load right here on the ice.

I forced myself to look away and skated over to the first of the traffic cones and took my frustration out on the puck.

"Save some of that aggression for tonight, Brewer," Coach said.

"I've got plenty to spare," I replied. I should dial it back though. Let the frustration bubble over when we faced off against the Kings. They were a tough team, but we'd shown them their asses before, we could do it again. I preferred it that way. The tougher the better. If we couldn't win against teams like that, we'd get smashed in the AIHL. I was fucked if I was going to let that happen.

I skated past Shaw and caught his eye. From the look on his face, he was moments away from planting a fist in my face. I wanted to flip him off, but I turned away instead.

I didn't need his permission to go near Cat. If he thought I did, he'd have to rethink. I was fucked if I was listening to anything he said. I respected his desire to keep her safe, but she didn't need protecting from me. I'd show her that. No matter what it took.

27
CATALINA

"I don't know about this." I leaned on my crutches, my eyes on the doors leading into the rink. They currently stood open to allow the crowds for tonight's game inside. Crowds who stopped to glance at me before they hurried past.

I never wanted to be a local celebrity like this. The fuss and gossip would pass, but for now it seemed like everyone knew who I was and what happened to me. One more pitying look and I was going home.

"It's a very good idea," Marley said. "What better way to prove you're not beaten than to come back here?"

"What Marley-Jane said," Eden said. "According to my therapist, facing the past is a good way to get past it."

I glanced over my shoulder to that corner of the car park. Since the attack, lights had been installed there.

The cars parked underneath were illuminated as bright as anywhere else. Would things have been different if those lights were there all along? If he couldn't attack me there, he would have chosen somewhere else. The clinic. My home.

Small mercies, I supposed. I had little reason to come here now. I could avoid the place and those memories if I wanted to. But Eden was right, I had to face what happened.

I turned back to my friends. "I didn't know you were seeing a therapist."

Eden shrugged. "I have been for a while now. I can give you her details if you like."

"That's probably a good idea. I can't keep dumping my problems on you two," I said.

Marley gave me a careful hug. "That's what friends are for, remember? To help you get through the bad times and celebrate the good shit. No matter what, Eden and I are here for you."

I hugged her back. "You're the best. Both of you." I hugged Eden too.

"Of course we are." Marley grinned. "Now, are we going inside?"

I took a deep breath and nodded. "Okay, let's do this." I lifted my chin, gripped my crutches and made my way through the doors and over to the stands.

I didn't want pity, but I was grateful to the people who moved aside so we could sit on the lowest row of benches.

"Front row." Marley sat beside me. "All the better for the team to see whose jersey you're wearing." She flashed a wicked grin.

I set my crutches down between Eden and me and grabbed the hem of my hoodie to pull it over my head. Underneath, I wore a white jersey with blue and grey, the Ghouls' colours. On the back was Shaw's number, seventeen. The defenceman gave it to me before the game, saying he wanted everyone to know who I was with.

By everyone, I assumed he meant Easton and Cruz.

Marley sat back and regarded me. "I never thought I'd see you wearing a hockey player's jersey."

I shrugged. "I decided to make an exception." Shaw wasn't like any other player I'd ever met. He was intense and had his share of arrogance, but he didn't run from my problems and my injuries. Not like Jason had.

I admit it crossed my mind that Jason was the one who attacked me. He was enough of an asshole to do something like that, but it didn't match up with the things my attacker said. Unless he was telling me to stay away from Melbourne.

In the end, I honestly couldn't see him bothering. He was too wrapped up in his own little world to give me that much thought or effort.

None of that stopped me from mentioning our past relationship with the police. I got a small amount of petty amusement from imagining the expression on his face when they approached him to ask him questions.

"You really like him, don't you?" Eden asked.

I blinked to bring my thoughts back to the present. "Yeah, I do," I said.

"That's good," Marley said. "Because I have a feeling you're not getting rid of him that easily."

I laughed. "I have the same feeling. That's better than a guy who runs at the first sign of trouble."

"Shaw would definitely not run," Eden agreed. "He'd stand between you and trouble every time."

I'd told them about the incident in the hospital with him, Cruz and Easton. They both agreed Shaw kicking the other guys out was hot as hell. In a platonic, they-would-never-go-there kind of way. I suspected Shaw would cut off his own cock before he cheated on me, especially with one of my best friends.

"The team is coming out." Marley elbowed me in her excitement.

I watched with a feeling of dread and anticipation.

The crowd cheered for the Ghouls. The cheer for the opposition was less enthusiastic, but I barely noticed. My eyes were on Shaw as he walked out with the other guys and started to warm up. He glanced at me and gave me a faint smile, but his attention was on the ice, specifically on Cruz and Easton.

The two wingers both noticed me sitting in the front row. They exchanged glances, which seemed wary.

Cruz flashed me a grin.

I flipped him off.

Easton laughed at him.

I grabbed my crutches, pushed myself to my feet and turned around so they could both see the back of my jersey.

When I sat down and put my crutches back beside me, I was in time to see both guys giving Shaw a dirty look.

Shaw smirked in response.

In the corner of my eye, I saw Dean practising groin stretches. At least, that was what he was supposed to be doing. He was glaring daggers at all three of the guys before he turned the look on me.

The coldness in his eyes gave me chills, even from here. A shiver went down my spine. Then a horrified flash of understanding.

Like a bolt of lightning right to my brain, I realised the truth. When I didn't think he could look colder, he did. His expression was one of pure hate. He curled his lip at me before pulling his mask down to cover his face.

"Fucking hell," I whispered.

"What is it?" Marley gripped my hand. "Are you okay? Is it your leg? Does it hurt?"

It ached like a bitch, but that wasn't what I was worried about right now.

"I need to get out of here." I gathered up my crutches and pushed myself back to my feet.

"Cat—" Eden started, but exhaled loudly. "We'll come with you."

I wanted to tell them to stay and watch the game, but the idea of being alone right now was terrifying. I nodded and hurried toward the door, leaving them to catch up.

I stepped out into the night, but the cold air did nothing to refresh me or clear my head. My whole body was trembling the way it did that night. In my mind, I relived every moment, second by second. Every punch, every kick, every word.

"Cat?" Marley said tentatively. "I know the memories of skating there must be difficult. We should have given you more time to—"

I cut her off. "No. That's not it. I mean, it is, but it isn't." I hadn't had a panic attack in years, but I was having one now. My heart was racing. My palms were slick with sweat. I wanted to throw up everything I'd eaten for the last week. I could barely put together two words, much less a sentence.

When I finally did, it was a whispered stammer. "I… I know who… Attacked me…"

"You know who…" Marley started. "Holy shit. For real?"

I nodded and swallowed hard. "There was a reason why I couldn't identify his voice. It's because I've never heard him speak."

Marley glanced around and pulled us further away from the door so we wouldn't be overheard.

"He who?" she asked gently.

"Dean Hayes," I whispered. "The Ghouls' goalie."

They both looked uncertain.

Eden asked, "Why would he do that?"

I shook my head slowly. "I don't know. I can't explain it, I just know it was him. The look he gave me a minute ago." I shivered to think of it. "I swear, it was him."

"We need to tell someone," Marley said.

"Tell who?" I asked. "What would I say? He gave me a look, therefore he must be guilty as shit? That's not going to be enough for the police."

"So you tell Shaw." Eden shrugged. "I get the impression he knows how to deal with Dean."

"He'll kill him," I whispered. "What if I'm wrong?" But I knew I wasn't. Not about this.

"He doesn't seem like the sort to kill first and ask questions later," Marley said. "He'll want to know why."

My breath misted the air as I exhaled heavily. "You're right. He'd want to know, even if it's only about Dean looking at me like that."

"If it was Dean, then you know it wasn't Cruz or Easton," Eden pointed out.

"So what?" Marley asked. "They still made that stupid bet. And talked about her behind her back. Who does shit like that?" She made a face.

She'd always been good at being pissed off at people on my behalf, right back to Ruby Fredrickson, who put yellow paint in my hair in kindergarten. Long after I put the incident behind me, Marley was still angry and vowed revenge. Which she got, by putting red paint in Ruby's hair. Sometimes I missed those simple days.

"They were assholes, but they didn't try to kill her," Eden said. "That's all I'm saying."

I pinched the bridge of my nose. "Can we stop arguing, please? I need to get my head on straight and go back in there." And find a way to stop my stomach from rebelling. I preferred not to leave lunch in the middle of the car park.

"You don't have to," Marley said. "We can take you home if you want. We don't mind missing the game. You're more important than hockey."

"I have to go back in and pretend I don't know," I said. "If anyone asks, I freaked out about being back in there. That's all. We'll go in, sit down and enjoy the game."

"For your sake, I can pretend to enjoy it," Eden said.

"Not just for my sake," I said. "If this blows up now, it destroys every chance the Ghouls have of joining the AIHL. For Shaw and for the guys who have nothing to do with any of this, we have to wait and deal with this quietly. For Opal Springs too."

The last thing any of us needed was for the crowd to turn into an ugly mob. If they knew what Dean did to me, and the way he risked the construction of the arena, they'd be furious. He'd be lucky to walk away from their anger. Opal Springs wasn't usually known for its violence, but too much was at stake for them to forgive his actions. Even if the townspeople didn't get involved, the team would.

Unless they decided to defend him and turn on me further. Fuck, this whole thing was a mess. For a couple of hours, I could act like nothing was up.

I hoped.

"That's why you're the brains around here." Marley pushed her glasses back up her nose. "Okay, let's lift our chins, walk through those doors and watch us a hockey game. All hell can break loose later."

All hell sounded about right. I felt like my hand was hovering over the button, ready to let a bomb loose on all of this.

Suppressing the panic as best I could, I walked between my two best friends and sat down again, keeping my eyes as far away from Dean Hayes as I could.

28
SHAW

Fuck team unity, harmony or whatever shit people went on about. The Ghouls decimated the opposition.

Cruz and Easton played like their lives depended on it. Dean didn't let a single biscuit into the basket. The Kings were aggressive and played well, but no matter what they did, we were right there, driving them back, stealing the puck, checking them against the boards.

Was it the best we ever played? No, but we destroyed them anyway. We did it so thoroughly their left defence picked a fight five minutes from the end of the third period and got sent to the penalty box. Bench, technically. The power play gave us another goal, leaving the score at eight to nothing.

I would have celebrated along with my team, but every time I glanced at Cat, she looked tense as fuck. More than I'd seen her before. She was hot as hell in my jersey, but her body was almost as rigid as my cock under my cup.

I would have put it down to her being back here, but her friends were tense too. They pretended they were enjoying themselves, talking and laughing, but that was all it was. A pretence.

The minute the horn went for the end of the third period, I was off the ice and showering in about thirty seconds flat. I was dressed when the guys were still patting each other on the back and hugging to celebrate the win.

I hauled open the door to the locker room and slipped out into the crowds. I scanned them quickly, searching for the most gorgeous redhead in the place. Was she still here or had she left when the game ended?

I'd almost decided she was gone when I caught a glimpse of her distinctive hair. As if she sensed my eyes on her, she turned around and gave me a nervous look.

I shoved my way through the crowd to her and cupped her cheeks in my hands. I didn't care who saw. I leaned down to kiss her mouth. She kissed me back, but she was trembling.

"Should we get out of here?" I said. I kept my tone light. As light as I could manage anyway, and curled my fingers around hers.

"Yes, we should." She looked relieved. She glanced at her friends who nodded their agreement.

Something was definitely going on here.

I ignored the congratulations and pats on my back and walked with the three of them out the doors of the rink and into the cool of the night. It was refreshing after a long, hard game, but Cat's hand in mine kept my blood hot.

I led them over to my car and helped Cat inside.

It wasn't until all the doors were closed and I turned the engine on to heat up the car that I turned to the three of them. "Okay, what the fuck is going on?"

Marley and Eden's eyes were on Cat.

She cleared her throat. "I think it was Dean who attacked me."

My blood was immediately on fire. Waves of fury washed over me. Not at her. Never directed at her.

I kept my voice even. "You think Dean attacked you. What makes you think that?" If that was what she thought, I believed her, but I needed to understand why.

"He gave me a look when he was warming up." She shuddered. "It was… I can't explain it. I just knew. I don't know his voice because I've never heard him speak, but I feel like… If he could punch me in front of all those people, he would have. I don't know what I did to him."

I sat back and rubbed a hand over the back of my neck. "He was pissed off at Cruz and Easton and our lack of team unity. I got the feeling he blamed you for it, but I never thought he'd do shit like that."

"He saw you in my jersey," I said slowly.

"So did Cruz and Easton," Marley said. "They looked pissed off. Then Dean looked pissed off at them. "

"Then at me," Cat said softly.

"That stupid fucking bet was the start of all of this," I said. "Because of Cruz and Easton, you were right in the middle of all of it."

"I'm sure they didn't mean for him to come after me," Cat said uncertainly.

"Whether they meant for that to happen or not, he did," I said. "They are almost as bad as he is." I wanted to punch both of them, but it wanted to hurt Dean so much more.

"What do we do now?" Eden asked.

"I need to hear Dean speak," Cat said. "Is there any chance there's an interview with him I can listen to?"

"The Ghouls don't have a high enough profile for people to bother to interview us, yet," I said regretfully. "If we were, Dean is the shy one. An interviewer would be lucky to get a peep out of him."

"Then we need to talk to him in person," she concluded.

"I don't want you anywhere near him," I said.

"It's not enough for the police to go on," she said. "I'm not sure they're allowed to take him in just to record him speaking. That would involve a lawyer, which would make trouble for the team. And I don't want you beating the shit out of him because of my suspicion. What if I'm wrong?"

I rubbed the heel of my hand up and down my forehead a couple of times. "Is this one of those things you have to do and I can't talk you out of it?"

"Yes," she said firmly. "But there's no way in hell I'm dealing with him alone. I'll need you close by to make sure he doesn't try anything."

"Fucking right you do," I said. If anyone suggested otherwise, they were out of their fucking minds. "For the record, I don't like any of this."

"Neither do we," Eden agreed. "But if Cat can confirm it's him, we have something to go on. I don't think we have any other choice. I mean, if you ask him to speak into your phone and take it back for her to hear, he's going to find that suspicious as hell."

"And if he gets suspicious, he might do something rash," I said.

"Exactly," Marley said. "He might try to leave the country. Then this whole thing ends up a movie of the week."

"I'm not sure it's not already movie of the week material," Cat said dryly. "Who would believe any of this?"

"I wouldn't," I admitted. "Everything apart from you feeling the same way about me. I thought those asshats might stand in our way for longer." I never had any doubts we'd end up together. She was always going to be mine. If it took years, I'd have fought for her. The universe couldn't have kept us apart forever. I wouldn't have allowed it to.

She managed a smile. "I'm sure you would have shoved them out of the way soon enough."

"That's right, I would have," I agreed. "Or if you decided you wanted them too, I would have shared you. Whatever it took to be with you, I'd do it."

Marley leaned over the seat and gaped at me. "You'd share her with two other guys?" She looked like she didn't quite believe what she was hearing.

Fair enough, it wasn't something a guy said every day. Cat wasn't an everyday sort of person. She was special. The most incredible thing about her was that she didn't seem to know that about herself. She had no idea she was drop dead gorgeous. Even when her face was bruised, she was still the most beautiful woman I'd ever seen.

"If that's what she wanted," I said.

"Would you share with them if she forgave them for being douchebags?" Marley asked.

I wanted to say that wouldn't happen, but I'd seen the electricity between Cruz, Easton and Cat. Did I like it? Not particularly. Was there anything I could do about it? That remained to be seen.

"If she forgives them, I'll support her, one hundred percent," I said, my eyes on Cat. "And if she wants to go on being pissed off with them forever, I'm behind that too."

I wouldn't mind having her and her glorious pussy to myself. My cock twitched at the thought of her. Okay, it didn't take much. A thought, a glance, a touch. My cock was as in love with her as I was. His favourite pastime was filling her body with my cum. Not surprisingly, so was mine.

"Can we deal with one thing at a time?" Cat asked. "Dean first, then Cruz and Easton." Her expression gave away nothing about the way she felt about them. She looked anxious to deal with Hayes. She didn't need to be. If he lay a finger on her, I'd rip it off and shove it down his throat.

I didn't hate the idea of her attacker choking on his own finger. If the police asked, we could tell them he accidentally bit it off. No big deal, it probably happened every day.

"To O'Reilly's?" I asked. "The whole team will be headed there to celebrate." I would have preferred to take her home, strip her naked and lick her from head to toe. Then fuck her until she couldn't remember her own name. Carefully, so I didn't do more damage to her leg. I meant what I said when I told her I wanted to drape her legs over my shoulders while I thrust into her, but I was patient.

Cat nodded. "Perfect. I can have a drink or two before I have to talk to him." She smiled faintly.

"You don't need Dutch courage," I told her. "You're the bravest woman I know."

"Marley and Eden are pretty brave too," she said.

"Yeah we are," Marley said. She was still draped over the seat. "But Cat is queen of being a badass."

"I don't feel very badass," Cat said in a small voice. "I want him dealt with before he hurts someone else. Off the ice."

Her tongue darted over her plump, luscious lips. I was looking forward to sliding my cock between them. When she was ready for that. We had all the time in the world to scratch every one of our itches. When it came to her, I had plenty of them. I wanted to have her in every possible way a guy can have a woman. On her knees, in the shower, on a blanket under the stars beside the lake. Everything.

"You don't mind people being hurt on the ice?" I asked, amused, but only slightly showing it. I'd never been inclined to smile. Never had much reason to. Cat might give me one. If anyone could, it would be her. But not tonight. Tonight was all about proving to her, and everyone else that she could be bent and battered, but she wouldn't be broken.

Dean on the other hand. Shame the Ghouls were about to lose such a good goalie.

"It seems to me like all's fair in love and hockey," she said. "Including punching the crap out of each other." She grimaced, but her eyes seemed to light up slightly when she said that.

"Is that your way of saying you want me to leave some opposition blood on the ice the next time we play?" I asked.

"I'd say it's hot, but don't tell my father. He wouldn't approve." She glanced at Marley.

Marley grinned. "I think you might be surprised what he'd approve of. If he knew about Dean, he'd be going for a scalpel already."

"Yeah, I guess he would," Cat said with a small shrug. "Let's get this over with."

29
CATALINA

I managed a few sips of wine before the rest of the team showed up. The crowd already gathered at O'Reilly's let out a cheer, welcoming the players like they were royalty or hockey gods.

Cruz and Easton led the way, the rest of the team behind them. Dean stepped in last, like he was trying not to be noticed. He succeeded, for the most part. Everyone else's attention was on the rest of the team.

I only glanced at him, confirming he was actually here. If I looked at him too long, he'd know something was up. I didn't want to see that expression on his face again. Not yet. There'd be time for that soon enough.

In the meantime, my gaze kept returning to the two wingers. Partly because neither seemed able to look anywhere but at me, and partly because, in spite of everything, I was drawn to them. I wanted to kiss them as hard as I wanted to slap them.

Side-by-side, they strode over to the table, both taking in Shaw's arm casually draped over my shoulders.

"Good game." Easton offered Shaw his hand.

Shaw looked at it for a moment before accepting and shaking. "Thanks. You too."

"I'm glad you came," Cruz said to me, emphasising the last word.

Shaw stiffened, but fortunately for everyone involved, didn't punch Cruz. Yet.

I shrugged slightly, not wanting to dislodge Shaw's arm. "I figured if you fell on your face, I should be there to see it. And video it. And share the video with the entire world. "

Easton grinned. "Nothing he wouldn't deserve."

Cruz elbowed him in the ribs. "Fuck off. If anyone is going to fall on his face, it'll be you. That'll give the Internet a good laugh."

"Did you clowns want something?" Shaw asked. "Because I'm enjoying a quiet drink with my girlfriend."

Girlfriend. I liked the way that sounded. And the way Cruz and Easton's eyes bugged out slightly.

Cruz recovered from his surprise first. "She can do better."

I raised my eyebrows at him. "*She* could do a whole lot worse."

Easton laughed and elbowed Cruz. "She's got you there, bro."

"She meant you too, bro," Cruz said.

Easton's smile faded. "You're really seeing this guy?" He jerked his thumb toward Shaw.

"Yes I am," I replied. "At least you two have each other."

That must have hit a nerve, because they turned and looked at each other. I'd sensed that vibe before, but this more or less confirmed it.

Cruz cleared his throat. "We don't—"

"Yes, we do." Easton grabbed the front of Cruz's hoodie, pulled him closer and kissed his mouth.

"Holy crap." In the corner of my eye, I saw Marley fanning herself.

I had to agree. Two hot as fuck hockey gods kissing each other had my pulse racing and my clit throbbing.

Cruz seemed surprised at first, but then he was kissing Easton back, hands curled around his biceps.

Finally, they broke off and stepped back from each other. Their faces were both pink, eyes dark. Neither seemed to regret the kiss.

"This doesn't mean I'm not into you too," Cruz said to me.

"Me either," Easton said.

"I still don't forgive you for what you did," I said slowly. "But you can help us with something."

"That depends on what that something is," Cruz said. He crossed his arms over his chest, bravado back in place. "Why don't you tell us?."

I gestured for them both to come closer so they

could hear better, and told them about Dean. They became more and more furious with every word.

"I'm going to rip his fucking arms off," Easton growled.

"Not if I rip them off first." Cruz locked his gaze on Dean and started over towards him.

"Don't—" I started. It was too late. Easton was on his heels and Shaw slipped his arm off my shoulders and followed a moment later.

Fuck.

"Should we?" Eden gestured to their backs.

"Yeah." I grabbed my crutches and limped after them as fast as I could go.

The three guys cornered Dean and all but dragged him outside to the beer garden.

"What the fuck are you doing?" The goalie struggled to push them off, but Cruz held one of his arms and Easton the other. They turned him around and pinned his back to the wall.

The chill that went through me was nothing to do with the cold air outside. It was the sound of his voice. He'd haunted my nightmares since the attack.

"What do you think we're doing?" Cruz snarled.

"Get off me." Dean struggled again. He kicked out at Easton, but missed.

Shaw glanced at me, questioningly.

My tongue swept across my lower lip and I nodded. "It's definitely his voice."

Before anyone else could move, Easton had his hand

around Dean's throat. He pressed him back hard against the wall and squeezed.

"Fucking prick." Easton's face was red with fury. "You fucking touched my woman. You attacked her. *You fucking broke her bones.*"

His tone made me recoil slightly. I'd never heard anyone so angry before, not even that night. Or so cold. The ice on the rink was warm in comparison.

Dean's eyes were wide. He struggled to breathe. In spite of that, there was no hint of regret or apology in his eyes. There was something else instead. Vindication. He completely believed what he did was right. He had faith the guys would understand his reasons for attacking me.

I didn't think I imagined him thinking he'd do it again given the chance.

He lifted his chin and stared Easton down.

"It was what you wanted," he rasped out. "All of you. You wanted her away from the team. Away from our rink. Away from all of us. You wanted her humiliated and broken. She was getting in the middle of us. Making us fight with each other. She was going to fuck up our chance with the AIHL. I did what no one else had the balls to do."

I wished he sounded unhinged, but he sounded like he knew exactly what he was saying and stood by every word. Cold, calculating, convinced what he did was somehow completely right. His conviction made me lose my breath for a few moments.

Cruz leaned in and spoke in a tone so menacing it made my spine tingle. "You could have killed her."

"I was going to, but Shaw came out of the rink," Dean said. "I fucking wish I had. Look at yourselves. She's done this to us."

"We did this to ourselves." Cruz stepped back and shook his head. "We did this to *her*." He glanced over at me. "Easton and I were assholes, that's what happened. If you wanted to hate someone, you should have hated us."

"Yeah," Easton agreed. "We did and said some bullshit things. Things she may never forgive us for. That doesn't give you an excuse for what you did. We never wanted anyone to lay a hand on her but us. If we gave you the impression this was what we wanted, then we screwed up even worse than I thought." His hand tightened around Dean's throat.

For the first time, I saw real fear in Dean's eyes. I saw the exact moment he thought Easton would actually kill him. I could smell it and hear it with each increasingly laboured breath.

"Easton, stop," I said softly.

Easton glanced over at me. "Why should I? Why shouldn't I kill him for what he did to you? He deserves it." His expression was one of fury, but it wasn't all directed at Dean. A lot of it was directed inward, at himself.

I heard what he wasn't saying. He and Cruz deserved it too. Dean looked up to them and they gave him the wrong idea about their feelings for me. Dean was far from innocent, but he didn't deserve to die. Not like this.

"If you kill him, you'll never forgive yourself," I said. "You'll be throwing away your life, your dreams and maybe the whole team. The AIHL won't choose the Ghouls with this kind of controversy hanging over Opal Springs. We've all lost enough, let's not throw away anything else."

Even if I was still as pissed off with him and Cruz as I was before, the rest of the team had nothing to do with any of this. Stealing their dream for something they weren't involved in, wouldn't be fair. They'd worked their asses off to get where they were. Pulling the rug out from under them like this would shatter them. I was fucked if I was letting that happen.

Easton let out a harsh breath, but finally stepped back, letting Dean slide to the ground. "He can't get away with what he did to you."

"He won't," Shaw said. "My phone was recording everything he said. I'll hand it over to the police. There's a possibility the AIHL won't touch us, but we can keep it quieter than if any of us murdered the prick." He looked down at Dean like he was considering doing just that.

"We could make it look like an accident," Cruz said darkly.

"And take the chance the police figure it out?" I asked. I bit my lip for a moment. "He took away my dream of going to the Olympics." Which right now seemed like such a trivial goal. I had the rest of my life in front of me, and an amazing career working with the animals I loved. Saying the words stung though. I'd lived that dream for so long, admitting I had to put it aside was difficult. It was something I had to do. Accept it and move on. Build my life around other dreams.

"All you guys want is to play professional hockey. Don't let him steal your dream too."

"That's not my only dream." Cruz looked from Dean to me, clearly conflicted. "I'm not giving up on finding a way to get you to see that too."

"Me either," Easton said. He was massaging his fingers with the opposite hand, loosening them from where they'd been so tight around Dean's throat.

Now was not the time to tell him how hot it was to see him like that. If I was going to forgive either of them, they had some work to do.

"Seems like you have some shit to work on together too," Shaw told them. He slid his arm around me. I nestled against him and exhaled softly.

"It seems like we all do." I glanced down at Dean, who was rubbing his throat. He looked so small right now. Scared the guys might change their mind and rip him apart after all.

I almost couldn't get my head around the fact he would have killed me if it wasn't for Shaw stepping out of the rink at the right time.

"You have some healing to do," Shaw said.

Marley stepped to the other side of me and gave me a careful hug, trying not to knock my crutches aside. "We'll be here to help her."

"Yes, we will," Eden agreed.

I hadn't realised they were both there, but they must have seen everything. They both looked at Dean in disgust.

"We all will," Cruz said. He gave me a look that said, 'you're mine and I'm going to prove it to you.'

The look I gave him in return said I wasn't sure if I'd ever forgive him or Easton, but I'd consider giving them the chance to try, as long as they stopped being assholes. At least, assholes towards me. More than that might be too far to stretch. In spite of everything, I liked them the way they were.

They were going to have to work fucking hard to get me to admit that.

30
CATALINA

"That feels better." I wiggled my toes and raised my leg. Without the cast, it was so much lighter. And I could finally scratch that itch that had been annoying me for days.

"You still have to take it easy," Dad said. "Don't go running any marathons just yet."

"I'll give it at least a day or two before I run any of those," I said. I laughed at the expression on his face. It would take a lot longer than that for me to be fit enough to run a marathon, but I wouldn't rule that out as my next athletic goal.

He shook his finger at me playfully and helped me down from the examining table.

Putting weight on my leg was tentative at first, but when it supported my weight, I let go of my father's arm and stood on my own.

"The scarring will fade in time," he said.

"Yeah, I know," I said softly. Both physical and mental.

Following Dean's confession in the pub, the police arrested him and charged him with my attack. The town was still reeling from the whole thing. If I had a dollar for the amount of times someone said, "He seemed so nice," I could have retired. That and, "It's always the quiet ones."

The Ghouls' backup goalie had filled in since then, doing almost as good a job as Dean had. While a couple of people muttered about losing someone so promising, no one blamed anyone but Dean. No one even glanced at me, or the rest of the team, and pointed fingers.

"I start work back at the clinic next week," I said. "They're happy to let me do the rest of my hours and take me on full-time."

"I had no doubt they would," Dad said. "Looks like your ride is here." He glanced toward the ute, not particularly approving, but he didn't say anything either. His expression spoke loudly enough, clearly warning Easton that if he put a toe out of line, he'd be answering to him.

In typical Easton fashion, the winger looked undeterred. He grinned at Dad and offered me his arm.

I gave him a similar look to the one my father had. "I still don't know if doing this is against my better judgement or not."

"Trust me, it's a great idea," Easton said.

"It might be the best idea ever, but trust you?" I raised my eyebrows at him. "We'll see about that."

"I've always liked a challenge." He led me out the door and over to his car. He opened the door and waited until I sat inside to close it behind me.

He climbed into the driver's seat and peeled the car away from the curb.

"Where are we going?" I asked.

"You'll see." He merged onto the highway out of Opal Springs and leaned forward to put on some music.

I thought it was random until the third song.

"How do you know my favourite music?" I asked.

"I spoke to Marley and Eden," he admitted. "They put together a playlist."

"I should have known," I said. "What else have you asked them about me?"

He glanced over at me and grinned. "Everything they'd give me. I now owe them about six favours each."

"Don't think they won't collect on every one of them," I said. "Because they will."

"I expect them to," he said. "I assume you'll be reminding them regularly and insisting on cashing in for all they're worth."

"Absolutely, I will," I agreed. "You might live to regret making any deals with them."

"Not a chance," he replied easily. "It's a small price to pay to learn more about you."

"Are you sure you shouldn't get a hobby?" I teased.

He chuckled. "Maybe this is my hobby?"

"I'm starting to think Coach Foster doesn't keep you busy enough. Or your work. I thought carpenters never ran out of things to do."

"We don't, but I always have time for you," he said.

"Smooth, very smooth," I said.

"You think so?" He glanced over again, then back to the road. "I might be in with a chance after all."

"Don't count your biscuits until they're all in the basket," I said.

"I wouldn't dare." He slowed the car and turned off the highway, into a small town.

I had no idea what he was up to until he pulled up in front of a small building. A sign across the front said Cosmo's Skating.

I felt the blood drain from my face. "Easton, I can't."

"Yes, you can," he said firmly. "But if you can't, no one knows us here. If you fall on your ass, I'll be the only one to see."

I frowned. "If you video it—"

He held up both his hands. "I'll personally pull out my own toenails. Better yet, I'll let you do it for me."

I narrowed my eyes at him. Part of me wondered if this was some kind of setup, but the expression on his face made me decide to give him a chance. A final chance.

"Okay, I'll try," I said finally. I was desperate to get back on the ice, but at the same time, I was terrified.

What if my leg didn't hold my weight well enough

for me to stay upright? What if it never did? I couldn't speak those fears out loud, but they'd circled in my head a hundred times a day since the attack.

Easton was right, no one knew us here. If I was going to make a fool of myself, it wouldn't be in front of his team or anyone who knew me. Unless Cruz was secretly waiting to do the videoing. That might be why Easton was so quick to swear he wouldn't do it.

As if he could tell what I was thinking, he said, "No one knows we're here except the guy who owns the place. I didn't tell anyone where I was taking you." He frowned briefly. "Except Shaw. He insisted on knowing. I think if I hadn't told him, he would have broken my kneecaps. He still might. He's very protective of you."

"Can you blame him?" I asked.

"Blame him? No. Envy the fuck out of him? Hell yeah, I do. If I was a better guy, I'd be in his place. I won't give up on you, on us, until I am." He let out a long slow breath, then smiled. "Shall we?" He pushed out of the car and came around to open the door for me.

I had to lever myself off the seat with my hands, but it was a lot easier than with crutches. When he offered his hand, I took it and we walked through the front doors and into the rink.

It was smaller than the one in Opal Springs, with no room for stands, or more than small change rooms, but the place was neat and the ice looked welcoming.

He led me over to a bench where skates waited for us.

"Are those—" I squinted.

"Yours," he said. "I figured you'd be more comfortable in your own than a hired pair. I brought them down here this morning. And the track pants. Courtesy of Marley. I wasn't sure if you'd be in pants or not." He gestured towards my skirt. "Unless you prefer to skate in that."

"No, track pants are perfect," I said quickly. What else had he thought of? I hurried in to get changed and came back to sit on the bench and lace up my skates.

"I feel like this should be strange, but it feels like I never stopped." I checked the laces and pushed myself to my feet.

"You've spent your life skating. It's like getting back on a bike." He was already wearing his skates. Also not hired one, by the look of them. He offered me his hand.

I swallowed hard and accepted it before wobbling a little on the walk to the gate leading out to the ice. Was I rushing this? Should I give my leg longer to heal before I tried skating?

"Are you okay?" he asked. "You don't have to do this if you don't want to, but I've got you. All you have to do is trust me." He turned to face me, gripped both my hands and stepped backwards onto the ice.

His hands were firm and strong, holding me carefully, his eyes watching every step while I joined him on the ice.

Moving very slowly, he skated backward, drawing

me with him so I didn't have to do anything but enjoy the feeling of sliding across the ice.

Gradually, I started to relax and move with him.

"Ready to go a bit faster?" When I nodded, he picked up the pace, glancing back over his shoulder every now and again so he didn't slam us into the boards.

Faster and faster, we circled the rink several times, him holding me steady the entire way.

"How's your leg?" he asked.

"Tender, but better than I thought," I said.

"Ready to skate on your own?"

I nodded slowly. "I think so."

He let go of one of my hands and turned so we were skating side-by-side, hand in hand. "Is there anything better than this?"

"Holding my hand?" I teased.

He dropped his head back and laughed. "That too. I meant skating. It's the closest thing to flying without actually having your feet leave the ground."

He sounded like a little boy who'd just discovered something incredible. Something that blew his mind in a way he'd never experienced before.

I could relate to that. I felt the same way when I first started to skate. And right now. This was something I'd never tire of doing. As long as my body would let me keep doing it.

"I missed this," I said. For the first time since the attack, I realised maybe I didn't need to race. I just needed to skate. He'd brought me all the way here to remind me of that.

"I know," he said simply.

We skated in silence for a while, enjoying the feeling of moving across the ice, and our fingers laced together. And each other's company.

Who else would have thought to bring me here like this? Anyone else I knew would have suggested I take my time and practise on the rink in Opal Springs. Not a private place where I could get comfortable. Easton seemed to understand what I needed before I did.

After ten or fifteen minutes of skating, he pulled us to a stop in the centre of the rink.

"I don't want you to overdo it," he explained. "If I let that happen, I have a feeling your father would do worse than pull out my toenails." He grimaced, but he didn't look particularly scared.

I laughed and let him take my other hand again, to pull me closer. "Chances are, you're right."

He was looking at me intently now, a smile hovering around the corners of his mouth. "You're so fucking gorgeous." He brushed hair off my cheek. He hesitated for a few moments before leaning in to kiss me.

I found myself kissing him back, my tongue sweeping over his lips and sliding inside his mouth. He tasted so good I wanted more. In a handful of moments, my panties were ruined.

He wrapped his arms around me and slid his hands

down to grip my ass. His growing erection pressed into the side of my stomach.

I was about to wrap my arms around his neck when he pulled away.

"I have another surprise for you."

"I can feel it," I teased.

He chuckled. "As much as I want to claim you here and now, I haven't earned you yet. Come on, I have something to show you." His hand in mine, we skated to the edge of the ice and stepped back off.

31

CATALINA

We drove back in the direction of Opal Springs without speaking. We sang along to the music pumping through the speakers, but didn't talk about the kiss or whatever his surprise was.

I let myself relax and enjoy his company. It could be all too easy to forget about the past and see what the future held with him and Shaw. Would Cruz fit into this equation? He'd have to work harder to gain my forgiveness. If he could put his ego aside long enough to try.

About ten minutes out of town, Easton turned the car onto a smaller road, then a dirt track. The going was rougher here. I clung to the handle as we bounced over dips and rises.

"Should I be worried about where you're taking me?" I tried to keep my voice light, but the further into the bush we went, the higher my anxiety rose. I pictured Dean bringing me out here in the boot of his car to kill me and bury me in a shallow grave.

My hands started to tremble.

Easton glanced over at me. "Fuck." He slammed on the brakes, making the car skid along the dirt until it came to a stop a metre or two from an embankment.

He threw off his seatbelt and leaned over the centre console to wrap his arms around me. "Cruz is right, I'm a fucking idiot. I'm sorry. I should have told you what was going on. I wasn't bringing you out here to do anything bad to you, I swear."

I leaned against him, inhaling his scent and taking comfort from the strength of his arms.

"I know you're not," I said in a shaky voice. "I just freaked out. I still have nightmares about that night."

He rubbed my back slowly. "I bet you do. Well, I would bet if I was a betting man. Which I used to be, but I've learned my lesson. Never again. Unless…"

I tipped my head back and looked at him. "Unless what?" I hoped he wasn't about to suggest some other stupid bet about some aspect of my life.

"Opal Springs has a yearly snail race," he said with a grin. "The team takes part every year, but the winnings go to charity."

I snorted. "I know all about the snail race. You can bet on that all you want." The Children's Hospital got all the money. And the snails went free after the race.

He stroked my hair softly. "I'm sorry I'm such a dickhead. I should have explained. I wanted to surprise you, not scare the shit out of you. We can go back if you want?"

I glanced out the front windscreen. The dust had almost settled from our skid, leaving the sight of huge gum trees and thick underbrush.

He sighed. "You don't trust me."

"I want to," I said slowly.

"Can you give me five more minutes to prove you can?" he asked. "If I can't do that, I'll…"

I waited for him to finish his sentence, but he didn't. "You can't bring yourself to say you'll back off, can you?"

He hesitated, but only for a moment. "Five minutes."

"Five minutes," I said softly.

He grinned and straightened the car to continue down the track.

A minute or two later, the trees gave way to an open paddock, filled with tall grass, a wide dam and several kangaroos.

Easton turned off the engine and pushed out of the car. He came around to my side and opened the door.

"This was what I wanted to show you."

"You wanted me to see you have a few roos loose in the back paddock?" I teased. I couldn't resist using the idiom that suggested he was a bit crazy. It was too perfect for the situation.

He laughed and grabbed my hand to pull me out of the car.

"I'm not saying you're wrong, but that's not the

point. I wanted to show you this place because it's important to me." He turned serious. "I grew up with six of us living in a two-bedroom house. It was so small, you couldn't turn around without falling over someone. We never had much money. I lost count of the amount of times I went without breakfast or lunch." His eyes glazed as he thought back.

"I started stealing things so I could eat. Then I graduated to beating up the kids in my class for their lunch. Me and Cruz. We'd split everything we got." He swung our hands between us as we walked to the edge of the dam.

"We were lucky to get the attention of one of the teachers. Instead of yelling at us and treating us like shit like the rest did, she got us involved in a program for kids like us, to do sport. We both played footy, but we got to try ice-skating one time and we both fell in love with it. She got us a scholarship to learn how to skate. She was the one who started the Ghouls. She said something about redirecting our energy to something productive. And we got to punch other kids once in a while and not get in trouble for it." He grinned.

I rolled my eyes. "You started playing hockey so you could punch people?" I squeezed his hand. I understood exactly what he was really saying. If not for that teacher, he and Cruz would have ended up in jail. Or worse.

"Cruz got into it for the women." Easton said jokingly.

"I'm not surprised one bit," I said. "You never thought you'd play professional footy?" There was violence and women in football, after all.

He shrugged. "Yeah, but we fell in love with hockey. And we were both good at it. We could have gone pro already, but we both feel like we owe the Ghouls. If it wasn't for the team, we'd be completely fucked."

He stared out at the dam. His Adam's apple bobbed as he swallowed back emotions that seemed to still be raw.

"We don't want any more kids growing up like that in Opal Springs. Not if we can help it. That's why Cruz and I are obsessive about the team. It's not just because we want to succeed. We want that too though, not gonna lie." He frowned briefly. "There's a saying. Something about leaving the world a better place than you found it. That's what we want to do, y'know? It doesn't justify being a prick to you."

"You were protecting what was yours," I said. "I get that."

He turned to me. "Can you? Because I think we could have done it better than being massive pricks."

"Yes, you could," I agreed. "I haven't ruled out racking you both in the nuts for it."

He laughed, but it ended in a sigh. "I'd hire a skywriter to write 'sorry' in the sky if I thought it would help. But all I have his this."

He gestured around us. "I haven't even told Cruz about this place. The first thing I'm going to do when we go pro is buy this place and build a house. Two houses. One for us to live in and the other to use as a place to support kids like I used to be. Kids who need a break from all the shit in life. They can come out here and…just be, y'know? With a gym to work out their frustrations. Maybe some gardens they can look after so they can feel proud of something. Stuff so they feel valued."

I looked up at him and smiled. "Easton Grant, if I didn't know better, I'd think you're a big softy."

He grimaced. "Fuck, don't tell anyone. I'm supposed to be a big, bad hockey god. Don't forget, I would have killed Dean for you."

"How could I forget?" I asked. "That was one of the hottest things I've ever seen."

Easton raised an eyebrow in surprise. "Really? There I was, thinking you were the softy."

"I'm a vet," I said. "I've had to euthanise animals for doing things like he did."

His other eyebrow rose. "That's dark, but I like it. Should I have finished the job? Don't forget, Shaw was the one who talked me out of it."

"You'd be in jail right now if you had," I said. "That wouldn't help the kids of Opal Springs. Or the Ghouls. There's still a chance you'll be chosen for the AIHL."

"We will be chosen," he said firmly. "You know what, I'm glad I didn't kill him. He can rot in jail, thinking about what he did, for a long, long time. He won't get to enjoy any of this."

The idea that Dean would be free again someday, gave me chills, but for now I was safe from him. If I thought that often enough, maybe the nightmares would stop.

"I love you," Easton said, breaking me out of the thought.

I blinked at him a couple of times. Had I heard him right? He loved me? Of all the things I expected him to say today, that wasn't one of them.

"You don't have to say it back," he said quickly. "I just wanted to say it. The moment I saw you, I was completely gone. Being a massive prick to you, some of it was a defence mechanism. I don't like feeling vulnerable. It leaves you open to bad shit. But I realised, if I'm not, then I'm missing out on a whole bunch of life. "

"Have you said the same thing to Cruz?" I ask bluntly. I knew he felt that way, I saw it when they were together. When they kissed. Thinking about that made me hot all over again.

Easton glanced down at the water. "No. This is where you tell me I should, isn't it?" He kicked at a piece of grass with the toe of his worn sneaker.

It was easy to imagine him as a kid, trying to get by from day to day. A lot of guys would have crumbled under that, but he hadn't. He was stronger than even he realised.

If the AIHL turned down the Ghouls, he'd find a way to do what he was determined to do. If he pulled it off, he'd make a real difference in Opal Springs. He made me realise I needed to up my game. I couldn't let what Dean did to me stop me from making a difference too.

"If you really want to live your life, then there comes a time when you have to stop holding back," I said slowly. "I've been doing that since the attack and I don't want to do it anymore. Skating with you reminded me of that. Being free, living in the moment. That's everything." I was done being scared and hiding from myself. It was time for me to reclaim who I was. From then on, I was going to live my best life.

"I feel like I'm standing at the edge of a cliff with you," he said. "Like you're telling me this is the moment where I either back away or jump off and see where I land."

"I feel the same way," I said. Did I dare to jump? Did I dare to let him in and live his best life with me? Could I really put everything behind me and be with him and Shaw? I wanted to. I looked deep inside me and found the sliver of fear had whittled away to almost nothing.

"Do you trust me?" he whispered.

I let that last shard of restraint wither away and die. From this moment on, I was giving life everything I had. That included giving Easton everything I had.

I looked him right in the eyes. "I trust you." I meant it. I was his.

He wrapped his arms around me and slammed his mouth down onto mine.

32

CATALINA

He scooped me up in his arms and carried me over to a patch of grass under a tree.

"Don't want you getting sunburnt," he said between kisses.

"How thoughtful of you." I smiled teasingly against his mouth before claiming his lips again and sliding my tongue between them.

He said something that sounded like, "I thought so," but it was muffled by our mouths.

He lay me down on the grass and slipped his hands under my jumper and shirt. "Your skin is so smooth." He pushed up the fabric and rubbed the heels of his hands over the lace of my bra, until my nipples hardened.

He pulled down the cup of one and licked my nipple before closing his lips around it and starting to suck.

"That feels good," I said breathlessly.

"Tastes good too," he said. He pulled down the other cup and suckled my other nipple. He did that for a few moments before moving down to grip the waistband of my track pants and tug them down my hips.

"Matching bra and panties," he observed. "Was that for me?"

I responded with a smile. "I always like to match." That was true, but in the back of my mind I knew there was a possibility we'd end up like this.

He made a noise in the back of his throat, like he didn't quite believe me but wasn't going to question it any further. Instead, he saved his energy to pull down my panties and slide a couple of fingers down my seam.

"Who are you so wet for?" he asked.

"For you," I said, already breathless. "I'm wet for you."

"Of course you are." He slid his fingers inside me, as far as they'd go. "You want me to fuck you, don't you?" He slid his fingers out and back in again. "You want my cock to slam into you and fuck you hard."

I moaned.

He fucked me harder with his fingers. "Tell me with words, Cat," he insisted. "Tell me you want me to fuck you with my cock."

"I want you to fuck me with your cock," I said. I wanted it badly. I had for so long. I needed to feel him inside me.

He slid his fingers out, lay down and rolled me over so my pussy was right above his mouth. My legs straddled either side of him, my weight on my hands and one knee. I didn't trust the other one quite yet.

He gripped my ass with his fingers and flicked my clit with his tongue. "This is the perfect view. Your pussy is incredible." He licked me more firmly, lapping at my clit and pulling it between his lips to suckle.

"Easton." I quivered.

"That's it, babe, say my name," he said. "Scream it."

I lifted my chin and shouted his name to the sky.

"Fuck, that was hot," he said breathlessly.

I dropped down beside him and manoeuvred myself so my pussy was once again in front of his face, but his groin was in front of mine. I undid his pants and pushed them and his boxers down to his hips. His erection sprang free, his cock huge and red, throbbing and leaking from his slit.

I cupped his balls with my hand and licked his tip before swirling my tongue around his head. When he groaned, I took the rest of him into my mouth.

We got into a rhythm of licks and sucks, the wet sounds from our mouths the only noises apart from the occasional insect or kookaburra.

He managed to unhook my bra and pull it down so he could roll my nipples while he lapped at my clit.

I couldn't stop myself from coming if I tried. I jumped right over the edge of the cliff and went into a freefall that could have gone on forever, it felt so good. I slid my mouth off him and screamed his name louder than before.

"That's it," he said. "Tell the world who you belong to."

I finally flopped back against the grass, puffing lightly. He sat up and shed the rest of his clothes before helping me out of mine. His body was a study in muscles and tattoos. With the additional scar here and there.

He was looking at me with the same admiration. "You are so fucking gorgeous." He grabbed my wrists and pinned them above my head before straddling my hips. "Now I'm going to claim you. I'm going to fuck that glorious pussy and make you mine."

He nudged my legs apart with his knees and positioned his cock before slamming into me.

We both cried out with the suddenness of his entry. A combination of pleasure and a hint of pain. Just the way I like it.

He pulled all the way out and thrust back in again, harder and harder. He held nothing back. He kept me pinned against the grass while he used my body, taking everything he wanted. Everything I gave to him willingly. Every thrust was pure heaven.

"Tell. Me. Who. You. Belong. To." He spoke a word with every thrust, his teeth gritted in concentration.

"You," I shouted. "I belong to you. Oh… Easton…" I tipped my head back. "I'm going to come again."

"Yes," he ground out. "Come around my cock. I want to feel your pussy coming."

I came again, harder than before, my muscles clenching around him, squeezing him tight, holding him hard so he could do nothing but come with me. His whole body went still, rigid as he exploded his orgasm into my body. Filling me with his hot release.

He slumped forward. "Holy shit, that was amazing. You're amazing." He squeezed his eyes shut for a moment before opening them and shaking his head. "Are you okay? Did I hurt you?" He glanced down to my leg. He wasn't putting any weight on it, he was supporting himself with his knees.

"Only the way I like to be hurt," I said.

"You are full of surprises," he seemed impressed. And pleased. Judging by the way his cock hardened again slightly, he was also aroused.

"You thought I was some soft, squishy marshmallow that would break if you looked at me the wrong way?" I raised an eyebrow at him. It felt good to lie here with his cock buried deep inside me.

He barked a laugh. "You're as sweet as a marshmallow, but there's nothing soft and fragile about you. You're probably tougher than I am."

"I don't know about that," I said.

He looked at me firmly. "Very few people can go through what you went through and come out the other side stronger than ever. You're the strongest woman I ever met. No one even comes close." He leaned in to kiss my mouth. "I love you."

I kissed him back. "I… I love you too." I didn't know when that happened, but I'd fallen for him. Arrogance and all. Underneath all of that was a heart. It might be a morally grey heart, but it was still a heart.

"Good, how do you feel about children?" he asked.

"Um, someday?" I said tentatively.

He made an indeterminate sound in the back of his throat and slid his cock out of me. He sat down beside me and bent my knee, opening me out to him. He pushed the tip of his finger into my pussy. "Don't want my cum coming out too soon. I want you pregnant."

I wasn't sure how I felt about that, but his finger felt good inside me. "If you keep doing that, I'm going to come again."

"I wasn't planning to stop." He looked up and flashed me a grin before going back to his work of plugging my pussy so his cum stayed inside.

"What if I'm on birth control?" I asked.

"Get off it," he replied. "I want you to have my baby. Or Shaw's. Or Cruz's. I don't care, as long as you're pregnant."

"If the AIHL accepts the Ghouls, and I figure things out with Cruz, I'll think about it," I said. I couldn't have guessed he had a breeding kink, but the way he talked about it, I was tempted to agree to try. In the meantime, we still had a lot of obstacles to overcome.

Before that, I was going to concentrate on the way

he was fucking me with his hand again. Thrusting roughly, driving his fingers into me and pushing me quickly towards a third orgasm.

"Deal," he said. "I don't suppose you want to make a bet on it?" He gave me a cheeky grin.

I grimaced at him. "Asshole."

He laughed. "That's me. Once an asshole, always an asshole. But I'm your asshole."

"And Shaw's. And Cruz's," I said.

His smile faded slightly. "Yeah, and his."

I should have added that to the deal, that he had to tell Cruz how he felt. I forgot to think about it when I came again, a wave of bliss washing all over my body and carrying me away.

33
EASTON

"Stop it." I poked Cruz in the knee to stop his leg from jiggling. He stopped for a few moments, then started again.

"I can't help it," he said. "How the fuck can you sit still?"

"Willpower." I sat back, knees and arms crossed and attempted to look cool, calm and collected. On the inside, I had an army of jumping frogs waiting to escape. Forget butterflies, these guys were leaping back and forth like they were on speed.

"You and me, we're kings of fake it till you make it." I glanced over at him.

"Yeah and it's about time we made it," he said. His bravado was back, but his eyes showed his continued nerves. A perfect match for mine.

Coach Foster strode over to the stands where we sat, waiting. "You guys did good out there. The AIHL reps were impressed with what they saw."

"Of course they were," Cruz said with all his usual swagger. "We're fucking awesome."

Coach snorted slightly, but he didn't disagree. His gaze returned to the reps, who were talking amongst themselves, conferring, making a decision that could change all our lives.

"What did they say about Dean?" Shaw asked, his voice low.

Coach's brow crinkled as he frowned. "A couple of them had concerns, but we had some support from…an interesting angle."

"Care to elaborate?" I asked.

"Aidan Draeger, the head coach of the Dusk Bay Demons didn't seem too concerned. He said it shouldn't reflect on the rest of you." Foster nodded slightly towards the other coach.

I hadn't met Aidan, but I'd seen him at games. He seemed intense but passionate about his team. He'd also dragged them from the bottom of the ladder to the very top. For that alone, he was well respected. The AIHL seemed to listen when he spoke. If that was the case, we were still in with a shot.

"He just became my favourite person," Cruz said. "Okay, third favourite person." He didn't look towards me, but I knew what he meant.

"He won't be in your top ten when the Demons are kicking our asses," I said.

"Who said they're going to kick our asses?" Shaw asked. "No reason we can't kick theirs."

"They have a proper arena to practice in," I said. "Legions of supporters and a shit load of merch." I couldn't wait for the day that was us. The first thing I'd do would be to buy Cat a hoodie with our logo on it. A big one so she could get lost in it. Her and her pregnant belly.

The idea of her carrying a child sent shivers through me. And a surge of blood straight to my cock. I didn't know what it was about the thought, just that I wanted it to happen. I didn't want to push her, but I did want to convince her.

"We have things they don't have," Shaw said. "The three of us, for one thing. Cat cheering us on."

"They probably have a goalie who's a normal dude," Cruz said. "I bet Phoenix DiMarco doesn't go around trying to kill people." He spoke lightly, but his eyes flashed with fury.

"Dean is locked away," I reminded him.

"Fucker should have—" Cruz shook his head and didn't finish. He didn't need to. We all felt the same way. More or less. I didn't regret not killing him, but only because of the repercussions I would have faced for doing it. The satisfaction wouldn't have been worth messing up everything for the rest of my life and for the team. And for Opal Springs. Not to mention I wouldn't have been able to fuck Cat. I wouldn't have missed that for anything. Words weren't enough to say how amazing her body was. How good it felt to be inside her. The sounds she made when I made her come.

If I kept thinking like this, I was going to blow my load in my track pants, in front of everyone.

I took a deep breath and put a hand over Cruz's. "We dealt with him. Just like we'll deal with anything else that gets thrown at us."

He looked down at our hands before turning his around to lace our fingers together.

I twitched slightly, but I didn't pull away. Something about holding his hand felt right. As right as holding Cat's.

No one on the team said anything or looked at us funny. The only one who looked at all was Shaw, and he wasn't even slightly surprised. He actually nodded slightly, which it was about as close to a smile of approval as anyone got from him. He was a judgy prick about some things, but he was a decent guy. We could share Cat with worse.

Cruz nodded. "Let anything try to stand in our way. We'll bowl that motherfucker down." He squeezed my hand.

"Yeah, we will," I agreed. I smiled at him, before turning my attention to the reps. They still stood with their heads together, talking and laughing. If I didn't know better, I'd guess they were off track.

"How long does it take?" I said in a low, harsh whisper. "Coach, aren't we the last ones they're seeing?"

"Yes we are." He was starting to look concerned. "It's

possible they made a decision before they walked through those doors this morning."

"That would be bullshit." Cruz leaned forward as though he was about to jump up and confront them.

I tightened my grip on his hand and held him back. "Don't do anything rash. We can't assume. If it's a no this time, then we'll convince them next time."

"Yeah, don't fuck it up for us," Shaw said. He looked about as ready to jump out of his seat as Cruz.

Cruz grumbled something under his breath, but sat back. "I hate waiting."

"Literally no one on the face of the planet likes waiting," I said. "Waiting is the suckiest suck to ever suck."

Cruz looked at me sideways. "Can you stop saying suck so much? You're making my balls hurt."

I smirked. "Suck." I hadn't told him Cat and I fucked. He guessed as much when I returned home with a grin on my face like Cat got my cream, but I was done bragging about her and sharing details like some dumbass kid.

Cruz groaned. "Bro."

I grinned, but my balls were aching as much as his must have been. I'd been thinking about him since that kiss and wondering how it would feel to touch him. I wanted to be with him, but I wanted Cat to be involved too. That meant her and Cruz resolving the shit between them. Which they had to, because if they didn't I'd be stuck in a very uncomfortable middle.

"They're coming," Mitch Ward said.

"We're not—" Cruz started before realising the alternate centre was talking about the AIHL reps. "Fuck."

We all sat up straighter as the six of them took their time to stride over to us. Five of them were dressed in suits, each looking expensive and official. Aidan was dressed in track pants and a hoodie with the Demons' logo on the front. He looked like the kind of guy who didn't give a crap if he was supposed to look dressed up and fancy today. He was going to be himself, no matter what.

I admired that. If I was going to choose a role model from these men, he would be it. Especially since he was a coach and former professional hockey player himself, not just a pencil pusher.

"Gentlemen, thanks for waiting," Herman Norris, the head of the reps, addressed us all. He was in his late fifties, and from what I could gather, he was the money man. If the Ghouls couldn't be profitable, he'd be the one to say so. He would have been crunching everyone's numbers for the last few months.

It wasn't him I was worried about. Opal Springs would get behind us, I was certain of it. So much was at stake for so many people. No, my eyes went to Larry Givens. His concern seemed to focus on us as a team. He'd been the one to scrutinise our skills the most closely. He'd come to a lot of our games and watched with eagle eyes and an unreadable expression. If we weren't up to scratch, it didn't matter how profitable we were, the AIHL wouldn't touch us. They could very well approve the Ghouls and replace the whole damn team. Not quickly, obviously, but they'd weed us out one by one.

That would be devastating, but in the back of my mind I'd considered the possibility for a long time. If that was what happened, I'd have no choice but to throw my support behind the team, even if I wasn't part of it.

"No problem." Kage Foster nodded to them. "We understand the importance of making the right choice."

"You also understand how complex this is," Herman said. "Especially in light of the actions of Dean Hayes. We need to consider the publicity that might be generated by his former association with the team."

"Former being the important word here." Aidan Draeger looked bored. Evidently he'd decided they'd discussed it enough, and that Herman was beating the proverbial dead horse.

Herman turned to him and pressed his lips hard together. "As you can see, we haven't reached a consensus on that matter. We don't want the AIHL being brought into disrepute by someone like that."

Dean was the fucking gift that went on giving. If he hadn't touched Cat, there'd be no need for any of these conversations. On the other hand, if he hadn't, he'd still be here with us, seething and hating. We were better off with him far, far away from any of us.

"We condemn the actions of Mr Hayes," Coach Foster said. "His actions towards Catalina Ryan were abhorrent. He in no way represented the Ghouls and what we stand for."

"Fucking right he didn't," Cruz said. "If any of us had any idea he was a psycho, we would have had him removed from the team."

"Yeah, we would," Shaw agreed.

A murmur went through the rest of us.

I cleared my throat. "If you don't mind me saying, I don't think it would be fair to judge all of us on the actions of one player. Cat Ryan doesn't. She's in a relationship with a couple of us. At first, she thought all hockey players were bad news. But then she got to know us and she learned we were decent guys. We make mistakes, like everyone else, but we've put *everything* into this. There's nothing we wouldn't do for the team and for Opal Springs. At the end of the day, this isn't just about us. It's about the whole town and the way we can inspire, y'know, the next generation to chase their dreams. Dean Hayes stole a dream from Cat. I hope you can appreciate that we don't want him to steal ours too."

I looked down at my knees as the guys clapped and Cruz patted my shoulder.

"Well said, bro. That's exactly how I feel, but I couldn't have said it as well as that."

I glanced over at him. "You could have, but you would have added a few more 'fucks.'"

He grinned. He was a good looking guy, but when he smiled, he made my heart melt a little more. I'd cared about him for a long time, but admitting it to myself was easier now than it had been. Denying it was a big part of my dumbass kid past.

Was there anything in my life Cat hadn't changed? She swept in like an ice storm, cleared everything in her path and made it better.

Aidan gave me an approving nod and another glance at Herman. One that seemed to say 'I told you so.'

Herman was unmoved. "Of course I can appreciate the sentiment. However, it's in the best interest of the AIHL that we don't make a decision today. It seems we have more to discuss." He raised his eyebrows at Aidan.

Cruz growled softly, barely loud enough for me to hear.

I patted his back. "It's not a no."

"It's very much not a no," Aidan said. He looked almost as frustrated as we felt. It seemed clear he'd made up his mind and he wasn't letting Herman sway him. Unfortunately, Herman didn't seem to be swayed by him either.

I leaned over to the side to look at Larry, but couldn't tell what he or the other three were thinking. None of them disagreed with Herman's decision. Apparently they were open to further conversation. I didn't like it, but I understood. The choice they had to make was a big one and they couldn't take it lightly. No matter what me or Aidan or anyone else said.

"Thank you gentlemen for your time," Herman said.

"We will be in touch as soon as we've come to a final decision."

Coach nodded and walked with them to the door.

"Fuck," Shaw said once they were safely out of hearing.

"What he said." Cruz jerked his head towards the defenceman. "They might decide to go with an easier choice than us. Fuck Dean."

I wanted to disagree, but I couldn't. In spite of Aidan's assurance, there were five more voices making the decision.

"It's lucky for all of us he's not right here in front of me," I said. "I might not let go if he was." I curled my hand in a fist as though I could squeeze his throat again, until he took his last breath.

"I might not regret it if you didn't," Cruz said. "The little prick would have deserved it."

The mood of the whole team had taken a nosedive.

It wasn't a no, but it sure as hell felt like one.

34
CATALINA

"So, everything is up in the air?" I slid into the passenger side of Cruz's car. He hadn't opened it for me, and made no move to help me inside. He did, however, watch me carefully and stay close enough that if I fell, he'd catch me before I face planted.

Fortunately, I got inside without incident and clicked on my seatbelt.

"It's bullshit," he grunted. He flopped heavily into the driver's seat and glanced over at me. "I suppose you think it's justice."

I smiled and held out my fingers slightly apart. "Just a little bit. You know what they say about what doesn't kill you."

"Yeah. What doesn't kill you pisses you off." He grinned. It quickly faded. "I'm glad Dean didn't... You know."

"Me too," I agreed. "Where are you taking me?"

"Nowhere until I say what I need to say," he said.

He sat around to face me, as best he could with the centre console between us. "It's taken time for me to work up to this. Taking you anywhere without Easton or Shaw lurking around like they were going to stab me in the ass if I looked at you the wrong way. Or in the cock if I said anything wrong."

He shuffled uncomfortably. "I was a fucking dickhead. From the moment I saw you, I screwed everything up. I'm not good at relationships that last longer than an hour or two. Easton would tell you I suck at anything longer than that too. I dunno."

He rubbed a hand over his head. "I've been doing a lot of thinking and talking to my therapist about why I'm so defensive. I figured it comes with the territory of being a hockey player. We're supposed to be aggressive or some shit. That's cool on the ice, but a dick move off the ice."

"You have a therapist?" I asked, not judgemental, just curious. We probably saw the same one.

"Yeah. Believe it or not I had issues to work through. The only one I care about is not fucking up with you anymore. Or with Easton. He hasn't said it, but I know he won't let our relationship go any further until I have my shit sorted out with you. I'm not saying that so you forgive me, that's my problem, and it's between him and me. But I do want to sort this out."

He nodded, turned away and started the engine.

"Are you going to tell me where we're going now?" I

wasn't going to address the rest of what he said, not yet. There wasn't much to say. I was giving him the chance to make it up to me. The rest was up to him.

"You'll see in a couple of minutes. But I want to explain something else. When I was a kid, I wasn't interested in playing sport. I did it because people said I should. Because I was good at it. I ended up loving it, but it wasn't my first choice back then."

He stopped the car in front of a small building on the main street of Opal Springs. He got out and waited for me to do the same.

"Let me know if you need to sit down or whatever," he said. He eyed my leg speculatively. "You have the best legs." He offered me his hand and led me inside.

I looked around. "You wanted to be an actor?" I'd gone past Opal Springs theatre millions of times, but I hadn't been inside for years.

"It's much worse than that." He guided me up the aisle and into a seat in the front row. "Have you got your phone ready? I want you to film what you're about to witness. If you want to share it with the world, you can. In fact, you probably should." He grimaced.

"Okay," I said slowly. I admit to being more than a little curious about what was going on. I slipped my phone out of my pocket and got it ready. "Are you going to strip for me?"

He snapped his fingers. "I should have thought of that. Wait, do you want me to?" He smiled slyly.

"I want you to do what you brought me here for," I said. "Let's put stripping in the 'maybe' basket."

"I prefer to put it in the 'later this afternoon' basket." He winked.

My heart skipped a beat, and my pussy throbbed. I couldn't help remembering the way he fucked me with his hand in the locker room. If my brain hadn't quite forgiven him, my body certainly had. I'd have to be careful not to let my clit do the talking and thinking until the rest of me caught up.

"Wait there." He trotted up the steps at the side of the stage and into the wings. He reappeared a few moments later with a bright pink feather boa around his neck and matching lipstick smeared across his lips.

"Before you say anything, I don't aspire to be a drag queen, although they are awesome. I embarrassed you with that video and I wanted to do something so absurd it might come close to making up for that. So you know, I don't just laugh at other people, sometimes I laugh at myself. You videoing?"

I wasn't, but I pressed the record button and nodded.

I didn't see the cucumber in his hand, but he raised it now and started to sing like it was a microphone. He sang loudly and with everything he had, but every note was off key and at the wrong tempo.

I'd heard people sing out of tune before, but he was something else. I wasn't sure if he was just that bad or if he was hamming it up for me. Either way, he sounded absolutely terrible. And absolutely hilarious. If I posted this online, it would go much more viral than my fall had. Especially if he went pro. Fans would eat up every moment of it.

He finished singing right before my ears started bleeding, and bowed, complete with a flourish of one hand.

I turned off the phone and stood to give him a round of applause.

"You're very sweet," he said, stepping down off the stage. "My teachers weren't so nice. I wanted to join the choir and sing, but they told me I sucked." He grimaced at the memory.

I winced. "That's harsh."

"It was, but it wasn't wrong." He flopped down beside me. "I was devastated. For the longest time, I thought it was because they didn't like me. Admittedly, I was a little shit. It wasn't until years later I realised they were right, I can't sing for nuts."

"So you got another dream," I said.

He ran a hand over the back of his head. "Some would say it's a better dream. Who wants to be a rock star when you can smack the crap out of a puck night after night? And skate. And hang out with guys like Easton and Shaw, and beautiful women like you."

"It sounds like you fell on your feet," I said.

"I guess I did, but I let it go to my head too. I'm sorry I was a fuckwit." He dropped out of his seat onto the floor in front of me, on his knees. He took my hands in his and looked me in the eyes.

"I'm just a humble mechanic and winger, begging you to forgive me for being an asshole." His brown eyes pleaded. He looked adorable like that, lipstick, boa and all. More than that, he looked sincere.

"If it makes you feel better, you can post that video," he said. "Let people laugh at me the way they laughed at you."

"I was showing off," I admitted.

He gestured to the boa and grinned. "So was I. I might not be able to sing, but I can wear a feather boa like a motherfucking bitch."

I shook my head at him and laughed. "Yes, you can." I grabbed the boa in both of my hands and pulled him forward to kiss his mouth. I didn't care if I got bright pink lipstick on my lips. I needed to feel his mouth on mine.

He kissed me back, his tongue dancing with mine, swiping across my lips and teeth.

"Does this mean you forgive me?" he asked. He wiped lipstick off the corners of my mouth with the pad of his thumb. "Before you answer, I want to tell you something I've never told anyone else before." He glanced down to the floor. "I didn't want to be a rock star. I wanted to be an opera singer."

He hesitated and looked back up. "You can laugh now if you like."

"Why would I laugh at anyone's dreams?" I asked.

"What's the point of life if we don't have them to reach for?" Tears started to gather in the corners of my eyes.

He wiped them away. "I'm sorry you didn't get to live yours. I would have been front row to watch you win the gold medal. I would have cheered louder than everyone else. If I could go back and stop Dean from doing what he did, I'd do it in a heartbeat. Even if it ended my career instead. Me being an asshole influenced him. Being a dumbass, I forgot that role models could be negative as well as positive. From now on, I'll keep being an asshole to a minimum and mostly in front of Easton. He's not as easily influenced as guys like Dean."

"Dean wasn't a kid," I pointed out. "The only person responsible for his actions is him."

"Does that mean you forgive me?" Cruz looked hopeful. "Wait. I shouldn't be pressuring you to answer that. You'll tell me when you're ready. Now that I've made a complete clown of myself, there's someone I'd like you to meet if you're up to spending more time with me?"

I appreciated his decision to give me some space and time. There was no rush to tell him what I'd already figured out. I had a feeling he already knew.

35

CATALINA

"You grew up here?" I asked.

Cruz kicked at a weed which grew in the middle of the gravel road running through the centre of the caravan park.

"Yeah this shit hole was home for the first ten years of my life." He stopped in front of one of the caravans and stared like he was looking at a ghost.

"There's worse things than living in a caravan." I kept my voice down, so a group of kids playing soccer at the end of the road couldn't hear. If this was their reality, I wasn't going to put it down in front of them.

"Yeah, I had a friend who spent a few nights living under the bridge leading into town," he said. "Others who lived in tents. A caravan was a roof over my head, but when you have friends who live in houses, with rooms of their own and a backyard for a dog, you kinda wish that was you. You know?"

I put a hand on his bicep. He went one better by draping an arm over my shoulders.

"Easton told me you guys wanted to make things better for kids, so they didn't have to live under a bridge or in a tent," I said.

Cruz glanced over at me. "We do. I don't want to make too much of a big deal of it. I'm not doing it for the pat on the back or any of that shit. I just think kids deserve better." He shrugged one shoulder.

"They do," I agreed. "Where would you be if you grew up in a fancy house with a backyard and dog?"

He grinned. "Still not singing. Maybe I could have afforded someone to be the front man and sing while I looked pretty."

I snorted. "You're pretty all right. Especially with a pink feather boa around your neck. Maybe you should start wearing one on the ice."

"Kage Foster would have a fit." He laughed. "I might have to try that sometime. Only if you're there to video the look on his face."

"He might ban me from all your games," I said.

"He wouldn't dare," Cruz growled playfully. "Me, Easton and Shaw would go on strike."

"If that doesn't piss him off, nothing would." I leaned against him.

"Seriously, I like to think I'd be playing hockey no matter what happened," he said thoughtfully. "It's the one thing I'm really good at. Everything else, I tend to fuck up. You've probably noticed that already."

"I'm sure you're good at lots of things," I assured him.

"I'm very good at being an asshole," he said. "I'm great at putting my foot in my mouth. I excel at making dumb bets. On the other hand, I'm very, very good at giving orgasms. In fact, I might be better at that than I am at playing hockey." He massaged my shoulder lightly with his fingertips.

My face heated from his touch and the memory of the locker room. "I can't argue with that. You do seem to know what you're doing with your fingers."

He leaned in to whisper in my ear. "It helps when you have a glorious pussy like yours. I haven't stopped thinking about touching you. The way you told me you hated me, and glared at me while I fucked you with my hand. It was awesome."

"Would you like me to tell you I hate you more often?" I asked.

"If I get to fuck you, definitely," he replied. He licked the side of my jaw and traced his tongue down to my throat.

I shivered. "In that case, I hate you very much. I hate you more than I have ever hated anyone else in my life."

"Mmmm, talk dirty to me, baby." He kissed my throat and crossed to the other side of my jaw.

"You're the biggest asshole I ever…mmm, we shouldn't do this here." I didn't want the kids playing nearby to see my panties burst into flame. Or flood.

Cruz glanced at the kids and took my hand. "I know a place. No one will find us there."

I hesitated for a moment, but let him lead me back past his car and onto the street behind the caravan park. The houses here were small, but looked cosy and well-loved.

The front lawns were all neatly mowed, some edged with flower beds which must be beautiful in spring and summer. Only the camellias were in bloom at this time of year. Every few houses had a tree with white or pink blooms, brightening up the neighbourhood.

"I used to walk this way to school," Cruz said. "I thought the people that lived in these houses were rich. Some of them even had two cars. How dumb is that?"

"It's not dumb," I said. "If you don't have much, anyone who has a bit more would seem as though they were rich. Compared to a tent or a bridge, these were castles."

"Yeah, they were. There was always friction between the kids who lived here and kids like me. Like somehow we were less because we lived in that." He jerked his head back to the caravan park. "I promised myself I'd buy one of these houses when I was rich."

He pulled his keys out of his pocket and started down the driveway of a cute, weatherboard cottage. The slats on the front were off-white, the window frames stained dark brown. Outside the front was a Camellia, bright pink flowers all over it.

He pushed the key into the lock and shoved the

door open. "Welcome to my castle. I'm not rich, but it's home for now. Easton lives here too, but he promised to stay away for the night."

I followed Cruz inside. The cottage was open plan, the living room to one side, a kitchen to the other. All of the furniture looked second hand and mismatched.

"When we go pro, I'm getting better shit," Cruz remarked. He tossed his keys down onto the dining table and his phone beside it.

"It's nice," I said. I glanced around, which didn't take long.

He crossed his arms and leaned against a wall. "You expected us to live somewhere fancy, didn't you? Big, bad ass hockey gods and all."

"I did," I admitted. "Which is stupid. I know how much money amateur athletes make. Or rather, how little."

"Tell me about it," he said. "I'm still living on a mechanic's wage. I only finished my apprenticeship a few years ago. That was shit money. The first thing I'm going to do when I get paid by the Ghouls is pay off the mortgage on this place. Fucking bank owns most of it."

"It's important to you isn't it?" I asked. "Making sure you have a solid roof over your head."

"It's everything." His lips pressed together in a tight line. "I'm never going back to living in a fucking caravan. I saved up everything I had to put a deposit on this place. I know too many guys who spend all their pay, or drink it all. Fuck that. A bigger place would be nice someday, but I'm never selling this. This is my assurance that I'm never going backwards."

"You own more houses than I do," I said.

I understood where he was coming from. They say money can't make you happy, but financial security must make life that much easier. I had a long way to go before I got there. I had to finish my degree first. And pay for it.

"If we keep talking like this, people might start to think we're responsible adults or some shit." He curled his lip.

I grimaced. "Ewww. Now who's talking dirty?"

He dropped his arms, grinned and sauntered over to me. "Babe, if you think that's dirty, you ain't heard nothing yet."

He grabbed my ass, picked me up and pressed me against the wall.

I wrapped my legs around his waist and kissed him, eagerly and hungrily.

One arm holding me in place, he slipped the other hand up the front of my shirt. He lightly ghosted his fingers over my stomach and cupped my breast. He pushed my shirt up higher until, between us both we took it off over my head and let it drop to the floor. He unhooked my bra and tossed it aside to join my shirt.

"Your breasts are fucking beautiful," he said.

"For someone you hate," I teased.

He chuckled. "Yeah, for someone I hate." He leaned

in and nibbled on my ear. "I'm going to fuck you like I hate you."

"I was going to say the same to you." I pulled up his shirt over his head and took a long moment to admire his bare chest and abs, decorated with an abundance of ink. "See how ridiculously hot you are?"

He glanced down at himself. "It's stupid isn't it? All those muscles."

"Definitely stupid," I agreed. I wriggled until my pussy was resting right against his cock, only layers of jeans between us. "I can feel how much you hate me." He was hard as a rock.

"So much." He palmed my nipples before leaning in to suck one, then the other. He put me down long enough for us to help each other out of our shoes and jeans. He picked me back up and rubbed the tip of his cock against my entrance.

"You hate me so much you're wet as fuck."

"If you don't put that inside me, I'm going to hate you even more," I growled.

"How much will you hate me?" He positioned his cock carefully and inserted just the tip.

"More than anyone I've ever met," I said. "I hate everything about you."

He slammed all the way inside me. "Do you hate that too?"

"Definitely." I was breathless with how good it felt to have him inside me all the way to his balls.

"Excellent." He gritted his teeth, pulled out and

pounded back in again, over and over like he was taking out every ounce of frustration he ever had, on my body.

I dug my heels into his ass and my nails into his back and rocked against him as hard as he was doing to me.

"Are you sure you hate me?" I asked. "It feels like you're being gentle to me."

He laughed-growled, held on to me and swung me around until my ass was on the edge of the table. He yanked my knees apart and thrust in all the way, as deep as he could go. Without restraint or mercy, he fucked me harder than I'd ever been fucked before.

I pressed the palms of my hands into the smooth timber on either side of me. I dropped my head back and closed my eyes.

"That better?" he asked. "Does that feel like I hate you?"

"Absolutely," I agreed.

"Good." He pulled out of me and stepped away for a few moments before stepping back, a vibrator in one hand and a tube of lube in the other. He rolled me over onto my stomach and opened the tube to slather lube over my rear hole.

"I'm going to fuck you in here." He slid a finger inside my ass and turned it around to spread the lubricant and stretch my muscles. He added another finger to the first, then a third.

"Has anyone ever fucked you here?" he asked.

"No," I said breathlessly. "Fuck my ass like you hate me."

He groaned, gripped my hips and pulled me slowly onto his cock. Every couple of seconds, he stopped to let my muscles get used to him. After a few moments, he was fully seated inside me. Like he had with my pussy, he started to fuck my ass hard, hard enough to bring tears to my eyes.

He angled me and bent my knees so he could slide the vibrator inside my pussy.

I moaned. The sensation of being filled like this was incredible. Like nothing I'd ever felt before. He fucked both my holes, deliberate and rough.

He thrust and thrust until I screamed out my orgasm, my cheek pressed against the top of the table.

He came a moment later, spilling hot cum into my ass. Grinding and thrusting, milking himself for every last drop. Finally, he slumped over me, panting.

"Fucking hell, woman. You're incredible." He slid his cock and the vibrator out of me and gathered me up to hold me on the edge of the table.

"You're not so bad yourself," I admitted. "I forgive you."

"I forgive you too," he said.

I drew my head back and frowned at him. "For what?"

"For being so fucking gorgeous and having the tightest ass I've ever fucked." He grinned. "And letting my cock be the first to fuck you there." He slapped my ass cheek.

"You're such a brat." I slapped his chest.

"That's undeniably true," he agreed. "Let's have a shower. I want to show you how much I hate your mouth."

36
CATALINA

"Are you sure I should be here?" I asked.

"We want you here," Easton said. He put a hand on my knee like he'd hold me down if I tried to leave.

"Yes, we do." Shaw put a hand on my other knee.

"You wouldn't miss us falling on our faces, would you?" Cruz asked. He sat behind me, his hands on my shoulders.

"When you put it that way, I guess I could stay," I said. Sitting in the stands with all three of them felt strangely right. Like somehow it was always meant to be this way.

"We are not going to fall on our faces, asshole," Easton said to Cruz. "If you think that, you can fuck all the way off."

Resting his wrists on my shoulders, Cruz flipped Easton off with both hands.

"Of course we're not, *asshole*," he retorted. "It's just

mine and Cat's love language. We love to hate each other, right babe?"

"Exactly," I said. "I only want Cruz to fall on his face." I turned and grinned.

He leaned forward. "Woman, you're going to pay for that. I'm going to fuck you like I hate you, even harder than before."

I lightly pressed my nose against his cheek. "Don't threaten me with a good time." I was sore for two days, but it was worth it.

"After this, I think a private celebration is in order," Easton said.

"Or commiseration," Shaw said quietly.

They both turned to glare at him.

He shrugged. "All we know is that Coach Foster said the AIHL has made a final decision. We don't know what that is. I bet he doesn't even know."

Cruz raised his hand.

"No," I told him. "He doesn't mean a literal bet."

Cruz lowered his hand.

Easton laughed and even Shaw chuckled slightly.

"You know what I think?" Easton asked. "I think they delayed on purpose."

"No shit, bro," Cruz said. "That whole thing with Dean—"

"Might have been just to push this whole thing into overtime, to build the suspense," Easton finished.

"This isn't a movie," Cruz said. "If it was, I forgot my

popcorn." He mimed sitting back with a bucket in front of him, eating.

Easton pretended to scoop out a handful and throw it at him. "You're such an idiot."

Cruz leaned over, lifted his hands and tipped all of the imaginary popcorn onto Easton's head, before shoving the imaginary bucket down and patting Easton on the top of his head.

"That would have been even better if it was real popcorn, covered in butter," Shaw remarked.

I giggled. "You guys are crazy."

"Of course we are, that's what you love about us." Easton mimed pulling off the bucket, tossing it aside and wiping butter off his face.

"If you decide to quit hockey, you could join the Opal Springs players," I said. "I've heard they could use a few comedians."

"I could sing." Cruz grinned. He gripped my chin with his thumb and forefinger and turned my face to his. "What did you do with that video? I assume by the fact I don't hear laughter, you didn't post it."

"I didn't," I said. "Not yet anyway. I figured I'd save it for another day, in case you decide to be a prick. It never hurts to have a bit of blackmail material."

"Huh, I didn't know you were evil. I like it." He kissed my mouth.

"Just keeping you on your toes," I said. I had no intention of sharing the video with anyone, unless he asked me to. I'd considered deleting it, but I'd watched it a bunch of times, when I needed something to smile about.

"It's about time someone got Cruz into line," Easton said. "I can't say I didn't try, but he's always been an unruly prick."

"Pot, meet kettle," Cruz said.

"I thought it was more *nail, meet head*," Shaw said.

Cruz flipped him off. "You two are assholes, you know that?"

Easton grinned. "Yeah, that's why you love us. Right, Shaw?" He offered Shaw a fist bump.

Shaw bumped. "I don't know about love, but Cruz is okay."

"I do." Easton looked at Cruz intently.

Cruz's Adam's apple bobbed. "Love you too, bro. Love you, Cat."

"I love you too," I told him. "All three of you." They weren't the easiest guys in the world, but I cared about them, nonetheless.

"We love you too," Easton said.

"Yes, we do," Shaw agreed. He gave me a soft look and even a faint smile. The first I'd seen from him.

My heart melted a little more.

We all startled and turned around as Kage Foster cleared his throat. None of us saw him approach, but he was standing in front of the stands now. He glanced at me, but didn't say anything. That was fortunate, because I suspected the guys would have argued if the coach wanted me to leave.

"I suppose you're all curious about why I asked you to come here," Kage started.

"We figured you missed us, since you haven't seen us since this morning," Cruz called out. "That's a whole bunch of hours."

Kage smirked. "Yeah, I've been crying into my coffee and watching replays so I can feel closer to all of you." His Canadian accent was stronger when he was sarcastic.

"I knew it." Cruz grinned. "It's unfair how fucking irresistible we all are."

"You want to shut up and let the man speak?" Easton asked.

"Yeah." I elbowed Cruz in the knee. I didn't know about any of them, but the suspense was almost too much for me. "Quiet."

"Yes, ma'am," Cruz said smartly.

I looked back over my shoulder at him and grinned. "I like the sound of that. It's better than Princess."

"You'll always be my princess," he said softly. He massaged my shoulders while I turned back around to face Kage.

Kage cleared his throat. "As I said, the AIHL has come to a final decision about the expansion team for the next season." He paused for about half a year. "Unfortunately…"

The whole team let out a disappointed groan.

"Fuck!" Cruz growled. "Why?"

"You didn't let me finish," Kage said. He blew a long

breath out his nose and continued. "As I was saying. Unfortunately… Opal Springs is going to have to deal with some construction for at least a year. The construction of the Opal Springs ice hockey arena."

His words were followed with absolute silence for at least two seconds.

The stands erupted with shouts of excitement. The guys were hugging each other and patting each other on the back.

"Fuck, yeah, I knew it!" Cruz shouted. He grabbed me, pulled me over the back of my seat and squeezed me so tight I thought I might pop.

At the same time, I was laughing, excited for them. My ice dream hadn't come true, but I was ecstatic theirs had. The whole town was going to be thrilled.

When they finally managed to quieten down, Kage was able to continue. "We'll be searching for a new goalie, but now we'll have the funds to headhunt one of the best. Before you say it, no, Phoenix DiMarco isn't available. Don't worry, I have some guys in mind."

The players groaned, but it was good-natured. They would have loved to have Phoenix, but they may find someone even better.

"The best news of all," Kage continued. "You all get lessons in dealing with the bunch of journalists who'll be coming to interview all of you."

This time, the groan was more sincere.

Before any of them could ask, Kage said, "Yes, you

have to talk to them. Get used to it. This is your life now."

"Fuck yeah," Easton said. "Bring it on. We can celebrate privately after that."

"Hell yeah, we can," Cruz agreed. His gaze lingered on Easton, hungry like a lion eyeing his next meal.

My panties were officially ruined. What was new these days? I couldn't get enough of any of them. My three hockey gods, egos, arrogance and all.

37
CATALINA

"Hey, how are you feeling?" Shaw placed a hand on the back of my neck and guided me through the front door, into his place. I'd only been here a couple of times, when he needed to get a few things to take back to my house. It was larger than Cruz and Easton's place, but not by much. The furniture was just as well-loved.

"I should be asking you that," I said. "I'm overwhelmed and I'm not even on the team."

"You could be our first Ghoul girl," Cruz said. He and Easton had found their way to the kitchen and helped themselves to bottles of beer. "I can see you in a cute little outfit with a short skirt and a top that barely covers your boobs."

"Every guy in the place would stare at her and not watch us," Easton said.

"Then I'd have to hurt them all," Shaw said. His grip

on the back of my neck tightened. "Cat's breasts are for our eyes only."

"We can get her an outfit for private times," Cruz conceded. "We could take turns taking it off her."

"That sounds like a plan." Easton toasted him with his beer.

I shook my head at them all and leaned my head against Shaw's chest. It might be fun to be a cheerleader for the team, but I had a long way to go before my leg was strong enough to support me all day, much less as athletically as a cheerleader needed to be.

"You three are about to be incredibly busy," I said.

"Fuck yeah we are," Cruz said. "First stop, putting in my resignation at the garage. No more fixing cars for this professional hockey player."

"I forgot about that," Easton said. "I don't mind my job, but it'll be a better hobby. Maybe I could build us all a house in a year or two. Cruz can fix all of our cars. Shaw can slice and dice all the meat."

"Cat can keep the dogs healthy," Cruz said. "You guys want dogs, right? If you don't, we might have a problem here." He looked around at all of us.

"I want a dog," I said. "When the time is right. There are a few things we need to figure out first."

"Four bedroom house, or five?" Cruz asked. "Somewhere big enough for us to have our own space, but be together when we want to."

"That might be rushing into things a bit—" I started.

"Nope," he said. "I told you how important it is to

me to have a place I can call mine. I want to share that with the woman I call mine." He hesitated for a moment. "And the guy I call mine." He glanced over at Easton and smiled tentatively.

"I want that too." Easton smiled back at Cruz, then at me. "And we all know Shaw goes wherever Cat goes."

"Exactly," Shaw agreed. "If being with my woman means living with you two clowns, then that's what happens."

"Is anyone going to ask what I want?" I asked. I cocked my head at them, as if it wasn't what I wanted as well.

"No, Princess," Cruz replied. He placed his beer bottle down on the kitchen bench top and strode over to me. He cupped my cheeks with his hands and pressed the tip of his nose to mine. "All three of us take what we want and what we want is to be with you. You can try to fight it if you want to, but we all know you don't want to." He claimed my mouth with his, kissing me hard, stubble scratching my skin.

Before I lost my breath, he pulled back. "I think we need to show this woman who she belongs to." He bent forward, picked me up and draped me over his shoulder.

"The bedroom is that way," Shaw pointed. He and Easton followed, both watching with tented pants as Cruz dropped me onto the middle of the bed.

Cruz started to help me out of my shirt and bra, while

the other two worked on my leggings, panties and shoes. In a minute or two, I was naked in front of all of them. Another couple of minutes later, they were all naked too.

I barely knew where to look. Three hot hockey gods, with muscles and tattoos and erections all pointing at me. I was a lucky girl.

Shaw knelt down between my knees, draped my legs over his shoulders like he'd always said he wanted to, and started to lick and suck my clit.

Cruz lay beside me and palmed his cock a couple of times before sliding it between my lips. "Holy fuck, your mouth is incredible."

While I licked and sucked him, he pulled Easton over and drew his cock into his own mouth.

Easton's eyes half closed with bliss. "Your mouth is pretty amazing too."

Between watching them, the taste and feel of Cruz, and Shaw's mouth on my clit, I came faster and harder than I ever had before. I bucked against Shaw's face and had to pull myself off Cruz's cock so I could cry out my release.

Shaw sat up and reached into the draw beside the bed for a tube of lube. "Because you're such a good girl, I know you can take all of us."

He gestured for Cruz to lie on his back and me to straddle his hips and lower myself onto his cock.

Cruz groaned. "Holy fuck, you have the best pussy ever."

Shaw handed Easton the lube to apply to my rear hole.

The winger spread it around liberally before tossing the tube aside. He slid a finger inside me, then another, stretching me out, readying me for him.

"That feels so good," I said breathlessly. "I want you inside me."

"Good, because that's what you're going to get." Easton positioned his cock between my cheeks and eased his tip into my ass. Slowly, carefully, he pushed in deeper.

Cruz's eyes widened. "Bro, I can feel you."

"I can feel you too," Easton said softly. He sounded awed

"Good girl," Shaw told me. "You take both of them so well. I know you can take me too." He pressed the head of his cock against my lips and waited for me to open so he could slide it in. "Such a good fucking girl."

I smiled around my mouthful and teased his tip with my tongue before taking him in deeper and sucking hard.

"I think she's starting to get the idea she belongs to the three of us," Cruz said. "She was made for us and our cocks. No one else is going to fuck her but us. We own her and she owns us."

"Yeah, she does," Shaw agreed. He half closed his eyes and slowly fucked my mouth, while Cruz and Easton fucked my pussy and ass.

Feeling all three of them inside me, thrusting at the

same time, was amazing. Even better than flying across the ice. Nothing could ever compare to the way this felt.

Easton set the rhythm for him and Cruz, who thrust up into me, his hands on my hips. Each time they were all the way inside me, their cocks must have tapped each other, only a thin wall of muscle between them.

"This is fucking next level," Cruz groaned. "I'm going to come inside your pussy."

"Come with me," Easton insisted. "I want to feel you come inside her."

Their words pushed me over the edge again, coming harder, clenching both of their cocks. They couldn't have held back if they wanted to. As deep inside me as they could get, they both came, flooding my body with their cum.

Shaw followed a few moments later, squirting hot cum down my throat.

I slid my mouth off his length and locked my eyes on his as I swallowed every delicious drop.

Still inside me, Easton whispered in my ear. "I think you can say we worked things out." He slid out of me and flopped down beside me on the mattress.

"We did." I lay over Cruz, his cock still in my pussy. "I'll think about it." I had four months left of my birth control pills. I knew he wanted me pregnant, but I wasn't sure I was ready for something like that.

He slid his hand between Cruz and I, to touch my belly. "Don't think too long. I want a baby in there before the arena is finished being built."

"A baby, hmmm?" Cruz asked slowly. "I don't mind practising as much as we can."

"Me either," Shaw agreed. "Cat is so fucking gorgeous and so fucking ours."

"And you're all mine," I said softly. We'd come a long way since we met, but I wouldn't give any of them up for anything.

They all held a piece of my pucking heart.

EPILOGUE

"He's in here." The corrections officer unlocked the door and gestured inside. "He hasn't been doing well."

"That's why I'm here to see him," I said lightly. "Thank you very much." I stepped inside the cell and waited until the door closed behind me.

Dean Hayes lay on the tiny bed against the wall, his face pale and covered in a sheen of sweat.

I clicked my tongue and pulled the chair over to sit beside him. "You're really not doing well, are you? What a shame."

He looked over at me. His eyes didn't widen, he didn't so much as twitch. Of course not, he had no idea what was really wrong with him, much less that I had something to do with it.

"Don't worry, I have some medication for you," I said. "Do you think you can sit up to take it?"

"Yeah." He struggled to push himself up on his

elbows and accept the cup of water I handed him, along with two pills. He threw them into his mouth and washed them down with the water.

"They should make you feel much better," I said. I took the cup from his hand and placed it aside. If they tested it later, it would contain nothing but tap water. The pills on the other hand, were tasteless and virtually untraceable. The coroner would find nothing more than the poor boy's heart stopped after a short illness. Terrible thing, the flu. Highly contagious, and deadly under certain circumstances.

Dean coughed a couple of times before curling up around himself and falling still. It was a shame he wouldn't suffer too much, but I had to cover my tracks.

I patted his shoulder before I stood and knocked on the door for the corrections officer to let me out.

"He should sleep for a while, but if he's not better in the morning, let me know and I'll arrange for him to be moved to a bigger hospital." He wouldn't be better in the morning; he'd be dead.

"Thank you. Is he still contagious?" The officer was careful to keep his distance from me.

"Very contagious," I agreed. I stepped aside to start removing my PPE. "Keeping him isolated for a while is the only option." I shoved everything into a bag, ready for disposal.

"I'll see you later," I said pleasantly.

The officer nodded. "Yeah. Thank you, Doctor Ryan."

I whistled softly as I walked away. No one fucked with my daughter. No one.

I wondered if Marley was available for a celebratory drink. She'd never know what I'd done. As far as she knew, I was nothing more threatening than her boss, and her lover.

Sooner or later, we'd have to tell Catalina. She was going to be pissed, but we'd deal with that in time. Cat would eventually understand.

I hoped.

The end. If you need to know how much Cruz hates Cat's mouth, you can find out here in this bonus scene. If you loved this book, please leave a review.

ABOUT THE AUTHOR

Maggie Alabaster writes reverse harem romance.

She lives in NSW, Australia with one spouse, two daughters, one dog, and countless birds.

Jo Bradley writes contemporary romance.

Sign up for Maggie's newsletter! Sign Up!

Join Maggie's reader group! Join here!

Follow Maggie on Bookbub! Click here to follow me!

Check out Maggie's website- www.maggiealabaster.com

Sign up for Jo's newsletter

ALSO BY MAGGIE ALABASTER

Pucking Dark Hearts

Pucking Hearts Collide

Pucking Forbidden Hearts

Dusk Bay Demons

Puck Drop

Breakaway

Power Play

Brutal Academy

Book 1 Heartless

Book 2 Cruel

Book 3 Vengeful

Court of Blood and Binding

Book 1 Song of Scent and Magic

Book 2 Crown of Mist and Heat

Book 3 Sword of Balm and Shadow

Book 4 Whisper of Frost and Flame

Dark Masque

Book 1 Bait

Book 2 Prey

Book 3 Trap

Saving Abbie

Book 1 Pitch

Book 2 Pound

Book 3 Session

Book 4 Muse

Book 5 Rhythm

Book 6 Encore

Novella Venomous

Saving Abbie books 1-4

Saving Abbie books 4-6 + Venomous

Ruthless Claws

Book 1 Ivory

Book 2 Crimson

Book 3 Elodie

Harmony's Magic

Book 1 Summoned by Fire

Book 2 Summoned by Fate

Book 3 Summoned by Desire

Shifter's Vault

Book 1 Discarded

Book 2 Deceived

Book 3 Disgraced

My Alien Mates

Book 1 Star Warriors

Book 2 Star Defenders

Book 3 Star Protectors

Academy of Modern Magic

Book 1 Digital Magic

Book 2 Virtual Magic

Book 3 Logical Magic

Complete Collection

Summer's Harem

Book 1: Shimmer

Book 2: Glimmer

Book 3: Flicker

Complete collection

Short reads

Taken by the Snowmen

Jingle All the Way

Also by Maggie Alabaster and Erin Yoshikawa

Caught by the Tide

Book 1–Pursued by Shadows

Book 2 Pursued by Darkness

Book 3 Pursued by Monsters

Milton Keynes UK
Ingram Content Group UK Ltd.
UKHW020225250424
441687UK00001B/11

9 781763 506312